A TURN IN THE ROAD

Recent Titles by Julie Ellis from Severn House

THE HAMPTON SAGA

THE HAMPTON HERITAGE
THE HAMPTON WOMEN
THE HAMPTON PASSION

ANOTHER EDEN
BEST FRIENDS
THE GENEVA RENDEZVOUS
THE HOUSE ON THE LAKE
SECOND TIME AROUND
SINGLE MOTHER
A TOWN NAMED PARADISE
VILLA FONTAINE
WHEN THE SUMMER PEOPLE HAVE GONE
WHEN TOMORROW COMES

A TURN IN THE ROAD

Julie Ellis

This first world edition published in Great Britain 2003 by
SEVERN HOUSE PUBLISHERS LTD of
9–15 High Street, Sutton, Surrey SM1 1DF.
This first world edition published in the USA 2004 by
SEVERN HOUSE PUBLISHERS INC of
595 Madison Avenue, New York, N.Y. 10022.

British Library Cataloguing in Publication Data

Ellis, Julie, 1933-
A turn in the road
1. Women lawyers - United States - Fiction
2. Birthmothers - United States - Fiction
I. Title
813.5'4 [F]

ISBN 0-7278-6044-5

Typeset by Palimpsest Book Production Ltd.,
Polmont, Stirlingshire, Scotland.
Printed and bound in Great Britain by
MPG Books Ltd., Bodmin, Cornwall.

For Kathy Keogh – and Yoshi and Eve and Nick

Prologue

The mid-January day was bone-chilling cold – gray and dismal. Slight, pretty, twelve-year-old April Bolton – dark hair cascading about her shoulders, blue eyes red-rimmed from tears – clung to her father's hand. A number of neighbors in this small upstate New York town gathered about the grave. Everybody had liked Mom so much, she thought defiantly. Why did God take her away?

She'd been here in the neatly kept cemetery only once before in her life – when her maternal grandmother died four years ago. Her other grandparents had died before she was born. Now, she thought in fearful anguish, only Daddy and she survived of their family.

At last the services were over. Walking from the site of her mother's grave, April knew her life would never be the same again. They'd done everything together – Mom, Daddy, and she. Memories of summer picnics, winter ski weekends, backyard barbecues assaulted her. But Mom would never be with them again.

It's my fault Mom was killed by that hit-and-run driver. If I'd taken the roast to Mrs Gorman instead of saying I had to do homework with Peggy next door, Mom would still be alive.

Daddy cried and said it was his fault. That he should have insisted Mom hire a woman to take care of the house. *'God knows, we could afford it.'* But Mom was born in the Depression – Daddy said she always worried they'd be short of money.

Nobody even bothered to get the license number of the car that hit Mom, she remembered – for a moment replacing grief with rage. Why wasn't he in jail? Daddy – who didn't believe in the death penalty – said he ought to be put away with no chance of parole. Daddy was a lawyer. Why couldn't he figure out some way to track down that man?

It had been a man driver – two people saw him run Mom down, though they didn't recognize him. How could people kill somebody and get away with it? One day she'd be a lawyer, she vowed. She'd help send murderers to prison.

She hadn't known then that her highly respected lawyer father would descend into alcoholism within a year, lose most of his clients, lose their house. It was as though he was waiting to die, she told herself in recurrent anguish that blended with anger.

They moved from their charming ranch house to a tiny ramshackle cottage in the rundown section of town. She bought her clothes at the thrift shop run by the Presbyterian Church. She cooked their meals, shopped for groceries – learning to watch for sales.

She drifted away from her friends at school. She was ashamed of the way they lived now. How could she bring girlfriends into their house? She became a loner, focused on earning top grades. She didn't know how it could happen, but she was determined to go to college, then to law school.

She began her senior year at high school, tried to blot out the knowledge that there was no way she could go on to college. Money was so tight that she couldn't afford to pay for the photographs for their yearbook. She didn't want to think about how she would acquire her graduation dress. The class had voted against caps and gowns.

She had no boyfriend at school. She ignored wary efforts by several to date her. Then she became aware of wistful glances from a classmate. Handsome seventeen-year-old Tommy Melrose – whose father was a judge and whose mother headed local volunteer groups, though folks furtively said the Melroses were stuck-up and arrogant – was clearly enamored.

She was quick to realize that not only was Tommy so good-looking that most of the senior girls were hoping he'd ask them to the senior prom when that time arrived, but he was warm and sweet and he didn't care that she wasn't part of the circle that attended all the teenage parties at the country club.

Soon they were together at every free moment. She discovered Tommy's relationship with his parents was hostile.

'They want to rule every little thing about my life,' he confided rebelliously. 'They want me to date Elinor Brady because her father will probably be our next mayor,' he blurted out. 'But I don't like Elinor. They worry that I won't make it into Harvard, and then into Harvard law. I don't want to be a lawyer – I want to go into theater. They made me drop out of the drama club – when they realized how much I loved it.'

She and Tommy didn't want to think about graduation – because that would mean separation for them. They talked about eloping – but they would require parental consent to get married. And how would they survive?

Then – on a snowy December evening when Tommy's parents were attending a social function in a neighboring town and the household staff were off – they spent a precious two hours together in the Melrose den before an open fire. It was inevitable, April thought years afterwards, that they would make passionate love – overstepping the boundary they'd set for themselves.

Tommy inherited his mother's car, and life took on a new dimension. They buried their hurt, their rebellion, in their love. The car became their home, their sanctuary, their refuge from reality. In shadowy corners of wooded areas – safe from prying eyes – they made love.

In early May – with graduation approaching – April realized that she was pregnant. Terrified, she told Tommy.

No thought of telling her father, who spent most days in a drunken stupor.

'We'll have to get married now,' Tommy said defiantly. 'Our folks can't say no.'

But Judge Melrose and his wife were outraged. They refused to believe that Tommy was the father of April's child. But to make sure Tommy could not disgrace the family with this admission, they shipped him off – in restraints – to a private sanitarium. The local newspaper carried an item that reported his 'sudden illness.'

'On the advice of the Melrose family physician, young Melrose is being treated in an out-of-state hospital specializing in his illness.'

The same day that the local newspaper carried the story of Tommy's treatment out of state, Evan Bolton suffered a fatal heart attack. April was left with nothing. Grief-stricken at the loss of her father, frightened of tomorrow, April turned to the compassionate social worker she'd met at the hospital when her father was dying.

The social worker arranged for her to go to a home for pregnant teenagers in a nearby town. Along with the other teenagers, April attended school, was awarded a high school diploma. Melrose and his wife had contrived to isolate Tommy from her. Still, at unrealistic moments she dreamed of his arriving at the home, to be with her when the baby was born.

She understood that she must put the baby up for adoption. What would she be able to do for her precious baby, whom she already loved?

'We have contacts who'll arrange for a private adoption,' the social worker explained gently. 'There are loving couples who can't have babies of their own, and they want so much to have a family. They'll raise the baby the same as they would their own.'

'How do I know that?' April was fearful. She remembered awful stories about stepmothers.

'The lawyer who'll arrange the adoption has handled many cases for us,' the social worker soothed. 'He investigates thoroughly before he agrees to bring them together with a birth mother.'

'I'll meet them?' Where was Tommy? By the time the baby was born, they'd both be eighteen – free to marry. 'How can I know they'll be good parents?' she demanded fearfully.

'The lawyer whom we work with is a father himself – a warm, compassionate man. He investigates thoroughly,' the social worker insisted. 'We've seen how our babies thrive with the adoptive parents he's brought in. And you'll meet them,' she confirmed. April understood that no names, no addresses, were to be exchanged. And the records would be sealed. 'He already has a young couple in mind. They're only twenty-three but so anxious to have a family. She lost their first baby – and they were told she could never have another. They're college educated, financially secure. And they're willing to be quite generous.'

'You mean they'll pay all the legal costs,' April interpreted, remembering what a recent young mother had confided.

'Not only that. We've discussed other arrangements for you. They know how well you did in high school, that you want to go on to college. They're putting funds into an escrow account that will see you through four years at state college.'

All at once April was ice-cold. 'That sounds as though I'm selling my baby,' she whispered.

'No.' The social worker was emphatic. 'They, too, were concerned about the parents of their adopted baby. They liked what they were told about you. They offered to set up this fund, to show their gratitude and to help you begin a new life.'

The baby – a girl – was born on November 22, 1977. April was told that it would be best if she never saw the baby, but she insisted on seeing her daughter. She would see the adoptive parents, too – as promised.

A nurse came into the hospital ward with the tiny bundle that was her daughter, placed her in April's arms. She gazed down at the small bundle in her arms with amazement. A tiny replica of herself. A mop of soft black hair, blue eyes like her own. One of the girls at the home said all babies were born with blue eyes. Would hers stay blue?

How sad that Tommy would never see his daughter. Where was he now? Did he think about her? Did he wonder about the baby? What would the adoptive parents name her? But this was best for her. She could give her daughter nothing – her new parents would give her everything.

But always she would remember these precious minutes when she held her daughter in her arms.

Chapter One

A murky sky tinged with deep red hung over Manhattan on this early November morning, in the first year of the new century. April Winston – nee Bolton – sat in the huge, elegantly furnished office of her boss at Addison, Richards and Friedman and made a pretense of listening to the lecture she was receiving from The Big Wheel – as the attorneys in the firm secretly nicknamed their founding father. A dressing down she had heard twice before in the past few months.

'April, you're so bright,' he said impatiently. 'Why do you persist in ignoring our need to eliminate pro bono work? Why do you keep dredging up these cases? Times have changed – we can't deal with them at the pace we're going. We're not a philanthropic organization!'

He scowled in reproach, but she was aware that his eyes were stripping away her designer suit, her smart silk blouse. He made a point of warning male members of the firm against 'hanky-panky' with female members – but he was addicted to choosing new female associates who were not only sharp attorneys but young and attractive.

'But isn't pro bono work good for our image?' she countered with a contrived sweet smile. Her expressive blue eyes exuding bewilderment. Her stock reaction. Her pro bono cases provided the few bright hours in her sweatshop-long day.

'Fuck our image,' he shot back. 'It's the hours we bill that concerns me. Get your act together, April.' His eyes now lingered on the expanse of silken thigh on display as she crossed her legs. It was an established fact that the women attorneys, paralegals, and administrative assistants at Addison, Richards and Friedman wore the shortest skirts considered decent. In the office, that is, April thought drily.

The women attorneys knew not to go into court with skirts that ended at mid-thigh. This might intrigue male jurors, but women jurors would be turned off. They knew, too, not to wear ultra-smart outfits or sexy shoes. At five three April was prone to wearing high heels in social situations. In court she wore low heels – which, she had decided, made men feel more protective. Male jurors more likely to vote in favor of her client. She wore her lush near-black hair in a deceptively simple short cut that emphasized her oval face and delicate features.

'All right, April. Remember what I said.' He glanced at his watch. The meeting was over. He'd had his morning allotment of office sex. 'We're cutting out all pro bono work. Focus on billable hours.'

April walked back to her own office with her usual fast pace. Perhaps she was especially upset this morning, she conceded to herself. November was always a bad month for her. Her precious baby had been born in November.

The inevitable questions haunted her. Is my baby happy? Is she well? Did I make the right move with adoption? Twenty-three years of painful questions.

Last month she'd hit 40 – though no man looking at her would take her for more than 28 or 29. She'd made a point of ignoring birthdays through the years. In truth, the only birthday she allowed in her life was her baby's.

In the privacy of her office she continued to fume that the firm was adamant about abolishing pro bono cases. This was what provided her with real satisfaction. All those years ago – before Mom died and he fell apart – Dad was so respected in town because he didn't focus on billing as many hours as he could. He cared about people. He wanted to help those who couldn't afford legal services.

The rules at the firm kept growing more restrictive, she scoffed in silent rebellion. Next thing, The Big Wheel would expect them to sign out before they went to pee.

She'd been with the firm for almost three years now. It was her fourth law firm since graduating law school. When she'd made the first change – two and a half years out of law school – Greg had warned this was not the way to go.

'You're not building anything that way,' Greg had objected. 'You stay with a firm, work your way up to a partnership – and eventually,' he pointed out with a gleam of triumph, 'you become an equity partner.' Sharing in partnership profits. But Greg had moved along with her. He, too, was restless. After the divorce he'd remarried, moved into politics – or so she heard.

Why had she married Greg right out of law school that way? Because she was scared and lonely. She was forever scared – since the day Mom died. Always scared of tomorrow. Except for that little while with Tommy. She'd suspected – after his parents shipped him off to that sanitarium – that she'd never see him again. But it was shattering when she discovered late in her freshman year at college that Tommy had died of an overdose. He'd never been into drugs. His parents drove him to that.

College had been secure financially, but she'd had to battle to make her way through law school. Scholarship, college loans, a stream of lowly jobs had seen her through.

She'd stayed with her marriage for seven years – though she knew by the end of the first year that it had been a serious mistake. Greg was super-ambitious – and he didn't care who was hurt while he made his climb up the ladder. The last three years had been a constant battlefield.

I hate my job – admit it. But don't most people feel that way? Maybe I haven't made it to the top – the way I vowed all those years ago – yet to most people I'm a success. I own a luxury condo on the colorful West Side. I drive a white Mercedes. I spend summer weekends – when

I can escape the office – in the Hamptons. Why am I so unhappy?

She was startled by the sharp ring of her private line. She reached to pick up the phone. 'April Winston, good morning.' Brisk, yet cordial.

'April, you always sound as though you're on the top of the world.' A warm, ingratiating – familiar – voice.

'Bob, how are you?' Bob Allen – and Nicole, his wife – had been at law school with Greg and her. She'd shared an apartment with Nicole.

'I've been better,' he admitted. 'My partner's finally made the firm decision. He's retiring.' April knew his longtime partner was practicing long beyond normal retirement age. At intervals Bob had hinted about her coming in with him. 'This is a lifestyle to love,' he'd declared. He had been practicing for a dozen years in Magnolia, a small upstate New York town.

'You knew it was coming,' she reminded, yet was sympathetic.

'I'm in town on business for forty-eight hours,' he said. 'What about dinner tonight? Or are you still working eighty-hour weeks?' Each time he was in New York they tried to meet for a couple of hours. There were times when she was chained to her desk.

'I'm still working eighty-hour weeks,' she conceded, 'but I'll take tonight off.' Her act of rebellion for the month, she told herself.

'I should be clear by seven thirty,' he said, a lilt in his voice. He insisted he loved that little town upstate, but didn't he miss the excitement of living in New York – where he had been born and raised?

'Fine. Where are you staying?'

'You know my budget,' he chuckled, and named a small hotel with modest rates. 'But I can splurge for dinner. Of course, I've been away too long to know the great places.'

'What about Lespinasse?' she asked. 'On my expense account,' she added hurriedly. 'It's superb.'

'Hey, if you can get away with it, terrific,' he effervesced. She'd taken him there for dinner a couple of years ago and he'd been awed. 'Lespinasse, seven thirty p.m.'

'How're the kids?' Marianne must be eleven by now, April calculated, and Neil nine. Each time she saw Bob and Nicole's kids she felt such a sense of loss. Would there ever be a time when she could think of her own daughter without anguish?

'Oh, they're fine.' Bob's voice was tender. 'Marianne is the captain of her soccer team – can you beat that? And Neil's all excited about becoming a Cub Scout.'

'I'll expect to see pictures,' she warned.

'Oh, I have a batch we took just last month. You haven't seen them in at least a year,' he chided. 'Nicole says we should kidnap you one of these days.'

April sighed. 'You know my crazy work schedule. Each time I expect to have some free time, something comes up.'

'That's got to change. Let's talk about that over dinner. See you at seven thirty – at Lespinasse.'

Off the phone April sat immobile, staring into space. Talking with Bob brought back so many memories. She'd suspected early on – though he gave no outward signs – that he disliked Greg. She'd told herself he'd envied Greg.

Everybody thought Greg was movie-star handsome, brilliant, destined for big things. They never encountered his violent rages, his incredible arrogance. They had no concept of the ruthless man beneath that charming exterior. But when he attacked her physically, she knew she was leaving him.

Bob and Nicole didn't know that she'd had a daughter. Not even Greg knew. She couldn't share that part of her life with anyone. She was ashamed that she'd given up her precious baby – and awash in guilt. But she'd had no choice.

God, I wish November was over! All these years later I feel the pain I felt then at giving her away. She'll be twenty-three on the 22nd of this month. And all I have of her is that snapshot my roommate in the hospital took of her in the hospital nursery.

Was it wrong of me to try to find her? But I knew so little – it was impossible, even in this Internet age. In my heart I knew I shouldn't try to find her. I would throw her life into turmoil. She might hate me. And I'd want to die . . .

Chapter Two

April arrived at Lespinasse at seven twenty-five. She was immediately seated in the elegant, high-ceilinged, gilded column room. She leaned back in her comfortable, oversized chair and began to relax. Three or four times a year she dined here – usually with a client to be impressed. Bob and Nicole were two of her favorite people. The closest she had to family. She relished being able to spend a couple of hours in Bob's company tonight.

Moments later Bob was being escorted to their table. There was something reassuring, she thought affectionately, about his small, compact frame, his penetrating brown eyes, his warm smile.

'Nicole always says you're the one woman she knows who'll always be on time,' he said, bending to kiss her. He chuckled. 'Something Nicole has never learned to do.'

'It's good to see you.' April glowed. Nicole and Bob had been the sole fixtures in her life since the beginning of law school. During the years with Greg she'd lived in New York, San Francisco, Dallas, and Atlanta. Throughout the moves she'd kept in touch with Nicole and Bob. Since moving back to New York after the divorce, she'd been too involved with career to have time to collect friends. And on the job she'd made a point of avoiding personal relationships.

'It's ridiculous that we get together so seldom,' Bob chided. 'You're the kids' godmother – and they've seen so little of you.'

They made a production of ordering – both aware that

dinner would be a culinary masterpiece. Both appreciative of the wide spacing between tables, which provided a pleasing privacy. Yet while they had bantered about choices as they ordered, April was conscious of an undercurrent of tension in Bob. Was he having problems? she worried.

'Still working those crazy hours?' Bob asked again as their impeccable waiter left their table. 'I suspect tonight's an aberration.'

April's face tightened. Tonight she'd hoped to forget about the office. 'The same,' she conceded.

'Something's come up.' He leaned forward with an air of urgency. 'You know about the great old guy who took me as his partner three years out of law school.'

'He's a darling,' she recalled. 'I met him twice. So bright, so devoted to his clients.' Her smile was wry. 'He's an aberration.' Like her father had been – before her mother died.

'As I mentioned, he's about to retire. He's close to eighty-three and ailing. Oh, he'll be around as a consultant. But I need a partner, April. Sure, Nicole puts in a few hours a week – but she's busy with the kids. She wants to be there when they come home from school, to be there when they're down with a cold. I need a full-time partner.' His eyes probed hers. 'Come in with me. Escape the rat race. We'll have the kind of practice we used to talk about late into the night back in law school. Not a lot of big-time corporate cases.' He chuckled. 'There're no big corporations in town. It's a varied practice – civil and criminal. Not that we have much crime in town. You know, it's a typical small town. There hasn't been a murder in six years – and that was a domestic violence case. April, in a town like Magnolia we make a difference. There's a great community spirit. When something's not working out well, people strive together to make improvements. We lost a major employer when Taylor Shirt and Jeans moved overseas – and left a falling-down factory and a huge unpaid tax bill.'

'You told me.' April smiled in sympathy.

'The Town Council is fighting to bring in new business. We've got young people – kids still in their twenties – who want to stay in Magnolia. They're bright and ambitious and determined to make a difference.'

Back in law school they'd been so earnest, so eager to 'make a difference,' April remembered. But the difference Greg had wanted was in his lifestyle. And after a while she'd told herself – remembering her rotten, growing-up years – that was the major goal in her life.

'Bob, I don't know . . .' She was startled. She'd never considered this. She hated working for the firm, yes – but practice in some small town? What was the population? Fourteen thousand, Bob said once. How would she fit into that scene?

'Yeah, I know – you won't earn anywhere near what you see now. No fancy year-end bonuses. But you'll have a life, April.'

'I've never thought about such a change.' She searched for words. 'I'm spoiled, I suppose. I don't know that I could survive in a small town.'

'So you live in a great city,' he challenged. 'How much time do you have to enjoy it? When was the last time you spent an afternoon at a museum? How many times do you go to the theater or the ballet?' He remembered her love of these in earlier years.

'I'm lucky to catch a figure skating event on TV,' she admitted. In the past ten years she'd become fascinated by the best of figure skating. There were skaters who were poetry on ice. 'The working hours are grueling.'

'You can watch all the figure skating you want up in Magnolia. We're fifty minutes from Saratoga – in the summer you'll be able to drive over for their ballet and theater and concerts. You'll have time to catch the really good movies. And—'

'Bob, I don't know,' she interrupted. Her heart pounding. Was she ready for such a drastic change? Where would it take her?

'It's a perfect time to sell your condo,' he reminded. 'Prices are soaring beyond what anybody thought possible. You'll make a killing.'

'Let me think about it,' she hedged.

Scott Emerson sat in his car in the parking area of the Magnolia town hall. One foot tapped impatiently as he checked his watch. Okay, another couple minutes and he could go in to present his deal to the Town Council. Ned Jenkins said, 'Come in at ten to eight – by then we'll be ready to hear your deal.' It was a mid-week evening – the meeting would begin at seven-thirty.

The weather was raw for the 1st of November, he thought as he stepped from the car into the night air. He hurried the short distance to the town hall. Lights glowed in the conference room where Town Council meetings were held.

Why in hell did David – his own father-in-law – refuse to come out and support him for a run on the council in the elections next spring? Wasn't a son-in-law more important than one of his reporters? But he knew the answer to that, he told himself grimly. David resented Beth's marrying him. David wouldn't think any man good enough for his only child.

I could have had my pick of women in this town – but right off I knew Beth was the one I wanted. Why won't Beth try to convince her old man to back me instead of Jamie Lawrence? Does she still have a thing for Jamie?

At the conference room door he knocked, waited.

'Come in.' Ned Jenkins' voice.

Scott walked inside, flashed the charismatic smile that had won him many friends in town. His eyes opaque for an instant as they grazed Jamie Lawrence. If he put this deal across with the Town Council, he'd be the town's fair-haired boy. Would it be enough to swing votes in a battle with Jamie for that seat on the council?

'Thanks for having me.' A deferential note in his voice

now. Except for Jamie, the council members were twice his age. 'I won't take up much of your time.'

He launched immediately into the possible deal he'd dug up. They were lapping it up, he told himself. Except for Jenkins, who had to throw his weight around. 'Kensington Womenswear can bring about seven hundred jobs into town. Permanent jobs,' he emphasized, 'if we can work something out. First, they're willing to buy the old Taylor factory. They're offering what I think is a fair price . . .' He paused, mentioned what he'd been told to offer.

'That's damn low,' one council member objected.

'They've seen the factory,' Scott pointed out. 'They know that heavy repairs will be necessary before the building can be used. They'll need to build an extension that will almost double the floor space – but they're willing to make that investment.' He paused. 'They're asking the usual perks. A twenty-year local tax abatement, plus a drop on the property taxes.'

'They're going to double the premises but expect a drop in the property taxes?' Jamie was derisive. 'That's a giveaway.'

Scott forced back a nasty retort. 'They'll bring in seven hundred jobs – full-time permanent jobs. And that could increase in time.'

'Why do they want to come here?' Jamie challenged. 'Aren't they somewhere out in the Midwest?'

'Texas. They weren't interested at first – I had to do a hard sell. I pointed out that with the whole country in a tight labor situation we could provide them with all the employees they'd need. I played it honest. I admitted we'd lost some large businesses. We had people anxious for jobs.' He paused, anticipating Jamie's next question. 'I explained that we lost companies that had been badly managed. Two had gone into bankruptcy – the others had internal problems at a top level. They figure that if we give them what they're asking for, they'll be in fine shape here.'

'We'll have to think about it,' Ned hedged. But Scott saw

avid interest in the eyes of several council members. *Damn, the town's starving for new jobs – and I'm throwing it in their laps.* 'We'll have a decision by our next meeting.'

But their next meeting wasn't until the beginning of the new year, Scott thought in exasperation. The whole deal could go sour by then.

At their table at Lespinasse Bob redirected the conversation. 'I gather you still don't ever hear from Greg.'

'No.' Her voice faintly sharp. 'And for that I'm grateful.'

'I just heard from him – the first time in three years.' He grinned. 'Yeah, he wanted something. He's about to run for the state legislature out there. He wanted a comment – favorable, natch – from a friend of law school days. I forced myself,' he said chuckling.

'He'll probably be elected.' Her smile was cynical.

Their first course arrived. They focused on eating. Always a magnificent experience here, April thought – willing herself to brush aside Bob's impassioned plea to join him in practice. This was one of those rare oases when she blotted out everything but the pleasure of dining in a lovely room that seemed to belong to an earlier, less prosaic era.

Conscious that tomorrow was a business day and Bob would have an early appointment, April insisted they call it a night shortly before ten p.m. She promised to think about his offer. Bob kissed her goodnight and put her in a cab.

In the cab April's mind turned to Greg. She'd lived with him for seven years, but it was rare that she thought about him. Their marriage had been a colossal mistake.

Still, it angered her that he'd been insistent that they have no children. Now he was remarried and the father of two.

'Children get in the way – they make such demands,' he'd argued. 'We'll want to travel – with kids that becomes a chore.'

She'd wanted desperately to have another child. But eventually she'd convinced herself she didn't deserve that.

She'd never even allowed herself to have a dog or a cat – though she adored almost everything on four feet. After the divorce she'd avoided any romantic entanglements, focused on career – trying to ignore the void in her life.

Pro bono work had been her escape – but now The Big Wheel insisted the firm had no time for pro bono cases. Dad had been famous for his pro bono work back home – in a small town probably like Magnolia, New York. He would have been proud of her involvement in those cases.

The cab pulled up before her building. As usual – because she considered driving a cab a painful occupation – she overtipped. With a friendly 'good evening' to the doorman on duty, she went up to her apartment, unlocked the customary double locks that Manhattan living demanded.

She felt oddly at loose ends. It was so rare to have time on her hands with no demands. She'd made a point of not bringing home work from the office – a rebellion against The Big Wheel. She glanced at the antique clock on the fireplace mantel. It was barely ten p.m.

She debated about starting a blaze in the fireplace grate – an occasional treat she allowed herself. She was proud of having a working fireplace – a rarity in Manhattan condos. No, she decided – a fire meant lounging before a blaze in delicious serenity. She felt far from serene this evening.

She tried to focus on television. Nothing held her attention. She flipped off the TV, made herself a cup of decaf coffee, sat down to drink it. Bob's plea kept darting across her mind. He'd said, 'You'll have a life.'

The next time she glanced at the mantel clock – bought on a brief trip to Switzerland with Greg, months before their break-up – it was almost midnight. She wavered. Was it too late to call Bob? He wouldn't mind if she awoke him – not when she wanted to say that yes, she was willing to join him in his law practice.

Her resignation elicited rage from The Big Wheel.

'After all we've done for you,' he reproached, 'you're leaving?' It wasn't her work that he'd miss, she told herself with brutal candor. He'd miss his eye-undressing sessions.

'I want a slower lifestyle,' she said. 'I'll find that in a small-town practice.'

'You mean you want to vegetate,' he said contemptuously. 'Don't expect us to take you back when you're dying of boredom.'

She agreed to remain for another two weeks – more than ample time to transfer her cases to a replacement. Still, she was startled to discover her replacement was a stunning blonde fresh out of law school – but the replacement, addicted to thigh-high skirts and low necklines, was more decoration for the firm than a legal star.

To her astonishment her condo was sold within a week – at $20,000 above the asking price. Bob was right – she was selling at a peak period. Even with the mortgage paid off, she'd had a substantial nest egg. At the price of houses in Magnolia, she suspected, she could buy a small house for cash. But first, she told herself with customary caution, rent an apartment. Make sure this move was to be permanent.

The day she signed the contract on the condo, Bob phoned in gleeful pleasure. 'You know we have only two garden apartment developments in town,' he reported. 'There's a first-floor two-bedroom available immediately.' He knew she would want a home office. 'Shouldn't you run up and have a look?'

'I'll take it,' she told him. She trusted Bob's judgement. 'Can you arrange the lease for me? I'll fax whatever information the owners request.'

Within twenty-four hours she had an apartment. The purchaser of her apartment was pleading for an early closing. She agreed, contacted a moving company, arranged for them to pack for her the day before the closing. She would spend her last evening in Manhattan at a hotel.

Now she focused on packing personal items. She'd stopped

being a pack rat years ago. She clung – admittedly sentimental – to a few things: a photograph album with snapshots of her parents and herself, the hospital bracelets when the baby was born, the Polaroid photo of the baby taken by her maternity ward roommate.

On the morning of the closing she awoke in her hotel room with the sense of embarking on a new adventure. Tonight she would sleep in the guest bedroom at Bob and Nicole's house in Magnolia. She arose, prepared for the day. The closing was scheduled for ten a.m. in her attorney's office. With luck she'd be at the wheel of her Mercedes by one p.m. and en route to her new life.

As she anticipated, the closing was uneventful. On schedule she picked up her car at the garage and headed for the highway. Was this a smart move – or a ghastly mistake?

All at once she was flooded with apprehension. November was always a rotten month for her. Had it been a mistake to make such a drastic change in her lifestyle in a month when her mind was always besieged with remorse?

Chapter Three

Settling herself in the guest room of Bob and Nicole's modest but cozy ranch house, April felt gratitude for such warm friends. They'd insisted that she stay with them this first night in town. Nicole had been at the apartment to receive her movers yesterday afternoon, had checked to make sure that each item was placed in the proper room.

'April . . .' Nicole hovered in the doorway of the guest room. 'I have to run over to pick up the kids from their after-school groups. I've put on fresh coffee – it'll be ready in a couple of minutes.'

'Oh, that'll be great. And I can't wait to see Marianne and Neil.'

She was curled up on a corner of the living-room sofa with a mug of coffee when she heard a car pull up in the driveway. Moments later she heard Bob in conversation with another man. It was barely five thirty p.m. Bob was right, she told herself in approval – he lived at a far more leisurely pace than she.

She glanced up with a smile when Bob strolled into the house in the company of a man perhaps five or six years their senior. His hair lightly streaked with gray, his blue eyes radiating warmth. Why did gray hair lend an air of distinction to a man – and did little for a woman?

'The closing was on schedule,' Bob guessed. 'Nicole told you, I assume – your furniture arrived late yesterday afternoon.'

'Right.' April was aware that his companion was awaiting an introduction.

'Oh, this is David Roberts,' Bob introduced. 'April Winston, my new law partner.' He turned to April. 'David is the publisher of the *Sentinel* – our local newspaper. Fourth generation Magnolia,' he teased good-humoredly. 'Not a newcomer like Nicole and me.' Bob and Nicole had lived here a dozen years – newcomers by local standards.

'Welcome to our town.' David Roberts radiated friendliness. 'It's been through a bad period – despite the great economy in the country – but it's coming out of it.'

'That was a terrific editorial in the Sunday paper about how the Town Council is working to attract new industry,' Bob told David.

'The *Ledger* wasn't happy.' David's smile was wry. 'They berated the hell out of the Town Council for thinking about offering tax abatements to a major company that would set up in town.'

'To the devil with them.' Bob dismissed this with a shrug. 'Most people in town wouldn't use that rag to take out their garbage.'

'The council's been cagey, though, about what's happening. I know Jamie feels awfully frustrated.' David's eyes were quizzical. 'What's happening, Bob? You're their attorney.'

'I'm their attorney,' Bob chuckled, 'because I don't bill the town. They're uptight about the deal Scott's been dangling before their eyes – because he can't give them a name until they agree to terms. And Jamie's breaking his back with some dot-com group that's after major venture capital – and they'd want the same premises. He says the dot-com people realize what a terrific savings they'll have on rent – and they can operate anywhere in the country. And they're not asking for tax abatements.'

'They'll rent?' David's eyebrows shot upwards. 'No property tax to come in . . .'

'They'll pay rent to the township – plus they're willing

to make the capital improvements they'll need. They figure in New York City they'll pay at least forty dollars a square foot for space. Jamie's talking to them about a seven dollars a square foot rental. Once they get their financing set – and that appears to be about to happen – they'll be great for the town.'

'A dot-com company will offer well-paying jobs,' April pointed out. 'They'll need skilled employees. With a factory it'll be little above minimum.'

Bob's face lighted at the sound of a car pulling into the driveway. 'That'll be Nicole with the kids. Stay for dinner, David,' he ordered. 'You know Nicole – she always cooks enough for an army battalion.'

'Not on such short notice,' David demurred, yet April suspected he'd like to stay.

The children charged into the house, rushed to welcome April. She saw so little of them, yet they always seemed so pleased to see her, she thought with pleasure.

'You're staying for dinner,' Nicole told David – her voice saying she'd reject any refusal. 'How's Debbie?' She turned to April. 'David has the most adorable granddaughter. How old is she now? Four months?'

'Five months,' he said tenderly. 'All she has to do is smile at me, and I'm her abject slave.'

Over dinner April learned that David's wife had died six years ago of ovarian cancer, that they had this one daughter – Beth. Her husband was with the local radio station.

'Scott is so good-looking,' Nicole told April. 'He and Beth make such a wonderful-looking couple. When he moved into town, every single girl – pardon me,' she drawled, 'every single woman was after him. But they didn't have a chance once he met Beth.'

'Scott does double duty,' David explained to April. 'He's a station announcer plus time salesman.' Yet April suspected he felt some reservations about his son-in-law of less than two years.

After dinner Bob took David to his basement office to discuss a legal matter. April settled with Nicole and the two children in the living room.

'One hour of TV,' Nicole decreed. 'Then homework time.'

By eleven p.m. April was in bed. The day had been exhausting, she conceded. Not physically – mentally. But she felt good about being here, she analyzed. She would enjoy living in a quiet, serene town like Magnolia.

In the bedroom of her charming colonial cape, Beth Emerson stirred into reluctant wakefulness at the sound of a car pulling into her driveway. Her head ached. She felt queasy. She forced her eyes open, glanced at the clock on the night table. She'd slept late – but Debbie had slept through, too.

She hadn't expected Scott home for at least another two hours, she thought, her mind hazy. He'd gone to a neighboring town last night to speak at a Chamber of Commerce meeting. He was sleeping over.

'Debbie?' She heard him in the adjoining nursery now. 'Debbie!' Alarm in his voice now. 'Oh, my God! Beth!' he yelled. 'Call for an ambulance!'

White and trembling – fully awake now – she reached for the phone on the night table, dialed 911.

'Send an ambulance to 921 Spruce Lane,' she gasped. 'Something's happened to our baby!'

She slammed down the phone, charged into the nursery. Scott leaned over Debbie in her crib – trying to breathe life into his tiny daughter. Beth watched, too terrified to ask questions. At last Scott straightened up in anguish.

'Scott, what's happened to Debbie?' Her eyes searched his as he turned to her. Seeming incapable of speech. 'Scott, what's happened?'

'She was on her stomach. Not breathing . . .' His voice was labored. 'Is this what they call SIDS?'

Beth stared at him in disbelief. 'She's alive!' She reached

to pull the tiny, inert form into her arms. 'Scott, she has to be alive!'

'She's gone,' he said in bewilderment, pulling Beth away from the crib. 'Why was she on her stomach?' A reluctant accusation in his voice. 'You know we never put her to bed on her stomach!'

'I didn't—' She gazed at Scott in disbelief. 'You know I never do that.'

They heard the sound of an ambulance shrieking close by. Scott rushed from the room, down the hall to open the door to admit the ambulance crew. A pair of medics leapt from their seats as the ambulance screeched to a stop, raced into the house.

Beth and Scott hovered beside the two medics – willing themselves to believe Debbie could be revived.

His eyes dark with compassion, one of the medics told them Debbie was dead.

'There's nothing we can do,' he said gently.

'Call the police,' the other medic ordered, terse and accusing. 'This isn't a case of SIDS. This is murder. Look at those marks on her throat,' he told his partner. 'She was strangled. Call the police.'

Chapter Four

In robe and slippers, Beth sat huddled at a corner of the living room sofa – vaguely conscious of the activity around her. Alarmed by her emotional state, Scott had summoned their family physician – a nearby neighbor – to administer a sedative.

A pair of detectives were shooting questions at Scott. Three others were involved in other activities relating to a homicide case. In a corner of her mind Beth realized her father had arrived.

'No,' she heard Scott reply in strained patience to one of the detectives. 'There was no break-in. I've told you that. I came home, unlocked the door, walked into the house.' All at once his voice broke. 'I went into the nursery to see my baby – the way I always do when I've been away overnight – and I saw her . . .' His voice trailed off in anguished recall.

'Who has keys to the house?' a detective asked.

'Just my wife and I.' Scott sounded bewildered.

'No sign of forced entry,' the other detective said, his tone almost casual. 'It was a cold night – all the windows were closed. And locked,' he emphasized.

'Any lock with a keyhole can be picked by an expert,' Beth heard her father point out. *Why does he sound so strange?*

'It would be helpful if we could question Mrs Emerson,' a detective said.

'She's in no condition to answer questions,' Scott reproached. 'Not yet . . .'

'What time did you arrive home?' the other detective asked.

'I told you.' Scott sounded annoyed. 'It was about eight thirty a.m.'

'And your wife was still asleep?' A note of surprise in the detective's voice. 'Not many young mothers get that chance.'

'Scott, help Beth into the bedroom,' she heard her father order. 'Later she can be questioned.'

'This is crazy, Frank,' David accused the older of the two detectives, whom he'd known since the early days of the newspaper. 'You're building a case against Beth!' No point in beating around the bush, instinct told him. Bring this out into the open.

'David, it sounds bad.' Frank Lorenzo was uncomfortable. 'I figure she didn't do it . . .' He paused in apology at David's grunt of rage. 'But the district attorney has to look at the facts. It's his job. She was alone in the house. No sign of forced entry.' He paused again, stared at the floor. 'I think you should line up a good lawyer for Beth.'

'Damn it, Frank, you know as well as I that an expert could easily pick both door locks.' *Why does he look so nervous? What does he know that he hasn't told me?*

'We may have to bring her downtown.' Frank was unhappy. 'It's the way the law works.' But for now they were leaving Beth here under what was unspoken house arrest, David interpreted.

The two detectives left, leaving behind three others still searching for evidence. Of an intruder they didn't believe could get into the house? David taunted himself. Moments later – as though awaiting the departure of the two detectives – Scott emerged from the master bedroom.

'She's sleeping,' Scott reported and dropped into a chair. 'Damn their hides! Lorenzo and his pal,' he said with contempt as David lifted his eyebrows in question. 'They tricked me, the bastards!'

David stiffened in alertness. 'Meaning what?'

'Lorenzo made some casual remark about checking the garbage can in the kitchen. Automatically – without thinking – I told them it was empty.' He tensed in anguish. 'But it wasn't. There was a pair of rubber gloves there. They're sure to have Beth's fingerprints on them. She probably did some last-minute cleaning. You know, she was alone in the house, nothing she wanted to watch on TV . . .'

David felt a wave of coldness sweep over him. He knew what the police would think. That Beth used the gloves to avoid leaving fingerprints on Debbie's throat. How could anybody believe Beth killed Debbie?

Frank was right. He should line up a lawyer for Beth. Call Bob, he ordered himself with sudden urgency. Call him right now.

'So what do you think?' Bob asked April with a broad grin. 'Does your office meet with your approval?'

'It's great,' April conceded. Winter sunlight poured into the large, square, high-ceilinged room. Bob's retiring partner lived on the second floor of the small colonial – the lower floor years ago converted into a suite of offices. 'I feel as though I've died and gone to heaven.'

'The old boy was horrified when we suggested redecorating a couple of years after I joined him in practice – but he adores Nicole, so we got away with it. She haunted every antique shop in the country before she was done.' He gazed with pride about the room – where only the large executive desk reflected beyond the nineteenth century.

A phone rang. A moment later Sandy – the secretary who had been with the firm almost as long as Bob – called out to him to pick up.

'It's David Roberts,' Sandy trilled. The pleasant newspaper publisher she'd met last evening, April recalled.

'Okay,' Bob called back and picked up the receiver. 'Hi, David.' Almost immediately Bob seemed shaken. 'My God, how did it happen?' His face drained of color as he listened. 'No! Nobody will ever believe Beth is involved! It's routine,' he soothed. 'The parents are always the first suspects – it doesn't mean anything.'

Something terrible had happened to David's granddaughter, April realized with shock. At dinner last evening he'd talked about his daughter and her baby with such love, and now that baby was dead. In this quiet town that hadn't seen a murder in six years, Bob had boasted. Without knowing David's daughter and son-in-law she felt their anguish.

'I'll be over in a few minutes,' Bob told David. 'It's awful about Debbie. What monster's roaming around this town? It's damn scary.' He paused a moment. 'David, cool it. There's no way Beth and Scott can be involved.' He glanced at April for a moment. 'Is it all right if I bring April with me? I'm sure she'll be helpful.' He listened to the voice at the other end. 'Yeah, we'll be right there.'

'What happened?' April asked fearfully as Bob put down the phone.

'Debbie was murdered.' Bob was ashen.

'When?' April asked after a stunned moment.

'Apparently in the course of the night. David's daughter and his grandbaby are the center of his world. I can't believe this!'

Driving to the house on Spruce Lane, Bob told April what David had said on the phone.

'He's terribly upset about the baby, of course – and he's shaken that the police are focusing on Beth as a suspect. Anyhow, we're her legal team now.'

'Does he think she'll be arraigned?'

'He's scared,' Bob conceded. 'David's one of the nicest guys in this world – always trying to do something good for somebody. Like his young managing editor – and prize reporter – Jamie Lawrence. Jamie's only 26, but he's on the

Town Council now – to a large extent because David put the newspaper behind him.' Bob smiled wryly. 'I know he was hoping Jamie would be his son-in-law one day. Of course, Scott charged into town, and he and Beth had a whirlwind courtship. Practically every girl in town – pardon me,' he drawled, reiterating Nicole, 'practically every young woman was out to catch Scott. But he chased after Beth. When Debbie arrived, they seemed the perfect family.' His hands tightened on the wheel. 'And now this horror.'

'Bob, did David go to law school? Or teach there?' April asked.

'He has a degree in journalism. Why do you ask?'

'I kept thinking last evening that I'd met him somewhere.'

'David does that to people. He's so warm and interested in everybody that people have a feeling they've met him along the line somewhere. God, I know how he's hurting now!'

Bob pulled up behind a pair of squad cars. A police officer was setting up crime scene yellow tape around the house. Bob and April left the car, approached the weathered-shingle colonial cape that sat on a modest plot.

The police officer greeted Bob with a smile.

'How're you doing?'

'Shook up,' Bob admitted. 'I can't believe what's happened.'

'Some nut case on the loose,' the police officer said with distaste. 'Nobody with kids will feel safe until that creep is caught.' He hesitated. 'You're here on official business?'

'David brought us in on the case. Oh, Jerry, this is April Winston, my new partner.'

The police officer grinned. 'Sure is lots prettier than the other one.'

Bob and April walked to the front door, rang the bell. Chimes tinkled within. Moments later the door opened. David rushed towards them with an air of relief, led them into the living room. A very handsome, distraught young man – the father of the murdered baby, April assumed – was in strained conversation with a pair of detectives. Even in these circumstances April noted his deep, charming voice and remembered he was a radio announcer.

'Beth's under sedation,' David told April and Bob. 'She can't be questioned until later,' he added with an air of apprehension. 'But I don't like the way the questioning is going.' He prodded them into the privacy of the den.

'It's probably routine questioning.' April tried to sound matter-of-fact. But in any case she handled where a child was involved, she became emotionally involved. Bad for an attorney, she always cautioned herself.

'They keep stressing that there was no forced entry – and I keep reminding them that the lock could have been picked.' He paused, took a deep breath. 'They don't expect to find fingerprints on Debbie's throat. She was strangled,' David explained in pain. 'And they found a pair of rubber gloves in the garbage. Kitchen gloves that are sure to have Beth's fingerprints on them.'

'There's nothing incriminating in that,' April soothed. 'Rubber gloves are standard kitchen equipment.'

'Nothing was in the garbage pail except the gloves,' David emphasized uneasily. 'The detectives were playing a game with Scott. They casually mentioned that it might be wise to check the garbage – but you know damn well they'd already done that. He told them he always empties the garbage before going to bed. But last evening he was speaking at a Chamber of Commerce meeting in a neighboring town. He and Beth had an early dinner. He emptied the garbage pail before he left. They want to know why Beth threw those gloves into the pail. They're like new.' David's eyes were tormented as they met first Bob's, then April's. 'It's a matter of time before they take Beth down for questioning.'

April understood he couldn't bring himself to say, *It's a matter of time before she's charged with murder.*

Chapter Five

Settling herself in the car beside Bob, April cautioned herself not to become emotionally involved in this first case as his partner. She knew that he, too, was struggling to deal with this shattering situation.

'In another few hours this whole town is going to be in shock. Everybody knows David and Beth. Nobody will believe Beth could be guilty of killing Debbie.'

'The district attorney doesn't have much of a case,' April said with involuntary defiance. But the vibes were bad.

If she hadn't met David Roberts last evening on a personal level, hadn't found him such a warm, compassionate man, she could be clear-headed, objective about how to handle this case. Little doubt in her mind that Beth – whom she was yet to meet – would be taken into custody, arraigned, and held for a grand jury trial.

'You'll want to have a look at your apartment,' Bob surmised, puncturing her introspection. 'But you'll stay with us for the next three or four days. And don't give me a hard time.' He tried for a light tone, but she knew part of him was back with David.

'I'm eager to see it,' she admitted and sighed. 'I'll have to start the madness of unpacking, settling in a routine.'

'You'll move in when it's liveable,' he said. 'Not a moment before. Nicole and I insist you stay with us until then. I'll leave you at the apartment. Your phone's connected. Call Nicole to pick you up when you've had enough of staring at all those cartons.'

'It's a few minutes' walk – I won't need a lift.' She hesitated, remembering the Mercedes parked in the garage beside Nicole's eight-year-old Dodge Spirit. 'Maybe I ought to sell my car, pick up something less ostentatious.'

'Keep it.' Bob grinned. 'Gives the firm a special touch to see one of the partners driving a Mercedes.' He took a deep breath, exhaled. 'This town is going to be in an uproar when the word circulates about the murder. Nothing like this has happened in years. And Beth and Scott are both very well liked around here.'

'Considering the likelihood of her being taken into custody, we ought to get a head start.' April stared into space. Her mind charging ahead. 'Tell me about her.'

'Beth has a degree in education. She was teaching high school English as a sub – waiting for a full-time opening – when she got pregnant. She figured on going back to teaching once Debbie was in school full-time.'

But Debbie would never be in school full-time. How awful for her parents. How awful for David. 'The police have a terribly weak case.' April brought herself back to the moment. 'I'm not even sure it's enough to have her go to the grand jury.' But both she and Bob knew that was grandstanding. 'The rubber gloves mean nothing. Beth was restless – she decided to do some spur-of-the-moment cleaning. The gloves leaked. She threw them away.'

'Maybe they leaked.'

April was startled. 'You don't for a moment believe she killed her own baby?'

'No way do I believe Beth is guilty – and that has nothing to do with the fact that David is one of my closest friends. But let's face it. We're going to have to prove that Beth is innocent.' He managed a lopsided smile. 'And don't give me that crap about being innocent until proven guilty.'

Bob swung off the road before an attractively landscaped garden apartments development.

'The garages are at the back. Nicole gave you the key, didn't she, along with the apartment key?'

'Yes, I have both.' The apartment would be far more modest than the one she'd left behind in Manhattan, she understood. But then the rent was less than one-third of what she'd paid in maintenance back in New York.

'Nicole said everything was placed as you instructed the movers. But it'll be a pain in the ass to unpack.' He grimaced as he considered this. Maybe I can rustle up a handyman to help.'

'I can handle it,' she insisted.

She needed that activity. Walking into a murder case like this – knowing Beth Emerson's pain – had thrust her back into her own grief at giving up her baby. *But I sent my baby on to a far better life than I could have provided. I did the right thing – didn't I?*

At agonizing intervals she'd ask herself how her baby had fared through the years. Had she gone to college? Did she have a boyfriend? Does she have children?

Am I a grandmother? But that's something I'll never know.

Alone in the apartment April moved from room to room. She'd lived in much worse, she reminded herself. In truth, the apartment was pleasant – though small compared to what she'd known these past few years. All right, she told herself – start opening cartons.

She reached into her purse for the box cutter placed there in preparation for this task. In that other life – as a highly paid attorney – she would have summoned a workman to handle this. But now she was a partner in a very small firm. Bob had made it clear – she'd be taking a tremendous drop in salary. Do her own unpacking.

As she worked, she found her mind focusing on the murder of David Roberts' tiny granddaughter. So young to die – and so brutally. Who had gained access to the house, crept into the nursery, and strangled Debbie Emerson?

The father spent the night in a town eighty miles away. He was in the clear. She worried about the pair of rubber gloves found in the kitchen garbage pail. The prosecutor would assume the gloves were used to avoid fingerprints. What other evidence would surface in the days ahead?

What kind of life had her baby had? she asked herself in fresh torment. Was she alive? A coldness shot through her as she considered this. So many unanswered questions. She'd spend the rest of her life in a kind of hell because she couldn't know. Since the day she gave up her child, she'd known no real peace.

Was the apartment awfully hot – or was it just that she was overheated from unpacking? She crossed to a window, opened it, breathed in relief as cold air assaulted her. She glanced about the bedroom. Almost human now, she thought with a flicker of approval. She'd filled the dresser drawers, hung away her expensive suits and dresses that belonged to that other life.

Lining up shoes and purses, she asked herself how she had accumulated so many. But the answer leapt into her mind. When she was uptight – and that was often – she became an obsessive shopper – as though buying clothes would make her feel better.

Early in the afternoon – with no pressing demands at the office, Bob returned to the Emerson house to talk with David about the course they must pursue. When David received an emergency call from his office, Bob left with him.

'I never thought we'd be running a story in my newspaper about my granddaughter's murder,' David said in anguish. 'We have to run the story, of course.'

'I'll talk with you later,' Bob said gently.

He walked to his car, hesitated. Why wait until tomorrow to start their probing? Talk to the neighbors today. Ask questions. Did they see a stranger – or strangers – hanging around?

He left the car, went to the house to the right of the Emersons, rang the bell and waited for a response. This wasn't just any murder case – David and his daughter were like family.

He heard footsteps in the foyer. People must have seen the squad cars, the yellow tape – they had to know something unpleasant had occurred.

The door swung open. A tall, spare, sixty-ish woman appeared.

'Yes?' She was wary – as though expecting a door-to-door salesman, Bob pinpointed.

'Please forgive this intrusion,' he apologized. 'I'm Bob Allen.'

'The lawyer?' Avid interest in her eyes now.

'That's right. You probably noticed the police activity,' he began.

'Was it a burglary?' she asked solicitously. 'I didn't think it would be right to go over and ask – but we noticed. My husband said to keep my nose out of it. Beth would tell me when she was ready. But I don't ever remember a break-in around here. Still Scott's away a lot – and Beth's alone in that house with the baby.'

'It wasn't a burglary,' Bob said, his face somber. 'I'm sorry to deliver such terrible news. The Emerson baby was murdered in the course of the night.'

'Oh, my God! That darling little baby? Oh, I can't believe it!'

'I'm representing the family,' Bob explained. 'Could we talk?'

'Come right in.' She gestured him into the tiny foyer and led him into a pseudo-Victorian living room. 'Just sit yourself down while I get us coffee. You've given me such a shock!'

Bob waited for Beth's neighbor – from the tiny sign on the lawn he gathered this was Mrs Comstock – to return. She returned in moments with a tray.

'I always keep coffee on hand. It's seen me through some real shockers – but this!' She shook her head in dismay.

'Did you notice any stranger around the area yesterday evening?' Bob asked, accepting a cup of coffee.

'Did I make it too light?' She asked. 'I'm so used to doing that for my husband. And you'll want sugar?'

'It's fine – and no sugar, thank you. Did you notice anybody unfamiliar yesterday evening?' he repeated.

'We were in the house all evening. We wouldn't know about what was happening outside.' She hesitated, seeming in debate. 'But I knew Beth was under some stress. She's always been so sunny and warm – but I suppose you could say she seemed almost distraught much of the time of late. Of course, with a young baby – especially a first one – there's a lot that's stressful.'

'Yeah, I have two kids.' Bob smiled in recall. 'I remember.'

'And then there were all the fights with Scott. Even with the windows closed, we could hear the arguing. They've been battling for weeks. Such a nice couple. I can't imagine what they'd have to fight about. But that wouldn't have anything to do with—' She paused, flinched. 'That wouldn't have anything to do with the murder.'

'No. All young couples fight now and then.' But Mrs Comstock said they'd been battling for weeks. Just the usual 'young marrieds' fights – or something more serious?

'I wish I could help you – but I can't think of a thing. I just hope the police catch that fiend fast. Nobody in this town will feel comfortable until he's behind bars.' She paused. 'Now wasn't that a sexist thing for me to say? I mean, until he or she is behind bars.'

'If you remember something later, would you give me a buzz?' He reached for his card case, extended a card. 'I'm sure the police will do everything they can – but Beth's father felt a little side help might be useful.'

Bob went to the house on the other side. Nobody was

home. Okay, go to David's office. What was that crap about Beth being distraught – and fighting with Scott? For weeks.

Bob sat across from David in his office and told him what Mrs Comstock had said.

'I should have realized they were having problems,' David reproached himself. He looked exhausted, drained, Bob thought compassionately. 'Every time I saw them, they seemed so happy. But I understand – Beth was too proud to admit it. I'd tried to persuade her not to marry Scott so quickly. She'd known him three months. Scott's a charmer,' David conceded, yet Bob felt reservations in him. That figured – his only daughter marrying so quickly, giving herself so little time to get to know the man.

'Every couple has problems somewhere in those early years,' Bob soothed.

'Scott's very well liked in this town. Everybody knows him – you know, from the radio station. And he gets involved in all the volunteer deals – along with Beth. For two years running he's headed the walkathon that benefits the hospital.' David was struggling to be fair, Bob sympathized. 'He walks three to four miles every day – just to keep trim.' David paused. 'He's very ambitious.'

'That's not bad,' Bob said gently. Would David be suspicious of any man Beth married?

'I know Scott's upset because I wouldn't consider having the newspaper support him for a seat on the Town Council. Jamie Lawrence is doing a great job in his first term. How could I oppose Jamie, even for my son-in-law?'

'I don't think we need to worry too much about what Mrs Comstock said to me this morning,' Bob began, 'though—'

'I can't go to her and tell her not to repeat that to anybody from the DA's office.' David was unfamiliarly brusque. 'But you know how a sharp prosecutor will turn that around.'

Chapter Six

April accepted Bob and Nicole's insistence that she remain at their house for her second night in town.

'We'll have a working session after dinner,' Bob decreed. 'David will be here. We have to focus on the probability of Beth's being taken into custody.' He sighed. 'We have to be realistic, plot our course.'

April was still amazed at leaving the office behind at five thirty. This was part of what Bob meant when he said, 'You'll have a life.' They'd been home only a few minutes when Nicole arrived with Marianne and Neil. The children knew about Debbie, April guessed. They were so solemn. Shaken.

'The whole town's in shock,' Nicole reported. 'That's all everybody's talking about – and they're scared. Some monster is out there on the loose – and nobody knows if – or when – he'll strike again.'

'Mommie, can I have the night light on when I go to bed?' Marianne asked.

'Of course, darling. But I was just being overly dramatic,' she apologized, exchanging a nervous glance with Bob. 'Nothing's going to happen to us. And soon whoever did this terrible thing will be caught.'

'Hey, you two . . .' Bob turned to Marianne and Neil. 'Go to the den and start doing your homework. Then you can have an extra hour of TV tonight.'

'Okay.' Marianne showed little enthusiasm. 'Come on, Neil. Let's hit the books.'

'I'll start dinner,' Nicole decided. 'David should be here soon.'

'He knows we eat early,' Bob told April. 'No fancy dinner hours like in New York.'

April managed a chuckle. 'I've had my fill of fashionable dinner hours. Too often I had dinner around eight or nine – at my desk.' She glanced towards Nicole's parting figure. 'I'll give Nicole a hand.'

'I feel so awful for Beth and Scott,' Nicole greeted April in the kitchen. 'Scott was upset before this happened. About his brother-in-law,' Nicole explained. 'Scott's sister Elaine – she's about seven years older than he – has lived here for a dozen years. She married a local boy she met at college. He's a popular teacher at our junior high.'

'What's happened to his brother-in-law?' April reached for the salad makings Nicole extended.

'Clark's very sick – something to do with his liver. His wife Elaine is down in New York with him now at Hamilton Hospital.' A hospital specializing in cancer cases, April recalled. 'He's undergoing all kinds of tests – and it doesn't look good. Their kids are in Marianne and Neil's classes. Beth offered to take them while Elaine's down there with Clark, but Elaine thought it would be too much for Beth with the baby so young.'

Does Elaine know that Beth and Scott were having marital problems? Was that why she didn't want her children to go with Beth and Scott? 'Where are the children?'

'They're with Elaine and Clark's next-door neighbor. Scott was already distraught about Clark – and now this horror about Debbie. You know that old superstition about bad things happening in pairs? I ask myself, what's going to happen next?'

Arriving for dinner, David brought a copy of tomorrow morning's *Sentinel*. In silence he handed the newspaper to Nicole. He was trying so hard to be cool, April commiserated – but she knew the anguish that hid behind that façade.

Nicole read the headline and winced. 'Oh, David . . .'

'I never thought my paper would headline the murder of my grandchild. But then the whole world lives minutes from tragedy. We just never know when it'll strike.'

'How're Beth and Scott holding up?' April asked.

'Beth's still under sedation. Scott's furious that the police haven't come up with any leads yet.' He took a deep breath. 'He's closing his mind to their suspicions about Beth.'

'Hell, we all know that's absurd!' But Bob seemed uneasy, April thought.

'This town will be in an uproar if—' David hesitated, as though what he was about to say was an effort. 'If they even hint at suspecting Beth. And I tell you right now,' he added defiantly, 'my newspaper won't carry anything they imply in that area.'

'And eighty percent of the people in Magnolia read the *Sentinel*,' Nicole reminded.

'I've been shuttling between their house and the office since morning. I had to make arrangements for the paper to run without my presence for the next few days. Jamie's taking over,' David explained.

'I'll get dinner on the table,' Nicole said.

'I'll help.' April rose to her feet.

With the children at the dinner table the others made a concerted effort not to discuss the tragedy that dominated their thoughts. Still, April noted, Marianne and Neil were abnormally quiet at dinner. They volunteered no contribution to the conversation, spoke only when questioned.

'All right, off to the den to do your homework,' Bob ordered when dinner was over. Nicole was a wonderful cook, April thought tenderly, but nobody ate with real appreciation this evening.

Nicole insisted April retire to the living room with the two men while she cleared away the dishes, stacked the dishwasher.

'I haven't been idle,' David told the other two with a wry smile. 'I went over and talked with Jeff Goodwin.'

'The district attorney,' Bob explained to April.

'He was real uptight. His wife was Beth's sixth grade teacher. We belong to the same church. Scott worked with the two of them on the committee that raised money for the Senior Center.' David's eyes were troubled. 'He reminded me he had a job to do. He indicated he understood Beth was in no condition to be questioned right now.' His eyes searched Bob's. 'Where do we stand?'

'I don't like this, David,' Bob admitted. 'If he talks about taking Beth into custody, we'll put up a fight – argue that he doesn't have enough evidence.'

'They have very little to back this up,' April said gently. 'So there was no evidence of forced entry – but somebody besides the two of them could have a key. A workman who made repairs and never returned the key. Perhaps a cleaning woman. We'll need to talk to Scott about that.'

'Let's go over to the house to talk with Scott now,' Bob said, then hesitated. 'If he feels up to it . . .'

'I'll buzz him.' David rose to his feet – seeming relieved by the need for activity. He punched in the number, waited for a response. 'Scott, I'm here with Bob and April. They'd like to ask you some questions if you feel up to it.' He listened, nodded to the other two. 'We'll be there in a few minutes.'

They were startled to see a squad car at the curb before the house as they arrived.

'Do the bastards think Beth is about to run off somewhere?' David exploded. 'They know the state she's in.' Still, April thought, he knew this was a kind of tacit house arrest. At least they weren't taking Beth into custody. Not yet.

'It's routine here,' Bob explained. 'The police leave a man on duty before the house of a – a crime if they have the slightest suspicion that someone there might be guilty. It actually means nothing.'

Bob went to the squad car, cleared their way. In grim

silence they walked to the door. Scott pulled the door wide as they approached.

'We've got a police guard.' He glared at the parked squad car.

'Bob and April have some questions,' David told Scott again. 'Beth's asleep?'

'She's out cold. The doctor sent over a prescription for her.' Scott gestured them towards the den – comfortably distant from the master bedroom. 'I'm glad you've come over. There's something that's been bothering me.'

'Perhaps we'd better begin with that,' April suggested.

They settled themselves in the cozy, wood-paneled den. April and Bob on the sofa, David in one of a pair of club chairs. Scott paced. He seemed to be searching for words.

'This may never come out – but I think you should know everything.' He stopped pacing, leaned against the desk. 'Beth's been stressed out since Debbie was born. I talked to the doctor about it – he dismissed it as post-partum blues. But Debbie is—' He paused, flinched. 'Debbie was five months old.'

'With a first baby it's fairly normal for a mother to be stressed out,' April said gently. But was this more than normal stress? She remembered now what a next-door neighbor had told Bob: 'I knew Beth was under stress. She seemed almost distraught much of the time.'

'She was upset every time Debbie cried. She – she was screaming all the time about how – how she wasn't doing things right. I was scared. I told her she had to see a psychiatrist. I made an appointment for her.' Scott paused. 'She broke it. Damn, I should have insisted she keep it – even if I had to drag her there physically.'

'Even if she'd seen a psychiatrist,' Bob pointed out, 'that would be confidential information.'

'But suppose the police dig up the information that she had this appointment – and broke it? Suppose the psychiatrist brings it up?' He closed his eyes for a moment as though to shut out this possibility. 'Maybe—' He paused, seeming to force himself to speak. 'Maybe she could plead temporary insanity?'

Startled, April turned to David. He was ashen.

'Are you saying you believe Beth could have done this horrible thing?'

Scott spread his hands in a gesture of futility. 'She hasn't been herself for months. It's been like living with a stranger. I don't know what to think anymore.'

Suddenly the atmosphere was super-charged. 'I know my daughter.' David was grim. 'She could not have done this. No way that—'

'We have a lot of work to do,' April broke in, anxious to ease the tension building between the two men. 'Much to learn about what happened that night.' Her eyes moved to David. 'We'll check on who might have had access to the house. We'll—'

'Nobody had keys,' Scott interrupted with an air of desperation. 'I'm a nut on security. The doors and windows were locked. But like you said, David' – he turned to his father-in-law, a hint of hope showing now – 'the front door lock – or the one in the back could have been picked. I'm just so scared for Beth . . .'

'There's a strong likelihood that the matter of the broken appointment with the psychiatrist will never surface,' Bob dismissed. 'What we must do at this point is search for clues that'll lead us to whoever managed to gain access to the house.'

'You mean, the police won't be doing that.' David was terse.

'They're convinced it was Beth,' Scott blurted out. 'Right now she's under house arrest. Why else is a cop car sitting out front?'

'In these cases, Scott,' Bob said once again, 'a parent is always the first suspect. They know you were out of town. That lets you off the hook.'

'By now I'm sure they've checked this out,' April confirmed. 'The pressure is on Beth. But they have the flimsiest of cases. Still, until we come up with someone else, they'll focus on her.' David looked so tormented, she sympathized. The familiar question shot across her mind: *Why do bad things happen to good people?*

'They may decide they have enough to take to a grand jury,' Bob conceded reluctantly. 'But considering your position in this town, David, they may hesitate.' He sighed. 'We just don't know.'

'What about a cleaning woman?' April probed. 'Would she have a key?' A key that could be passed along.

'Beth just brought some woman in now and then – when she felt overwhelmed. But she was always here. There was no need to give out a key,' Scott explained.

'Were there people here in Magnolia who knew you would be away overnight?' April pursued.

Scott seemed bewildered for a moment. 'I guess so . . .'

'Work up a list for us,' Bob ordered. 'We must chase down any lead.'

'I think I'll have another talk with Jeff Goodwin,' David said. 'First thing tomorrow morning.'

But all that would accomplish, April thought, would be to delay Beth's being officially charged with murder. For all her talk about the DA's flimsy case, she feared in two or three days Beth would be taken into custody, held for arraignment. It would be the worst day of David Roberts' life.

She was doing what she always vowed never to do – becoming emotionally involved in a case.

Chapter Seven

After a conference over breakfast April and Bob went their separate ways. Bob would begin a background check on the handful of people Scott listed as having known he'd be out of town the night Debbie was murdered. April would call on other neighbors.

She drove to Spruce Lane, parked across the street from the Emerson house – conscious of the squad car on duty. Questions forming in her mind, she walked up the flagstone path to the miniature white colonial that faced the Emerson house. A cordial smile in place, she rang the doorbell.

She heard footsteps in the hall. The door swung open. A small, slender, white-haired woman, who appeared to be somewhere in her seventies, gazed inquiringly at her. A widow, Bob had told her – a woman active in community affairs.

'Good morning. I'm sorry to intrude at this early hour. I'm April Winston, in law practice now with Bob Allen, and—'

'Oh yes, I heard Bob had a new partner. I'm Celia Logan – in case you didn't know.'

'How nice to meet you, Mrs Logan. Bob and I are representing Beth and Scott Emerson. Bob suggested that I talk with you about the—'

'About the murder,' Mrs Logan picked up, her face etched with pain. 'What an awful shock that was to all of us! Please, come in. And call me Celia – everybody does.'

Celia Logan led her into a comfortable, eclectically furnished living room that conveyed an air of friendliness.

'Make yourself comfortable while I get us coffee – or would you prefer tea?'

'Coffee would be great.'

Minutes later the two women were seated on a low, comfortable sofa and sipping coffee.

'That morning – it was just the day before yesterday, wasn't it?' Celia said with eyebrows lifted in astonishment. 'Well, it was a traumatic morning in more ways than one for me. I live here with my sister-in-law – we've both been widows for years. I'm seventy-nine – Marcia's a year older. She's a night owl. She stays up reading suspense novels till three a.m.' Celia paused, her smile wry. 'Sometimes she reads the same book over and over again. She's developed a memory problem. But she still functions all right.' Celia was all at once defensive.

'That's what counts.' It was clear, April thought, that Celia Logan was a compassionate woman.

'Well, in the middle of the night – I was sound asleep – she had to go to the bathroom. She has the bedroom across from mine. When she left the bathroom, she felt a draft from the guest room in the front. She figured a window had been left open and went to close it. And – half-asleep – she tripped in those silly slippers she wears that she says make her feel glamorous. She fell so hard, made such a thump, that she woke me up.'

'Was she hurt?' April was solicitous. At eighty falls could be serious.

'She fractured an ankle and suffered a mild concussion. I went with her in the ambulance and stayed at the hospital while they did all kinds of tests. Thank God the concussion wasn't serious. By the time I got home it was past eight a.m. – and I saw the police cars in front of Beth and Scott's house.' She winced in recall. 'I never suspected something so awful had happened.'

'Mrs Logan – Celia,' April corrected herself, 'in the course of the evening before, did you see anybody who was a stranger to the neighborhood approach the Emerson house?'

'Now that you mention it, yes.' Celia's mind was following this. 'A shabbily dressed woman was hanging around about five p.m. or so. And it was strange – she was about to walk up to the door, and then Scott pulled up at the curb. She left real fast once she saw him.'

'Nobody you knew by sight?' April pressed.

'No, a total stranger to me. But then I'm very near-sighted. Oh, there's more,' Celia recalled with sudden urgency. 'When I returned from the hospital, I saw that woman again. She was walking towards the Emerson house. When she saw the police cars – and all that action – she beat a fast retreat.'

'Would you recognize her if you saw her again?' April probed.

Celia frowned in thought. 'I think so. I was upset on the second round – but I got a good look at her the afternoon before. Is that important?'

'It could be.'

'I just hope they catch that monster fast. I know they've lost their darling baby, but let Beth and Scott at least have the satisfaction of knowing he's behind bars.'

'For the next day or two I'll be staying with Bob and Nicole. But let me give you my phone number – and our office number. If anything else comes to you, please call.'

In her car again April called Bob on her cell phone – impatient to report what she'd learned from Celia.

'He's not in yet,' Sandy told her.

'I'll talk to him later.'

Anxious to have confirmation from others about the woman at the scene, April left the car and rang doorbells at every house on the block. There was nobody home at three of them. Residents of the other houses had seen no one suspicious lurking in the neighborhood – not even the woman Celia had noticed.

April drove into town, stopped to pick up a turkey sandwich and a container of coffee and went to the office.

'Bob just came in, too,' Sandy reported. 'He wants to see you right away.'

Brown paper bag in tow, April hurried to Bob's office.

'Hi.' Bob sat behind his desk, feet propped on an opened desk drawer while he consumed his lunch.

April briefed Bob on her meeting with Celia Logan. 'She's confident she'll recognize the woman if she sees her again. What about you? Anything new?'

Bob nodded. His body language said it wasn't good. 'I persuaded David to let me speak with the district attorney – Jeff Goodwin. He knows about the broken appointment with the shrink. It's a small thing – but not good.'

'How did he latch on to that?' But before Bob could reply, April supplied the answer. 'The shrink had some axe to grind,' she guessed.

'He hates David. His brother ran for the legislature a couple of years ago – the *Sentinel* supported his opponent. Not only that, the *Sentinel* dug up damaging dirt. It caused a real uproar in this town.'

'Did the DA give you any hints of how they were thinking?'

'He intimated that they might take Beth into custody tomorrow. They've stalled to give her time to get off the sedatives. David's out of his mind.'

'I can imagine.' What a nightmare this whole period must be for him. 'But nobody in this town will believe Beth killed her baby. And that's where your jury pool comes from.' April struggled to sound optimistic.

'Don't count on that.' Bob was grim. 'Almost everybody in town loves David – but that bastardly shrink couldn't wait to hurt him with that story of Beth's broken appointment. The inference is that she knew she was in need of help. In a lot of minds that'll label her as disturbed.' He paused. 'Capable of murder.'

'How do we find this woman who was hanging around the house?' It was as much a question to herself as to Bob.

'We need her,' Bob said. 'Goodwin's betting he'll get Beth before a grand jury.' He hesitated, grimaced in distaste. 'Maybe we'll have to go for a temporary insanity plea – as Scott suggested.'

'No!' April was surprised at the strength of her rejection. 'Bob, I go a lot on instinct. And my instinct tells me Beth Emerson is innocent.' *Am I letting my compassion for David rule my thinking?*

'I'm praying the grand jury will have the same instinct.' Bob sighed, reached for his container of coffee. 'This case could split this town right in two. Through the years David has built up a small group of haters – like that shrink. He's always fought for what he felt was good for this town – but in doing that he stepped on a lot of toes. Let's pray those haters don't latch on to this as payback time.'

'We have to find that woman.' April abandoned eating. 'Why did she run away from the house when she saw Scott approach? Why did she return in the morning – and disappear when she saw the police cars?'

'You said Celia Logan would recognize her.'

'Right. Should we have Celia look at mug shots? The district attorney couldn't object to that. The woman might have a record.'

'Let's talk to David.' Bob reached for the phone. 'Also, if it's possible to talk with Beth . . .'

Bob tracked David down at the Emerson house. He gestured to April to pick up the extension.

'Beth was questioned for almost two hours this morning,' David reported tensely. 'She's too shaky to be questioned.'

'Something's come up. It's important for us to talk with Beth.'

'I don't know,' David hedged.

'Celia Logan saw some strange woman hanging around

the house the evening before and the morning after,' Bob explained.

'Come on over,' David agreed after a moment. 'Nothing's going to be easy for Beth.'

At the house April and Bob found David pacing in the living room.

'Scott's all upset that Dr Harris – the psychiatrist – told the detectives about the broken appointment. I told him it was ridiculous to go over and argue with him about that, but he insisted. I don't know what he expects to accomplish.' David paused. 'And then he's going over to the coroner's office. Beth and Scott want to bury Debbie. They're sick at the thought of her lying there in the morgue.'

'The coroner won't release the body for another couple of days,' Bob pointed out. 'You know the routine, David.'

'Yeah,' David acknowledged.

'About Celia Logan,' April began.

'A detective questioned her, too,' David picked up. 'After your meeting with her. They know about that woman. Celia thought it was important they follow up.' David shrugged. 'Maybe they will.'

'You don't think it's important?' April was startled.

'Maybe Beth will have something to add,' Bob said quietly.

'I'll ask her to join us,' David agreed. 'She can't hide away forever.'

Moments later David returned with Beth, introduced her to April.

'April is in practice now with Bob,' David explained. Beth seemed bewildered that she was being questioned by a lawyer. 'We know the police are working on the case, but we want to help.'

April gazed with compassion at the pretty young woman who was David Roberts' daughter. What an awful ordeal she'd been through – and here they were intruding on her grief.

Beth listened to Bob's report on the strange woman who'd

hovered about the house the night before and the morning after Debbie's tragic death.

'Beth, have you any idea who this woman might be?' Bob probed.

'No,' Beth whispered. Her eyes clung to Bob. 'Do you think she killed Debbie?'

'We have to follow every lead,' Bob said.

'Could she be someone who worked for you at some time or other?' April probed. 'Somebody who might have a key to the house? *Does Beth realize how close she is to being taken into custody? Poor baby – she's still in shock.*

'Beth, think hard,' David urged. 'Who could that woman be? It's our strongest lead to date.'

'I'm sorry,' Beth stammered. 'I don't know.'

Chapter Eight

April and Bob sat in somber silence while David walked with Beth back to her bedroom. It was uncanny, April thought, the way she kept feeling she had known David somewhere in earlier years. But perhaps Bob was right. It was just that David was so warm and friendly that he made people feel they'd known him in the past.

David walked back into the living room. 'I made Beth take another pill.' His eyes were troubled. 'All that questioning this morning was bad for her.' He paused, seeming to be in some inner struggle. 'The DA can't seriously be thinking of taking her into custody?'

Bob exchanged an anxious glance with April. 'It can happen. As early as tomorrow.'

'They have no evidence that warrants that!' David's voice shook with rage. 'Why don't they check out Scott? You said that parents are always the first suspects. Why don't they question Scott?'

'He was out of town,' April reminded gently. 'I'm sure the police must have checked the motel where he stayed last night.'

The phone was a jarring intrusion. David frowned. 'Will one of you take it, please?'

April reached for the phone. 'Hello?'

'This is Celia Logan. I saw Bob's car outside. Is this April?'

'Yes.' April was all at once alert. 'Did you want to speak with Bob?'

'I can tell you,' Celia said. 'Two detectives were just here to question me. I told them about that woman. They've asked me to go down to the precinct and look at mug shots. I thought you should know.'

'Thanks, Celia. That could be very helpful.'

'I'll be leaving in a few minutes. I'll call you when I get back.'

April repeated what Celia had told her. 'The woman may not be the killer – but she could be involved somehow.'

'Beth's in no condition to be taken into custody.' David rose to his feet, began to pace. 'I'll talk to Dr Franklin, have him explain. And damn it, the police have nothing to warrant taking her into custody!'

David made several impassioned phone calls, put down the phone at last. 'It's okay – she'll stay here for now. But she's not to leave the house. Not that she's likely to be doing that.'

'I'll be checking on the list of people who knew Scott was going to be away overnight,' Bob reminded and sighed. 'That's not much to go on.'

'What was the motive?' April probed. 'Who would want to kill a five-month-old baby?' She felt sick as she said this. 'But it wasn't Debbie the murderer was after,' she pinpointed. 'He was out for vengeance against Beth, Scott – or you, David.' Her voice a blend of compassion and apology.

'More lists to make – and follow through.' Bob reached into his jacket for a notebook, rummaged in another pocket for a pen. 'Let's start with you, David. Who's been nursing a hate for you – maybe for years?'

The three focused on compiling a list of possible suspects. David searched his mind for enemies he'd made through the newspaper.

'Everybody loves Beth,' he said defiantly. 'She's always involved in doing good. And Scott's very well liked. I suppose there might be some who're envious of his standing here in town – but I've told you that I've stepped on a lot of toes through the years.' He paused, took a deep, painful breath. 'But I never expected a payback like this.'

Scott returned shortly – enveloped in an air of frustration. 'That bastard Harris – he gave me a load of shit about it being his obligation to admit Beth broke her appointment with him. He didn't admit it – he volunteered it!' He dropped into a chair in exasperation. 'And we're not allowed to schedule Debbie's funeral just yet. Her – her body's still being held by the coroner.'

'It'll just be a matter of another couple days,' Bob surmised – his face compassionate.

'Dr Franklin talked with Jeff Goodwin,' David told Scott. 'There's no question of taking Beth into custody as yet.'

'But she's still under house arrest,' Scott pinpointed. 'The police car still sits outside.'

'It's just a routine deal,' April tried to mollify him.

'This is the evening I was supposed to drive down to New York to meet with the Kensington Womenswear people,' Scott said in sudden recall. 'I've got to make them understand the Town Council needs time to work out a deal. All the council has to do is to agree to a sensible tax abatement – and to guarantee to lower the property taxes. It would mean seven hundred new jobs in this town.'

'Kensington will understand the situation,' Bob soothed. He glanced at his watch with an air of apology. 'I have to be at the office for a real estate closing in twenty minutes. I'd better take off.'

'I'll check later with Celia Logan.' April tried to sound matter-of-fact. 'We may be on to something with that woman.'

While Bob conducted the closing in his office, April conferred with Sandy in the outer office. She shot a barrage of questions at Sandy in an effort to get a feel of the town. What had caused someone to kill a five-month-old baby? *Was* it revenge against Debbie's mother, father, or grandfather? What was the motive for this horrendous act?

The phone rang. 'Excuse me.' With a wry smile Sandy reached to respond. 'Smith, Allen, and Winston, Attorneys at Law. Oh, hi, Celia. Yeah, April's right here.'

April took the phone. Instantly alert. 'You made an ID from the mug shots?' she asked.

'No.' Celia sighed. 'But I have this weird feeling now that I know that woman from somewhere.'

'Would it be all right if I dropped by in a few minutes to talk with you?'

'That would be fine,' Celia approved. 'But I don't know how much help I'll be.'

As April hurried up the path to the house, Celia pulled the door open.

'I've been searching my brain – but as Hercule Poirot would say, the little gray cells aren't working. Still, I know I've seen her before.'

'We'll sit down and go over places where this could have happened.' April tried for an optimistic approach. 'Perhaps it'll come to you.'

Celia prodded April into her cozy living room, left her briefly to bring in a coffee tray. 'It's freshly ground beans – but they're decaf,' she warned. 'I don't keep real coffee in the house because Marcia would never get a night's sleep. Though with Marcia,' she said with a chuckle, 'it's more daytime than night sleep that she thrives on.'

'How's she doing?'

'Ordering me to go over to the library to get her a batch of suspense novels. Complaining about being kept there in the hospital. She's over the concussion, but the ankle has to heal.'

'Could you have seen this woman at the library?' April probed.

'No, not at the library.' Celia was positive. 'But I was so disappointed not to see a mug shot. Nobody in this town will rest until that fiend is arrested.'

'About this woman – could she work at the supermarket here in town?'

Celia frowned in thought, then shook her head. 'It'll come to me – but when?' She grunted in frustration. 'What about Beth? Was she questioned about this?'

April nodded. 'She hasn't the faintest idea who it could be.'

'Poor baby – she must be in such pain. And such a little while ago David gave that wonderful surprise birthday party for her. Scott had to be out of town on radio station business on her birthday, and David thought a surprise party would make her feel better. I couldn't believe she's twenty-three. It seems such a little while ago that I remember David and Jane coming home with that precious little bundle.' Celia glowed in recall.

'In those days,' April said whimsically, 'the hospitals were not shipping new mothers home in 48 hours.'

'Oh, Jane wasn't Beth's birth mother,' Celia explained. 'They adopted her. Beth knows that. But nobody could ever have loved a child more than Jane and David loved Beth. It was like she was their own.'

April sat frozen. Facts leaping up in her mind. Beth was twenty-three. She'd been born in November. She had been adopted. All at once she understood why David Roberts seemed familiar. The faces of her baby's adoptive parents had been etched on her brain in that brief meeting. All these years later David's face was known to her.

Beth is my baby. Debbie was my granddaughter – whom I never saw, never held in my arms. And now my precious baby faces a murder charge.

I must prove she's innocent. I must do this!

Chapter Nine

'April, are you all right?' Celia's solicitous voice intruded on her tumultuous thought.

'I'm so sorry,' April stammered, conscious now of her trembling hands. Of the coffee that had splashed over her cup, over the saucer and on to the floor. 'I've spilled coffee on your rug.'

'It'll come right out,' Celia comforted. 'I'll just get some paper towels from the kitchen.'

April struggled to deal with the dizzying emotions that flooded her. She'd found her baby. After all these years! Her baby had grown into a beautiful young woman. She'd had a loving family. She was married – and for a little while she'd had a much loved daughter. My granddaughter. But now this horror.

Grief for the grandchild she'd never known swept over her. What anguish Beth must be feeling now. She remembered her own anguish at giving up her baby – but she'd lived with the hope that her baby was being raised with loving care. Beth had lost her child forever.

And now Beth is suspected of murdering Debbie. At this point the only suspect. The evidence against her is so slight – yet a strong prosecutor can build a case with tiny bits of evidence. New York is a state that can demand a death penalty. This is my baby! I have to clear her! Am I good enough? Can I do it?

Celia returned to the living room with a roll of paper towels in one hand and a carafe of coffee in the other.

'Let me fill up your cup again,' she said, approaching April. 'There's more milk – half-and-half actually, but Marcia and I always refer to it as milk – and more sugar, if you like.'

'Just coffee, please. I'm sorry to be so awkward – but my mind was racing.' April fabricated. 'I was trying to pin down some place where you might have seen that woman. You said she was shabbily dressed. Perhaps some place where you're a volunteer?' Bob said Celia was active in the community.

All at once Celia seemed transfixed. 'Oh Lord, I remember!' Her smile was brilliant. 'I saw her at the food pantry! My church has a food pantry that helps poor families in crisis. She's too proud to go on welfare, but she runs short on food at times. She's a widow of a migrant farmer. He died in an accident during a harvest season, and she stayed on with her two young children. She cleans houses, babysits. Whatever comes along.'

April leaned forward urgently. 'Do you know where she lives? Her name?'

'She lives in a trailer on the other side of town. I don't know which one, but we could find it. I think her name is Rosita.'

'Could we go there now?' *Please God, let this be a lead.*

'Finish your coffee,' Celia ordered. 'I'll go get my coat.'

The two women left the house. April suppressed her surprise that Celia didn't lock the front door. But then this was Magnolia – not Manhattan.

'Let's take my car,' April said and gestured towards the white Mercedes at the curb.

'That'll be an eye-catcher at the trailer park.' Celia allowed herself a whimsical smile. 'We don't see many foreign cars here.'

'It was a bonus.' All at once April felt self-conscious. She'd bought the car with her Christmas bonus – after being instructed to divest herself of her six-year-old compact. 'In more affluent times.' Was Celia curious about why she'd come here to join Bob in his practice, where she'd probably earn little more each year than her Christmas bonus?

While they drove, Celia talked about the grief felt by the townspeople.

'Everybody knows Beth and Scott – and admires them. Both of them so involved in local needs. Scott came into town four years ago. His sister and her family live here. Right away Scott got a job at the radio station. He started a reading group at the senior citizens center. Started a campaign to provide twice-weekly playgroups for the under three age group at the library. And that Debbie . . .' Celia's voice revealed her own grief. 'Debbie was precious. This town is hurting. Hurting real bad.'

Did Beth ever wonder about her mother? April agonized. Did she ask herself, *What kind of a mother could give away her baby?* Did Beth ever try to find her? Adopted children did that these days – though it wasn't easy and not many succeeded.

No, she rebuked herself. Beth wouldn't have tried to find her. Beth loved David and his wife. She would have only contempt for a mother who would abandon her child.

'The trailer park is just ahead.' Celia broke into April's introspection. 'There're no more than a dozen trailers there. I'll just ask somebody which is Rosita's.'

The trailer park sat in a clearing of a wooded area – its trees drab and barren, reflecting the desolate appearance of the trailers that sat in an abject row. The day was cold. There was no sign of life outside except for a young black Labrador that sprawled asleep on the ground.

'I'll knock on the door of that trailer there,' Celia said as April pulled to a stop in the parking area, home to half a dozen decrepit vehicles.

April waited while Celia approached her destination. An

elderly woman opened the door, stared past Celia for an instant at the white Mercedes that seemed an alien among the other cars. April couldn't hear what Celia was saying, but the woman was pointing to a trailer at the far end of the row. That would be where Rosita lived, April interpreted.

She left the car to join Celia.

'The last trailer,' Celia confirmed, and they headed in that direction. A radio or TV was playing. 'She's home.'

In response to Celia's knock, the door opened. A small, painfully thin woman somewhere in her thirties gazed at them with an odd wariness.

'Yeah?' Her eyes swung from April to Celia. All at once she smiled. 'You're the lady from the church pantry.' Her accent indicated a Hispanic background.

'That's right. How're you doing, Rosita?' Celia's voice said she understood life was tough for Rosita and her two children.

'We're doing okay. My little one had a cold for a while, but she's all better.' She hesitated. 'Would you like to come in?' But she was still fearful, April sensed.

'Thanks, Rosita. Oh, this is my friend April. She's just moved to Magnolia. We thought you might be able to help us with something . . .' Celia and April walked into the tiny trailer, where efforts had been made to make it appear homelike. It was immaculate, April noted.

'Please, sit down.' Rosita pointed to an improvised loveseat. Still nervous, April sympathized.

'You know about the Emerson baby,' Celia began.

'Oh, I feel so bad for Beth. She loved that baby so much.' Rosita's voice broke. 'And she's so good, the way she tries to help people. Why did such a terrible thing happen to her?'

'We understood you were in the area of their house the evening before Debbie was murdered,' Celia said, almost matter-of-fact. 'Rosita, did you see any strangers loitering near the house? A drifter perhaps?'

'I was there . . .' A terrified glint in her eyes now. 'But I didn't see nobody. Beth had told me to come by and pick up a bundle of clothes for my kids – she'd got them from her sister-in-law. But then I saw Scott arriving – and I left.' Her eyes opaque now. What wasn't she saying? April asked herself.

'You were there the next morning,' April reminded and Rosita flinched.

'I saw the cop cars, and I knew something bad had happened. I knew I couldn't go in then . . .' She turned from April to Celia with a look of horror on her face. 'Nobody thinks I had somethin' to do with what happened to that sweet baby?'

'No, of course not,' Celia soothed. 'We'd just hoped that you might have seen somebody there.'

'I keep a light on all night now – the kids are scared. They know about the baby.' Rosita hesitated. 'The cops – they don't know nothin' yet about who done it?'

'Not yet – but they will soon.' April tried to sound reassuring. 'And thanks for your help, Rosita. We appreciate it.'

April and Celia were silent until they were in the car again.

'I like Rosita – she's a good person.' Celia seemed to be in some inner debate. 'But I have the feeling that she was hiding something from us.'

'Something that frightens her,' April pinpointed.

'She's had rough times,' Celia commiserated. 'At one time she and her husband were migrant farmers somewhere down south – Arkansas or Texas. Then another migrant family told them about working in New York state, and they traveled up here in a ramshackle car that fell apart when they arrived. They worked on local farms in season until her husband died in some freakish accident. Of course, there was no liability insurance,' she said drily. 'Rosita and the kids scrape by on whatever jobs come along for her.'

'What is she hiding?' April pondered. 'Does it have something to do with Debbie's murder?'

Jamie grunted in annoyance when his intercom buzzed. He had no time for anything except bringing tomorrow's newspaper together. He pushed the button on his intercom. 'What is it?'

'There are two detectives here who want to talk to you.' Iris, the *Sentinel*'s long-time secretary, sounded unnerved.

'Send them in.' He mentally rebuked himself for sounding so harsh – but Iris understood, he told himself. They were all uptight right now.

He sat back in his chair, searched his mind for a reason for this intrusion. The door swung open. Two detectives he knew from the force walked into the office.

'So, what can I do for you?' He was puzzled. Why pretend otherwise?

'Jamie, uh – we have a couple of questions.' The older of the two detectives cleared his throat in a gesture of discomfort. 'It was reported to us that you visited the Emerson house late in the evening before the baby's murder was discovered. How late?'

'I didn't visit the house.' All at once Jamie was receiving disturbing vibes. 'I stopped by after a meeting of a civic group we'd formed – to give Beth notes on the meeting.' He gazed from one detective to the other. 'It was a few minutes before eleven – the meeting ran long that night.'

'When did you leave?' the other detective asked.

'Three minutes after I arrived.' Jamie glanced from one to the other. 'I didn't go into the house,' he emphasized. What the hell was going on here? So some neighborhood busybody saw him drive up – and knew Scott was out of town. Hell, that was why Beth couldn't make the meeting. Scott couldn't babysit.

'Anybody see you leave?'

'How the hell do I know?'

'Where did you go from there?' one of the two asked.

'Home.' They knew he lived in his parents' house. They knew, too, that his parents had left for Florida a week ago, would be down there till April. 'I watched the eleven p.m. TV news, then hit the sack. What's this all about?' Exasperation crept into his voice.

'There was a murder in this town. We have to check everything out. Just routine.'

When the two detectives left, Jamie leaned back in his chair and tried to follow their thinking. So somebody saw him drive up – in the company car he was using while his own was in the shop. They hadn't seen him drive away, he assumed. Did they think he was having a thing with Beth behind Scott's back? The bastards!

Sure, he'd figured he and Beth would get married in time. They'd gone together their last year in high school, through the college years. Then Scott came into town – and Beth couldn't see anybody else. He didn't have a chance after that. They saw each other at community meetings – worked together on committees. Crumbs, but he was grateful just to be near her at times.

Could the cops be thinking Beth had killed Debbie? And he was involved? God, they were off the wall!

Chapter Ten

After an hour-long – unproductive – conference, April and Bob sat in his office in somber silence – each in a mental search for some elusive clue that would lead to the fiend who had killed Debbie Emerson.

'Hey, it's past six.' Sandy hung in the doorway to Bob's office.

'Then what are you doing here?' Bob clucked. 'Go home.'

'You two want more coffee before I beat it?' Sandy was solicitous. Little happened in this office that skipped past her. She knew they were concerned about Beth's being arraigned.

'No thanks,' April replied for both. 'We'll be leaving in a bit.'

Bob rose from his chair, began to pace. 'Okay, what has Jeff Goodwin got so far?' he challenged. 'The house was locked tight. So somebody was able to pick the lock.' He paused, an uneasy glint in his eyes. 'I wish Scott hadn't said Beth was a light sleeper. Goodwin's going to ask himself, how did Beth sleep through while her kid was murdered?'

'Scott didn't say that to the detectives,' April reminded. 'He was horrified that he even mentioned it to us.'

'A prosecuting attorney will ask her.' Bob was grim. 'And he'll point out that she was under enough stress to consider seeing a shrink.'

'But she didn't,' April pinpointed.

'This Dr Harris already reported she broke the appointment – which sets her up as having emotional problems. Harris could claim confidentiality if she'd had a session with him. He's under no obligation in the present circumstances.'

'And you're sure the Comstock woman reported Beth's marriage was in trouble,' April added. 'Then there's the pair of discarded gloves – new gloves,' she emphasized, 'in the kitchen garbage pail – that are sure to have Beth's fingerprints.' It was an old story – they had to prove who killed Debbie if they were to clear Beth.

They heard voices in the reception room. Sandy about to leave. Somebody had just arrived.

'It's David,' Bob realized, and moments later David burst into the room.

'I want to sue the fucking *Ledger*!' David bellowed, and waved the evening's edition before Bob's eyes. 'Look what the lying bastard is spreading around town!'

April stared in shock as Bob held the newspaper so that the two of them could read the headline: BABY-KILLER SUSPECT AND LOVER IN SECRET TRYST.

'Oh, my God!'

'Police uncover secret meeting between Beth Emerson and *Sentinel* reporter Jamie Lawrence on the eve of her baby's murder.' Terror ripped through April as she read the lurid account that followed.

'The son-of-a-bitch is out to crucify Beth to get back at me!' David's voice trembled in rage. 'Bob, I want to sue that rag!'

'That'll get you nowhere,' Bob rejected.

'Find out the truth behind this allegation and print a retraction in tomorrow morning's *Sentinel*,' April instructed. 'Talk to Beth and to Jamie Lawrence. And do it right away. The retraction must be in tomorrow morning's paper,' she reiterated.

'I know there's some innocuous explanation for why Jamie happened to be at Beth's house that evening,' David blustered. 'The damned newspaper took some innocent encounter and labeled it a "secret tryst." Like some sensational tabloid rag!'

But this unexpected accusation would guarantee that Beth

would be taken in for serious questioning. April's heart began to pound. Beth would be arraigned, held for a grand jury hearing. No matter how sympathetic, the district attorney would have to take action.

David groaned. 'How can I ask Beth if she was having an affair with Jamie? I know it's a lie.'

'Let me talk with her,' April urged. It would come more easily from somebody who seemed a stranger. *How would Beth feel if she knew that half of her defense team was her birth mother?*

'David, you talk with Jamie,' Bob picked up.

'We'll have Jamie write the story – first person,' David decided with an air of defiance. 'People in this town like Jamie. He's been active in the community since he was sixteen. Our local Wonder Boy . . .' David's voice softened. 'People trust Jamie. He won his seat on the Town Council with a tremendous majority.'

'All right. I'll go over now and talk with Beth.' April saw the glow of anguish in David's eyes. 'Beth has to realize what's happening.' April's voice was gentle. *How can I talk this way about my precious child? Her life is at stake.*

'Where's Jamie right now?' Bob asked.

'At the newspaper.'

'All right. You and I will talk with Jamie,' Bob decreed. 'April will talk with Beth.'

'Let's get cracking.' David was terse. April realized he understood how damaging the ugly accusation – even though untrue – was to Beth. 'We have a newspaper with a revised front page to get out by early morning.'

Driving to the Emerson house, April searched for words to convey the situation to Beth. Face it – Beth would be stunned by such an accusation. There must be some simple explanation. Something the district attorney would understand.

Beth and Jamie Lawrence were both engaged in community activities. April clutched at this explanation. But people would remember, she forced herself to acknowledge, that once Beth and Jamie had been romantically involved.

Pulling up before the house she noted that the garage door was open, the garage empty. That meant Scott was not at home. The police car still sat out front. Did the local townspeople realize that Beth was under house arrest?

She crossed to the police car, identified herself as the Emersons' attorney. The police officer seemed self-conscious in his role.

'It's okay. Bob Allen called on the cell phone to say you were coming.' His smile was admiring.

April walked up to the door, rang the bell. Was Beth awake? When would Scott understand she couldn't be kept under constant sedation? She heard footsteps in the foyer. Beth was awake. Her throat tightened as she geared herself for this encounter with Beth.

The door opened. Beth stood there – fearful, wary.

'Beth, I'm April – remember me?' She contrived a reassuring smile. 'I'm Bob Allen's new partner.'

'Yes.' But Beth's voice was uncertain. April saw her apprehensive glance towards the police car at the curb. She was coming out of her state of shock – she understood the situation, April realized.

'May I come in?'

'Yes, of course.' Beth pulled the door wide. 'Scott isn't here – he's gone to talk with the coroner again.' Her voice dropped to a whisper. 'We want to bury Debbie.'

'I'd like to talk with you, Beth.' No time now for Beth to grieve. They must build a strong defense for her. To do that they needed her help. 'Your father sent me over.'

'Would you – would you like some coffee? Or tea?' Beth was struggling for composure.

'Thank you, no.'

Beth led her into the living room, sat at one end of the sofa. April felt a rush of compassion as she sat beside her. Poor baby, she was so distraught.

'We know this is all a terrible lie,' April began, 'but Bob and I need specific facts to clear it up.'

'What's a terrible lie?' Beth seemed wary again.

'Your father's competitor – that slimy rag in town – has run a headline story that claims you and Jamie Lawrence are—' April took a deep breath, forced herself to continue, 'are having an affair. That Jamie was here with you on the evening when—' She paused before the outrage in Beth's eyes. But it was good, she told herself, that Beth could feel something besides grief at her baby's murder.

'Jamie dropped by to give me the notes from the meeting of a civic group we'd formed. He didn't even come into the house! How could they tell such lies?'

'Jamie will confirm it,' April soothed. 'Right now your father and Bob are talking with him. The newspaper will have a retraction out in the morning.' She hesitated. How to make this easier for Beth? There was no way. 'I know it's a horrible injustice – but we suspect that the district attorney will insist on bringing you in for questioning. He—'

Sudden realization drained the color from Beth's face. 'He thinks I killed my baby?'

'In any case where a child is involved, the parents are the first suspects,' she explained. 'But we'll find Debbie's murderer,' April said with sudden intensity. I promise you that.'

David and Bob charged into the small red brick building that housed the *Sentinel*. The reception area was deserted. With grim determination on their faces they headed through the newsroom, back to Jamie's private office. Sounds from the composing room told them a segment of the morning edition was going to press.

As usual, the door to Jamie's office was open. He glanced up from the copy he was checking.

'Jamie, we need to talk.' David was fighting for calm. 'That rag – the *Ledger* – is out for blood.' He unfolded the newspaper, laid it across Jamie's desk. 'I know this is a damn lie,'

Jamie scanned the headline, turned pale with shock. 'That's why those two detectives dropped by a little while ago.' He took a deep breath. 'They asked what time I was at Beth's house, when I left.' He gazed from David to Bob, back to David. 'I stopped by to give her the notes from a civic group meeting – I was there maybe three minutes.' He hesitated. 'I can't prove that – unless somebody saw me leave.'

'Not the snoop who saw you arrive,' David surmised. 'All right, you have to write a first-person story denying this. It goes front page,' he ordered. He frowned at the shrill ring of Bob's cell phone.

Bob reached in his jacket for the phone. 'Hello?' David noted his instant alertness. 'Yeah, we heard. But—' Bob tightened his free hand into a fist. 'Look, David Roberts is here with me, Jeff. He'd like to talk with you.' Bob covered the phone. 'Jeff wanted to warn us that he expects to charge Beth tomorrow morning.'

David reached for the phone. 'Jeff, you know that headline is a damn lie!' He paused for a moment. 'I know you're in a rough spot, but at least let Beth bury Debbie before you take her in. The coroner keeps giving Scott a bad time – he won't release the body.' Bob saw a tic quivering in David's right eyelid as he listened on the phone. 'Jeff, you know she's not going anywhere!' His face etched with pain, David listened for another few minutes. 'Of course, I'll be responsible.' He hesitated. 'Thanks, Jeff.'

David handed the cell phone back to Bob, struggled for composure. 'Jeff's ordering the coroner to release Debbie's body. We're to arrange a quick funeral.' He took a deep, anguished breath. He dreaded the days ahead. 'Then Jeff will charge Beth.' His eyes met Bob's. 'Unless you and April can perform a miracle, she'll be arraigned, held for a grand jury hearing. Oh God, I can't believe I'm saying this!'

Chapter Eleven

After what seemed to be endless claps of thunder, flashes of lightning that made the night appear to be day, rain began to descend from the sky in torrents, attacked the windows with ominous force. For the first time April lay in her bed in her new apartment – knowing sleep would elude her.

They'd gathered together for a late conference at Bob's house. She, Bob, David and Jamie. Nicole, too – as a part-time attorney – had joined them. At moments – fearful of the task ahead – April asked herself if Bob and she should retire in favor of some big-time defense attorney. Neither Bob nor she had heavy criminal case experience. She shuddered as she realized the fees such attorneys demanded – in the neighborhood of a quarter-million dollars. Between them she and David could probably raise the funds to handle this – though both would be almost stripped of all assets.

She wavered about discussing this with David. How could she explain her willingness to put up everything she owned to help defend Beth? Not without revealing herself as Beth's birth mother. And instinct told her that David would insist that she and Bob handle the case. He wouldn't allow himself to think that they couldn't clear Beth. That her defense was so fragile.

Three times in the course of the evening David and Bob had talked with Scott. On tomorrow morning's radio news – with the approval of the management – he would chastise the *Ledger* for its attack on Beth and Jamie. Tomorrow morning he would make the necessary funeral arrangements. Debbie would be buried the following morning.

She'd liked Jamie Lawrence on sight. She was touched by the closeness – the mutual respect – between David and Jamie. Their families had known each other forever, David said. He'd hoped – expected – that one day Beth would marry Jamie, she gathered. This emerged in so many little ways.

She'd never felt so drawn to any man as she was towards David, she realized in astonishment. Was she wrong in sensing he was drawn to her? But how could she think this way in the midst of their nightmare? It was just that she was so grateful that he had been such a wonderful father to Beth, she told herself defensively.

She abandoned thoughts of sleeping just yet, reached to turn on the bedside lamp, rummaged on the shelves of the table for a magazine to read. But her mind refused to cooperate. How were she and Bob to convince a grand jury that Beth was innocent? That she shouldn't go to trial?

She suspected that both David and Jamie were lying sleepless now – haunted by Debbie's murder and by the suspicions that hung over Beth. Day after tomorrow Debbie would be buried. Her granddaughter. She dreaded attending the funeral, though she must – because it would be an agonizing task to conceal the depth of her own grief. In that tiny white casket would be the grandchild she'd never known.

David stared out into the rainswept night. No point in going to bed just yet – he'd just toss and turn. How had they been thrown into this nightmare? A few days ago he was a happy man – enthralled with his tiny granddaughter. Her arrival had made him less hostile to Scott, he conceded.

Maybe it had been wrong of him to be upset that Beth had married Scott rather than Jamie. It was Beth's decision to make – not his. Everybody – well, almost everybody – in Magnolia thought Scott was special. The others, Beth said, were envious of Scott.

Traitorous remarks made to Bob by Della Comstock crept into David's mind. Why were Beth and Scott fighting? For weeks, Della told Bob – and probably by now she'd told the police. Folks said Della had a motor-mouth. Why hadn't he realized something was troubling Beth?

Beth had always been the focal point of his life. His treasured child. It was Beth who'd held his marriage together. He and Jane had married too young, had grown apart when Beth was small. But they'd remained together for Beth's sake – to provide a family for her.

He couldn't erase from his mind the ugliness that the *Ledger* had so blatantly implied. He felt a tightness in his throat as he envisioned that headline. People would remember that Beth and Jamie had once gone together. And his own defense of Beth in the *Sentinel* would be suspect, he warned himself. He wasn't just the publisher – he was Beth's father.

He kept telling himself that the case would never go beyond the grand jury, that Beth would be cleared. But in a deep corner of his mind he was scared. Damn the *Ledger*! That bastard Tim Lott was out for his hide. Lott wanted Beth to go to trial. He wanted to see her convicted – because that would be a slow, torturous death for *him*.

Should he consider going out for a big-time criminal lawyer at this point? He could raise a good chunk of cash on the newspaper, borrow against the house – the mortgage was more than half paid off. Sure, he'd feel like a traitor if he dumped Bob and April. But this was Beth's life at stake. Tomorrow talk about this with Scott. Scott was the husband – he was the one to make the decision.

His face softened as he thought about Bob's new partner. April was such a charming woman. He'd felt such warmth in her. It had taken guts to walk out of a top-drawer New York law firm and come here to practice with Bob. But did she and Bob have the criminal law experience needed to clear Beth?

Tomorrow I'll sit down and talk with Scott. We must make a decision about Beth's defense. I'm her father – I have a right to share in that decision.

Normally Beth enjoyed the night sounds of rain beating down on the roof, pounding the windows. It was a relaxing symphony. But not tonight. She sat with feet tucked beneath her in the lounge chair across from the queen-size bed that dominated the master bedroom and tried to bring order to her mind.

Scott thought she was still taking the sedative Dr Raines had prescribed. Not anymore, she told herself defiantly. She had to get her head together. That woman lawyer – April – who was Bob Allen's partner now had made it clear that the police considered her their suspect. They were building up some insane case. *I can't let people believe I killed my baby!*

Did Jamie know what was happening? She shuddered, hearing April's voice again: *Your father's competitor – that slimy rag in town – has run a headline story that claims you and Jamie are having an affair.* Dad always said they were out to cut his throat – but to spread such lies?

She started at the sound of the knob on the other side of the master bedroom door being turned. She'd locked it – as though protecting herself from the detective who sat outside the house. Ever since April told her what was happening she was haunted by horrible visions of being dragged from the house in handcuffs.

'Beth?' Scott sounded uneasy. 'Open the door . . .'

'No.' When they were alone she didn't have to pretend everything was all right between them.

'We need to talk.' He sounded exasperated now.

'We have nothing to talk about.' Did he know about the story in this evening's *Ledger*? He had to know it wasn't true.

'Beth, I spoke with your father a little while ago.' A

cajoling tone in his voice. 'He's talked with Jeff Goodwin – the district attorney,' he reminded. 'The district attorney will order the coroner to release Debbie's body to us tomorrow. We can bury our baby,' he soothed.

Beth leapt from her chair, charged towards the door, opened it. 'You're telling me the truth?' Her eyes searched his.

'You know I've been trying for that. Your father has more drag with people than me.' A touch of rancor in his voice now. 'I'll be at the office when it opens in the morning. I'll make all the arrangements for the funeral.'

'I want her to wear the little white dress that Melanie Woods at the Senior Center made for her,' Beth whispered. 'With a tiny white ribbon in her hair.'

'Whatever you say,' Scott soothed.

'Scott . . .' She hesitated. 'Do you realize the police think I killed Debbie? How can they think that?'

'It's normal police procedure,' he soothed.

'Will they keep me from being at the funeral?' All at once she was ice-cold. 'Am I going to jail?'

'Debbie will be buried day after tomorrow – and we'll be there. Together,' he emphasized. 'We don't want the police to suspect we've been – been fighting. That won't look good for you.'

'I want to know who killed my baby!' Beth's voice was suddenly shrill. 'I want to see him in prison for the rest of his life!'

April turned on her bedside radio the moment she awoke. Her eyes fastened on the clock. In moments the seven a.m. news would come on. It would be the first time Scott was on his job as newscaster since Debbie's murder.

April pulled herself into a semi-sitting position against a pair of pillows and waited for the music segment to be over.

'Good morning. This is Scott Emerson with your morning

news and weather.' His deep, charismatic voice sounded almost normal. 'But first, on a personal note, I must express my shock and revulsion at the libellous headline and story that appeared on the front page of last evening's *Ledger*. As you all must know, my wife Beth and I are mourning the murder of our daughter Debbie.' His voice choked on the last three words. For a moment April thought he would be unable to continue. 'And now that newspaper has the audacity to spread lies about my wife Beth and a highly respected local journalist, Jamie Lawrence. Beth and I have a strong and healthy marriage. We have total trust in each other. What you read were contemptible lies. But let me bring you the morning news. The temperature in Magnolia is—'

April switched off the radio. Her mind assaulted yet again by Mrs Comstock's remarks about how Beth and Scott had been fighting for weeks, that Beth seemed under deep stress. Thank God, Jeff Goodwin had agreed not to bring Beth in for arraignment until after Debbie was buried.

All at once restless, April flung aside the covers, left her bed. Prepare for another agonizing day. Every day would be agonizing until Beth was cleared. She couldn't allow herself to believe that she and Bob could not accomplish this.

David said the DA was uncomfortable at what lay ahead – but he had no doubt that Goodwin would fight for a conviction. 'It's his job,' David had pointed out. 'He'll fight to win his case.'

Why didn't Goodwin pursue other leads? April asked herself in a surge of frustration? But she knew the answer to that: slim though it was, the evidence pointed to Beth. In her mind – again – she explored that evidence. No way would she believe that Beth was guilty.

She fought against a surge of fear. How were she and Bob to clear Beth? They must! It was not an unfamiliar story – she'd encountered this in her pro bono criminal work. To clear Beth they must pin down the real murderer, provide evidence strong enough to convince the district attorney that he was in pursuit of the wrong suspect. *Are we good enough to do this?*

Bob had to go to court this morning in a civil case, she remembered. They'd confer later in the day about how to proceed in defending Beth. Her poor baby – Beth realized now what lay ahead. What pain she must be feeling.

All right, what to do today? In little more than forty-eight hours – unless she could accomplish a small miracle – detectives would arrive at the house and charge Beth with murder. Beth would be held for arraignment. She'd thought that the day she gave up her baby was the worst in her life. The day after tomorrow would be worse.

Chapter Twelve

April lay awake until the first gray streaks of dawn crept between her bedroom drapes, then fell asleep from exhaustion. She came awake with a sense of falling through space, frowned in rejection of the sounds that had awakened her. A stupid car alarm – the noise loathed by city-dwellers. She'd thought she'd left that hideous awakening behind when she moved here.

From habit she glanced at the clock while the discordant noise of the car alarm played out its message. All at once she was ice-cold despite the warmth in the room. Her heart pounded. This was the day Debbie was to be laid to rest.

In three hours she must be at the church. She felt exhausted, sick at heart. The right to show the depth of her grief was denied her. Nobody in this town must know she was Beth's birth mother. Debbie's grandmother. A strange but beautiful word, she thought – one she didn't deserve to claim.

It's my tiny granddaughter that's being buried today – and I never once saw her, never held her in my arms.

She felt Beth's pain, David's pain. And she'd hurt for Scott when she'd heard him on the radio yesterday morning denouncing that scurrilous story in the *Ledger*.

With a sense of being drained of all strength she left her bed to prepare for this worst of all days.

In the kitchen of the barnyard-red ranch house where he'd lived for almost twenty-four years, David Roberts poured himself yet another cup of strong black coffee. He'd made no pretense of going to bed last night. He'd paced about the house, stared out into the night at intervals as though the town had become an alien place to him. And at regular intervals he returned to the kitchen and the coffeemaker. It was in the kitchen where momentous family revelations occurred, he thought in a corner of his mind. It was here that Jane had told him she'd received word that the baby they were to adopt was about to be born. Here that Jane agreed he would quit his job as a teacher in the local high school to use their savings and her small inheritance to start a newspaper. Here Beth told him she'd decided that she wanted to become a teacher – after an adolescence filled with the usual thoughts of fanciful professions. Here she told him she was engaged to marry Scott – and when she was pregnant with Debbie.

And now they were about to bury their baby. The hardest day of his life, he thought. He'd grieved for Jane, but somehow it seemed more tragic that at five months Debbie's life had been snuffed out. And now he must face the brutal fact that tomorrow morning Beth would be taken from her house and placed behind bars.

Oh God, I feel so damned helpless! Should I confess to Bob that I'm afraid Beth needs more experienced defense than what he – and April – can provide?

Beth hovered before the medicine chest mirror in the master bedroom and gazed at her image. She mustn't fall apart today. For Debbie's sake she must hold herself together. Her head ached. At moments she fought against light-headedness. But Dad would be with her – she clung to this thought. That would help see her through the pretense that she and Scott mourned as one.

She started at the knock on the master bedroom door.

'Yes?'

'I've made breakfast for us, Beth. It's on the table now.'

'I'm not hungry.' How could Scott talk of food this morning?

'You have to eat. You don't want to pass out . . .' He hesitated a moment. 'There're still pills left in the—'

'I don't want a pill,' she broke in ferociously. She couldn't live in a constant daze.

'Come to breakfast,' he ordered. 'You'll need all your strength today.'

And what about tomorrow – and all the tomorrows afterwards? It wouldn't matter to her if she was sent to prison – her life was over. But it would be such a disgrace for Dad. She loved him too much to see him have to face that.

Who came into the house in the middle of the night and killed Debbie? *Why didn't I hear him? Or her? Was it a woman?* April – that lawyer who was working with Bob – seemed so warm, so bright. Would she and Bob find Debbie's killer?

'Beth!' Scott was grim now. 'Get your act together. You don't want the whole town to know you've trashed our marriage. It won't look good for you,' he emphasized.

Reluctantly she reached for her robe, walked to the door. Did Scott think she'd killed their baby? How could he think that? She unlocked the door, pulled it wide. For Dad's sake she had to walk through today without falling apart.

From the line-up of parked cars April realized the church would be packed this morning. She pulled up at the curb, sat gripping the wheel as she tried to gear herself for what lay ahead. She hurt for herself and for Beth and David. Today was a respite, she reminded herself – a day to mourn. Tomorrow she and Bob must accelerate their fight for Beth's life. Or talk to David about bringing in a new defense attorney . . .

She saw Celia emerge from a car just behind her. Celia spied her, waved, waited for her to approach.

'This is a sad day for the whole town,' Celia greeted her. 'I can't believe this is happening.' And her eyes said that she was worried about Beth. Everybody in town must realize that it was a matter of hours or days before Beth was taken into custody, charged with murder.

'How's your sister-in-law?' April asked as they walked towards the church.

'Oh, she's doing fine. But wouldn't you know it? She came down with a touch of pneumonia yesterday. You go to a hospital with one thing and pick up another. At her age the doctors insist she'll have to stay a while – they won't say how long. Thank God for Medicare.' Celia managed a whimsical smile.

'I know she'll be glad to get back home,' April sympathized.

'Marcia's an ex-New Yorker like you. She lived smack in the middle of Manhattan until her husband died. But without his pension and social security she couldn't handle living there.'

'It's an expensive city to live in,' April agreed.

'I had the house – but I was missing Joe's social security and pension, too – so I persuaded her to come here and live with me. Together we manage.' Celia's eyes were reminiscent. 'That first year was rough on Marcia. I remember how she'd complained through the years about the city noises – garbage trucks grinding away in the middle of the night, new construction never stopping, the nastiness of the subways. But when she moved here, she missed the city conveniences. The supermarket around the corner, the take-out meals, the coffee shop across the street.'

'It's a trade-off,' April said. *How can I carry on this casual conversation when I know what lies ahead?* 'I hear birds singing instead of garbage being ground up – and it's heavenly.'

'Living in the city Marcia never bothered to learn to drive. Now she has to wait for me to drive her to the supermarket if she discovers she needs a jar of spice. She's a gourmet cook.' Celia paused. 'When she remembers her recipes. Cooking and reading suspense novels make life possible for her here in Magnolia.'

They were approaching their destination now. Hordes of people were filing into the church. She should have arrived early, April reproached herself. There was probably only standing room now. Fighting for composure she walked inside. The worst day of her life, she thought yet again.

She spied Nicole and Bob in a pew up front. Nicole held up a hand – she'd been saving a seat. April hurried down the aisle – conscious of the almost sickening sweetness of flowers. Already she saw handkerchiefs dabbing at moist eyes. To lay to rest a young child – and after such a horrendous death – was devastating even to people who knew Beth and Scott only slightly.

Nicole reached out a hand to April as she joined them. They couldn't know the anguish she felt, April thought. She yearned to hold Beth in her arms and comfort her – but that she couldn't do. She was suddenly conscious of a low murmur and turned to gaze up the aisle.

Flanked by Scott and David, Beth was walking towards the pew reserved for them. How pale she was – but determined not to break down, April interpreted. David looked exhausted. When had he last slept?

After the services April left her car in the street to drive to the cemetery with Nicole and Bob. Until the day she died, the image of that tiny white coffin that held the body of her granddaughter would be etched on her brain.

Beth clung to her father, his arm about her waist. Scott seemed to be fighting for composure. There were audible sobs from those gathered about the grave. Mercifully the graveside service was brief. April's vision was blurred as her eyes focused on Beth. Her poor baby. Her darling baby was in such pain.

At David's urging she – along with Nicole and Bob – agreed to follow him, along with Beth and Scott, to the Emerson house. April understood. Now they must focus on Beth's defense. Tomorrow she would be behind bars – awaiting arraignment.

They couldn't file an application for bail before a grand jury indicted Beth. And Beth would go before a grand jury and be indicted, April tormented herself. Bob said Jeff Goodwin was like a tiger when it came to major cases. This was a major case.

At the house Beth went to her room without a word. Before the funeral several neighbors had brought platters of food – though it was understood there were to be no visitors. The *Ledger* had made it clear that Beth would be taken into custody. But no one thought about food in this traumatic hour.

Surely nobody believed Beth could be guilty, April told herself yet again. But even in the church she'd been aware that there were some among the mourners who avoided glancing in Beth's direction – though she'd felt overwhelming sympathy for Scott. Did they believe that horrendous story about Beth and Jamie? It was a disconcerting question.

David slumped in a corner of the living room sofa. He seemed in deep debate.

'I don't like what that rag is saying,' he said, clutching and unclutching one fist. 'They're taking a few tiny bits and trying to make a strong case. Because they hate me!' His voice soared in frustration.

'David, perhaps you ought to consider bringing in a top-drawer defense attorney,' April said slowly. 'I know it'll be terribly expensive, but—'

'Absolutely not!' Scott broke in. 'You and Bob will handle Beth's defense. To go out and bring in some fancy lawyer now is like saying we think Beth's guilty.'

'We owe it to her to provide the strongest defense team possible.' David took in a deep breath. 'Bob and April plus some superstar. I know it'll be wildly expensive, but I can borrow on the house, on the paper . . .' He seemed apprehensive. He knows how much he'd have to ante up, April thought. He's apprehensive about raising that amount. *How do I tell him I'll contribute?*

'No,' Scott rejected. 'I consider that a wrong move. It would look bad for Beth if we appeared to panic.' He paused, seeming to search for words. 'I'm her husband. It's my decision to make.'

The atmosphere was suddenly heated. Scott and David stared at each other in hostility. David was fighting for calm. April remembered that Bob had said David had never liked Scott – had admitted he'd had his heart set on Beth's marrying Jamie.

'Yes,' David said tersely after a moment. 'But she's my daughter – and I want her to have the best defense possible.' His eyes were challenging.

'We'll stay with Bob and April.' Scott defied contradiction. 'I'm sure Beth will agree with me.'

He didn't realize the case that the prosecution was building up, April thought in exasperation. This was a charge of murder – not a parking ticket. Let David talk with Beth. Let him convince her to bring in help. The ultimate decision should be hers.

'Tomorrow morning she's going to be charged with murder.' A vein pounded in David's forehead. 'Tomorrow night she'll sleep behind bars. We need to provide the best defense possible. Can't you see that, Scott?'

'I have to go to the station now.' Scott frowned. 'The big boy said he expected me to return to work after the funeral. I can't afford to be fired at this time.' The inference being, April thought, that he expected to pay Beth's legal expenses.

'I'll stay here with Beth,' David said. 'Until you're off duty.'

'Yeah.' Scott sighed. His eyes said he knew this would be Beth's last evening at home – until she was cleared. 'Thanks.'

David sat grim and silent until they heard the front door opened, then closed. Scott was out of earshot. 'What is the matter with the young bastard?' he demanded. 'Why can't he understand that Beth's life hangs in the balance?' Without waiting for a reply, he continued. 'I'm talking to Beth. She's the one to make this decision.' He took a deep, agonized breath. 'I'll talk to her later – before Scott returns.'

'David, would you like me to talk to Beth about adding to the team?' Not dumping Bob and her – adding a star attorney. 'I can be more factual, less emotionally involved.' She stumbled now. It was impossible for her to be more emotionally involved. 'I can explain that Bob and I feel that Scott is not thinking clearly at this moment. That would explain his rejection.' This was not the time for townspeople – prospective jurors – to recognize a rift between husband and father.

'It's my responsibility.' David stared into space. 'Maybe Scott's right. Maybe it would send the wrong message. No!' he refuted instantly. 'Beth deserves the best possible defense. Oh God, how did we get into this nightmare?'

'Let April talk with Beth,' Bob urged. 'It has to be Beth's decision – not ours, not Scott's.'

'All right,' David agreed after a moment. His eyes rested on April with disconcerting intensity. 'It's terrible to frighten her even more – but make her understand the situation.'

'Yes,' April said gently. 'We know she's innocent – and according to law she's innocent until proven guilty beyond a shadow of a doubt.'

'But already I feel vibes I don't like,' David broke in – his voice a blend of anger and apprehension. 'People know Scott was out of town that night. The glare of suspicion is falling right on Beth's head. They read all the innuendos that are being spewed out, and they ask themselves, how much of this is true? People who wouldn't have been caught dead reading that rag before now are devouring it.' He closed his eyes for a moment. 'I can't lie. I'm scared.'

Chapter Thirteen

'I suspect that none of us has eaten today.' Bob's tone was matter-of-fact. 'That's unproductive.'

'Suppose I check the kitchen?' April turned to David with a tentative smile.

'Sure. Several people brought care packages. You need any help, just call.' He tried for humor. 'I hope you don't think we're being sexist?'

'Never crossed my mind.' He was such a warm, sweet man, she thought. It would kill him if Beth wasn't cleared. She felt a sudden knot in her stomach. It would kill *her*.

April set three places at the dining table, put on coffee, brought in platters of food. She hesitated a moment, then prepared a tray for Beth – suspecting Beth would reject this. Still, she made the effort. There was no reply to her light knock. Perhaps Beth had fallen asleep from exhaustion.

April summoned David and Bob to the table. She ached to be able to console David, to tell him with confidence that she and Bob would clear Beth. But she, too, was scared.

'You really picked a rough time to join Bob in practice.' David was making an effort at conversation. 'This has always been such a pleasant, quiet town. Oh, we've had our financial problems,' he conceded. 'But we're beginning to come out of it.'

'Scott's been fighting hard to get the Town Council to offer concessions to that clothing company . . .' Bob frowned. 'What is it? Kensington Womenswear?'

'That's right. They want a hell of a lot of concessions,'

David recalled. 'Jamie's been working on another deal with a dot-com company. They're struggling to raise more capital, but he feels that once they do this they'll be able to offer substantial jobs.' He paused. 'The kind of jobs that'll keep our young people here in Magnolia.'

'Has he presented his deal to the Town Council?' April asked. For a little while, at least, let them move David's thoughts from the more painful subject of Beth's future.

'No. He's still trying to pull it together. But once he does' – defiance lent strength to David's voice – 'you can be damn sure the *Sentinel* will get behind him. And that, April thought, would create much bad feelings between him and Scott. Did this all go back to David's disappointment that Beth married Scott rather than Jamie? Natural enough to cause this dissension, she conceded. But for Beth's sake David and Scott should present a united front.

Bob insisted on clearing away lunch dishes. 'See if you can talk to Beth now,' he ordered. 'Make her understand we want a stronger team.'

'Right.' April's gaze rested for a moment on David. 'I'll give it a try.'

Focusing on this effort – searching her mind for effective arguments – April approached the master bedroom door, knocked lightly.

'Yes?' Polite but a plaintive reproach.

'Beth, we need to talk.' April kept her voice casual. 'It's important . . .'

A moment later Beth opened the door. Deep shadows beneath her eyes, her face devoid of color. April aborted a yearning to draw her daughter into her arms, to make an effort to comfort her.

'We must talk about your defense.' Her eyes apologized for this intrusion.

'With my baby gone, I don't much care,' Beth whispered, but she pulled the door wide to admit April. 'Except for Dad.' She crossed to sit on an edge of the bed. 'He's always been so good to me – and now I may be ruining his good name in this town.'

'Beth, you're not guilty.' She couldn't bring herself to expand on that. 'We have to prove that in court. Your father feels that it would be wise to bring in another lawyer. Someone who specializes in – in cases like this. With much more experience. But Scott believes that would be wrong – that it would look as though we expected to lose.'

'No more lawyers. Just you and Bob.' Beth's face tensed. 'It's the first time in months that Scott and I agreed on anything.'

April debated for an instant. 'Would you like to talk about that?'

'Sometimes I think he believes I killed Debbie . . .' Her voice dropped to a whisper. 'We fought so much these last weeks.'

April remembered what Scott had said: *Beth's been stressed out since Debbie was born. She was upset every time Debbie cried. She was screaming all the time about how she wasn't doing things right. I was scared. I told her to see a psychiatrist.* But Beth had broken the appointment he'd made for her.

April forced herself back to the moment. 'What did you fight about, Beth?'

'It was always the same thing. He wanted me to prod Dad into supporting him for a run for the Town Council next fall. He said it was only right his father-in-law's newspaper should be behind him. Scott's so ambitious it scared me sometimes. He's got this blueprint in his head. By forty-eight, he kept saying, I'll be in the White House. You'll be First Lady.'

'Ambition is a good thing,' April conceded. 'Within bounds.'

'I don't want another lawyer,' Beth repeated. 'I know about fancy lawyers – about the insane fees they demand. Scott and I can't afford that. Dad can't afford it,' she emphasized. 'I won't put him through that.'

As though suddenly drained of strength, April sat on the

bed beside Beth. 'You understand the situation?' Her eyes searched Beth's. She must be brutally truthful. 'Tomorrow morning you'll be taken into custody.'

'What happens after that?' Beth's air of acceptance frightened April.

'You'll be taken to night court for arraignment. Probably in another day or two.' April forced herself to speak calmly. 'At the arraignment it's fairly certain that you'll be ordered held for a grand jury hearing. Unless we can come up with the real perpetrator . . .'

'Who could have killed Debbie?' Beth exuded bewilderment. No way could she be guilty, April told herself. 'Who would do such a thing?'

'We mean to find out,' April told her. 'But we'll need your help.'

Beth gazed at her in bewilderment. 'How can I help?'

'By answering some questions. Beth, we're convinced this was a grudge murder – somebody with a sick mind who harbored an insane hostility towards you or Scott or your father. Knowing what pain this would inflict. I want you to think very hard – going back as far as high school,' she said urgently. 'Try to remember someone who was very angry at you. It could be someone who nursed that anger for years.'

'I can't think of anyone,' Beth stammered.

'Maybe not at this moment,' April said gently, 'but if someone comes to mind, make sure you tell me.'

'All right.' It was a disconcerted whisper.

'Now a few more questions. That night – you heard no sounds of an intruder?'

'Nothing.' Beth closed her eyes for a moment in anguish. 'I didn't want to move Debbie's crib from our bedroom into the nursery – she was so young. But Scott thought I was being paranoid. He put in an intercom system so that we could hear any tiny whimper,' she conceded. 'But if she'd been in our bedroom, I would have heard any slight intrusion!'

In a corner of her mind April could hear an accusing

prosecutor: *But this mother – admittedly a light sleeper – heard no intruder in the nursery, right next to her own bedroom?* He would take a dramatic pause. *And remember – every window in the house, the front and back doors, were locked.*

'Bob and I are tracking down every possible lead. We want so much to find him – or her.'

The following morning was cold, blustery. April awakened almost an hour before her alarm was set to go off – after a night of broken slumber. Instantly she was conscious of what lay ahead. Each day seemed a little more painful than the one before.

She'd found her baby – only to discover her in this precarious situation. She was constantly tormented by the fear that she and Bob – with limited criminal case experience – were not up to clearing Beth. And Beth refused to consider bringing in someone else.

She prepared for the day with a feeling of unreality. She and Bob were accomplishing nothing. Bob had checked out all those who knew Scott would be away the night the murder was committed. Everyone with a solid alibi. Though she had admitted this to no one, she'd checked out the motel where Scott said he'd spent the night. He was there.

Bob arrived to pick her up. It was minutes before seven a.m.

'We'll have coffee first,' April said. She didn't want to arrive at the house before Scott left. She was still inwardly furious at him for rejecting their request to bring in another attorney.

As prearranged, she and Bob arrived at the Emerson house well before the hour when they'd been told Beth would be taken into custody. They saw David's car at the curb as they emerged from Bob's ageing Dodge Spirit. Scott's car was gone.

Haggard and unnerved by what lay ahead, David opened the door in response to Bob's ring.

'I can't say good morning.' David was defiant. 'What's good about it?'

'How's Beth?' April struggled for calm.

'At moments I don't think she understands what's happening. Maybe she's blocking it out. The first thing she asked me when I arrived this morning was, what do you hear about Elaine and Clark?'

'Elaine is Scott's sister,' Bob explained. 'Her husband Clark is down in New York for all kinds of tests at a hospital down there.'

'Beth worries about everybody's problems.' David prodded them into the living room. 'She's always been that way. Clark's been at Hamilton Hospital almost a week now. In these days when hospitals have a revolving door, it sounds bad for Clark. He's a young man . . .' David was talking compulsively, April realized – to avoid what was haunting him. 'He's just thirty-six. He and Elaine have two young kids.'

'Have you tried to talk to Beth again – or to Scott – about bringing in another attorney?' Bob asked.

'Neither one will give an inch.' David paused, seemed to be trying to deal with some inner apprehension. 'They don't exchange a word between them now. I cringe at the hostility I'm feeling between them. Damn, how is that going to look to outsiders? Some might take it to mean Scott thinks Beth is guilty.'

'I'll talk with him,' Bob promised. 'It's important for them not to show a rift in their marriage. Not at this time . . .'

'Where do we go from here?' David lowered himself on to the edge of one of the two living room club chairs while April and Bob settled on the facing sofa. His eyes moved from Bob to April – pleading, it seemed to her, for some word of reassurance.

'We have to stall for time,' April said. 'Delay the grand

jury hearing as long as we can.' She took a deep breath. Be realistic – without a miracle Beth would be held for trial. 'Once we're past the grand jury hearing we'll file for a bail hearing.' She saw David flinch. 'The police are focusing on proving Beth's guilty. Our job is clear – we need to track down the real perpetrator.'

David rose to his feet in impatience, began to pace. 'How do we do that? What leads do we have? That woman who was hanging around the house – you say she's in the clear. There are no outstanding keys to the house. Bob, you've admitted you're getting nowhere tracking down the handful of people who knew Scott was going to be out of town that night.' Alarm lent an aura of anger to his voice. 'Where do we go from here?'

'We need to find out who in this town harbored a grudge – a sick, insane grudge – against one of the three of you.' April repeated an earlier resolve. 'Either against Beth, Scott, or you.' She exchanged a swift glance with Bob. They'd discussed this at length. 'We need the three of you to sit down with us – one at a time – and explore this.

'For me that's a long list,' David warned and grimaced. 'How could somebody be so sick as to take out a grudge against me on a sweet, innocent five-month-old?'

'We start with you at dinner at the house tonight,' Bob told David. 'April will talk again with Beth. Or try to,' he said wryly. 'And I'll set up a time to talk with Scott.'

'It's against all my instincts, but I'm going to have to get back to the newspaper,' David admitted. 'Jamie's working almost around the clock. I'm needed there. I feel so damn guilty, to be going to the office when – when Beth is going to be sitting there behind bars.'

'You'll be able to present a sympathetic front for Beth in the *Sentinel*,' Bob pointed out. 'That's important.'

'But I'm the father.' An edge of desperation in David's voice now. 'There'll be those who won't believe I won't lean over in Beth's defense. I've told you – already the circulation at the *Ledger* has gone up.' He snapped his fingers in sudden recall. 'Tell me where this Rosita woman lives. Beth asked me to have Scott arrange with her to come in to clean the house once a week. I doubt that she's concerned about the state of the house. She wants to know that Rosita will have a little extra cash each week.'

David left them to go down the hall to the master bedroom. April and Bob heard him coaxing Beth to come out and have some breakfast. Moments later they heard her voice. She was allowing her father to prod her into the kitchen.

'Coffee for you two?' he called to April and Bob.

'Nothing for us,' Bob called back.

Twenty minutes later David returned to the living room with Beth at his side. Seeing her this morning – knowing what lay ahead – April felt a frustrating inadequacy. Her precious baby – but she could only comfort her as a stranger. As part of her defense team, April derided herself.

With an air of ambivalence David flipped on the radio. It was time for Scott to deliver the eight a.m. news. His voice filled the room – a warm, charismatic presence. April remembered what Beth had told her about Scott and his soaring ambition. She sensed that Beth was steeling herself to listen to him now.

Scott reported nothing about the murder case, though this was the news that dominated the town this morning. The station management arranged for another announcer to report on this – being as brief as possible. Last night's *Ledger* had been blunt in reporting that Beth would be taken into custody this morning.

With the eight a.m. news completed, David flipped off the radio. Why had he turned it on? April asked herself. Had he expected – hoped for – some reproach for what was happening? But then Scott was held to station rules, she conceded. He didn't write the news. He read it.

To fill in the time until the detectives arrived to take Beth into custody, the other three talked about the weather

– growing colder and more blustery. David made one ill-timed plea to Beth about expanding her defense team – but her blunt rejection again aborted pursuing this.

April's eyes moved compulsively to Beth at intervals. In truth, she tormented herself, Beth was emotionally removed from the charges about to be pressed against her. Only for her father did she worry about this.

April was assaulted by recurrent fears that Bob and she would not be up to the task of clearing Beth. Instinct told her they needed Beth to fight with them. Would she do this? Was she so disconsolate as to accept whatever came along?

The moment the car with two detectives pulled up before the house, David was on his feet – his face betraying his anguish. He reached for Beth's coat and held it for her.

'I'm going with you,' he told her tenderly. 'We're going to win this fight.' But April knew his optimism was fragile.

The doorbell rang. David seemed frozen. Bob went to the door, pulled it wide. Two detectives – Frank Lorenzo and another detective, new to the force – walked inside. Both were visibly uncomfortable.

'Sorry, David,' Frank Lorenzo mumbled and turned to Beth. 'Elizabeth Roberts Emerson, you are under arrest for the murder of your daughter, Deborah Jane Emerson . . .'

Chapter Fourteen

In grim silence April and Bob – in his car – followed the police car into town. As they approached the small business area, she recoiled from the sight of Christmas lights being hung at intervals across Main Street, Christmas trees being set up before each shop. Only now did she realize that Christmas was barely two weeks away. What should have been a time of joy was darkened by horror and fear.

April reminded herself that she was here at the police precinct as Beth's attorney. Her personal feelings must be put aside if she was to perform efficiently as part of Beth's defense team. Beth was her client – hers and Bob's.

She heard herself perform as she should, was ever conscious of David's agony as an onlooker. So quickly Beth was booked, taken away. And she was frightened that Beth seemed reconciled to these happenings. Beth, she tormented herself, couldn't move beyond the knowledge that Debbie was dead.

How was she to pull Beth from that frightening apathy? One way, she told herself yet again: through David. Beth loved him so deeply – she didn't want to see his name besmirched by a daughter convicted of murder. Make her realize she must help in her defense – for her father's sake she must do this.

Later Beth and she would talk. Beth must search her mind for someone who harbored a psychotic rage towards her. But she and Bob mustn't lessen their pursuit of someone with a terrible grudge against Scott or David, she warned herself. That was the motive for Debbie's murder.

'I have to be in court this morning,' Bob said as he headed along with April and David for the parking area beside the precinct. He glanced at his watch. 'Damn, I'm late.'

'I'll drive April wherever she wants to go,' David offered, then hesitated. He turned to April. 'You know I'm anxious to do anything I can to help. Would you like to come up to the office with me and thrash things through a bit? I'm warning you,' he reminded with a rueful grin, 'I've got a long list of people who hate my guts.'

'Let's do that,' April agreed.

In the short drive to the office of the *Sentinel* David talked compulsively about what a wonderful daughter Beth had always been. He admitted that perhaps he had been harsh in his feelings about Scott.

'I didn't show my inner hostility. At least, I don't think I did. But Beth scared the hell out of me when she married Scott just three months after he arrived in town. She'd grown up knowing Clark, of course – and she's always been very fond of Elaine. There was a time,' he reminisced with tenderness, 'when she was a steady babysitter for Elaine and Clark.'

'Clark is down in New York on some health problem, isn't he?'

'It's terribly serious. Something about his liver. Beth was so concerned about them. She offered to take the two kids while Elaine is down there with Clark, but Elaine thought it would be too much for her. You know, with Debbie so young and demanding so much attention. I kind of thought Scott ruled that out.' He paused. 'Scott supposedly came here to Magnolia because of his sister and brother-in-law – but Scott and Elaine were never very close. I don't know . . .' David frowned in thought. 'Maybe I imagine things.'

At the newspaper office David was caught up in business for a few minutes. There was an urgent call to be made, a decision about the following morning's editorial.

'I'll have Iris bring us coffee,' David broke in while Iris gave him a breakdown on problems in the pressroom. 'She makes the best cup of coffee in Magnolia.' His eyes apologized for the delay in settling down to what was uppermost in their minds.

'For that,' Iris joshed, 'I'll grind the best Colombian beans,' she promised and turned to Beth with a glint of approval. 'Milk and sugar?'

'Black, no sugar,' April told her.

'Got it.' Iris flipped and left David's office. He settled in his chair with an air of dismissing newspaper problems for now.

'I don't have to tell you how much Beth means to me,' he said quietly and hesitated. 'There's no reason for you to have known it, but she's my adopted daughter.'

'Oh?' All at once April was ice-cold. Would he one day look at her and know she was Beth's birth mother? Would he regard her with contempt for giving up her baby? She didn't want him to feel that way about her. *What's the matter with me? Why do I feel this way about David?*

'Jane and I were married during my senior year in college. She was pregnant – and we were happy about it. Then she lost the baby. The doctors told us – and we tried half a dozen – that she could never conceive again.'

'Beth was lucky to have found such loving parents.' That was true, April told herself. All those years she worried about her baby. David and his wife were wonderful parents.

'It was Beth – bless her – who held Jane and me together. We married so young – after a few years we drifted apart. But Beth held us together. We were a family. And during those painful years when Jane was so sick, Beth was wonderful. How could something like this happen to somebody like Beth, whom everybody loves? It's someone after me,' he said in anguished self-reproach. 'She's paying for something I did.'

April dug into her purse for a notebook. She was shaken by the unfamiliar emotions that surged in her. She was vulnerable now, she taunted herself – because of Beth. And David had been so good to her precious baby.

Yet a moment later she conceded that what she was feeling for David was apart from what was happening with Beth. That first evening they met she was drawn to him – before she knew about Beth. And she'd sensed, too, that he was drawn to her. But this was no time for such emotions.

'Shall we start with the major vendettas against me – and work our way down to the minor ones?' He was striving for a touch of humor.

'Start with the most obvious,' she said. 'And work back through the years. This could be a grudge that took root when you were a little boy.'

'You may be here for a long time,' he warned.

'As long as is needed,' April said. The original plan was for Bob to work with David and Scott. She would work with Beth. But time was of the essence. Deal with this now. Bob wouldn't object.

Iris tapped at the door, walked in with two mugs of coffee.

'There're refills if you're in the mood.' She placed the two mugs on David's desk and left. Her eyes told them she knew this was an important conference.

At intervals as David and she talked, April was disconcerted by the intensity of his gaze. It was nothing more than gratitude – a soaring hope that she would be able to clear Beth. But there were moments when their eyes met and she was conscious that he was seeing her as more than a partner in Beth's defense team. She didn't realize the passage of time until Iris came into the office to ask if she should order lunch sent up for them.

'Are you willing to go another inning?' he asked April with a wistful smile. 'I know I'm monopolizing you today.'

'I'm willing. The only case I'm handling is Beth's,' she reminded.

They focused for a few moments on ordering lunch, then returned to delving into who among David's enemies was most likely to be responsible for Debbie's murder.

'It's going to be heavy digging for you and Bob,' David warned and paused in troubled thought. 'When do you expect Beth to be arraigned?'

'I was told it was tentatively scheduled for tomorrow evening,' April said. 'We'll receive confirmation late today.' Bob felt it best that she should represent Beth at the night court hearing. But they both knew there was no way she could manage a dismissal. 'There's no point in burying our heads in the sand,' she said with a blend of compassion and apology. 'Beth will be held for a grand jury hearing.'

'When?' David probed, a tic in one eyelid revealing his anxiety.

'Probably within a week or so. Bob and I will work hard to present a strong case for bail – but I don't know. In cases like this' – she couldn't bring herself to say *in cases of first degree murder* – 'bail is rarely granted.'

'But people in this town know Beth,' David said in fresh frustration. 'They know she can't be guilty.' He paused. 'But I'm getting weird vibes. People I've known all my life seem to be avoiding me. Damn it, April! It's the slimy stories the *Ledger*'s running!'

'And we can't sue them for libel.' April read his mind. 'They've managed to keep themselves in the clear.'

But the stories were so damaging, April told herself. The newspaper had managed to interview the psychiatrist that Beth was supposed to see. They'd dug up the fact that Beth and Scott had been battling furiously for weeks. They'd even elicited the information that new rubber gloves had been thrown away the night of the murder – the implication being that those gloves had been used to strangle Debbie – and Beth's fingerprints were on them. They knew that the doors and windows of the house had been locked against any intruder. And no sign of a break-in. These small bits of evidence haunted April in most of her waking hours, inflicted her with insomnia.

'Damn them!' David pounded on his desk with one fist.

'The evidence against Beth is absurd! Nothing that could convince a jury that she's guilty.' But he was terrified – as she was – that the prosecution would bring together enough to sway a jury to convict. 'Why the hell aren't they out there looking for other suspects?'

'That's up to us.'

'Debbie's dead because of me,' David accused himself. 'Beth's accused of murder because of me! This has to be a sick grudge against me,' he reiterated yet again.

'Let's be specific. What enemies have you made here in town? Let's focus on names.' April reached into her purse for a notebook and pen.

'April, I've told you . . .' David sighed. 'I've stepped on a lot of toes in this town. Fighting for causes some didn't like.'

'Most recently,' she pinpointed and glanced up at the light tap on the door. It swung open to admit Jamie.

'We're short a photographer on this shift,' Jamie told David. 'I had to send Nicky over to cover a fire we just got a call about, but he has his cell phone in case we need to reach him to cover something else.'

'Okay.' David dismissed this with a frown. 'Sit down with us for a few minutes. You've met April?'

'Yes.' Jamie smiled warmly.

'We've just about decided that whoever killed Debbie was out to hurt one of three people: Beth, Scott, or me. I can't believe anybody would harbor that kind of grudge against Beth. I'm doubtful that it would be a deal to get back at Scott. You get around this town a lot. Do you know anybody who hates Scott? From what I hear, he's damn popular.'

'That's right.' But it was a reluctant admission. 'Except with you and me,' Jamie added with a wry grin. 'But I suppose it's natural that Scott and I aren't exactly buddies.' His eyes were somber. *He's thinking about Beth – he's still in love with her.* 'I mean,' he added awkwardly, turning to April, 'we're both aiming for a political career in this town.

I'm on the Town Council – and he wants to replace me. I guess he can't figure out why the newspaper supports me when he's David's son-in-law.'

'Where's the fire?' David seemed anxious, April thought, to move away from this touchy subject.

'Over at the trailer park,' Jamie said.

All at once April was uneasy. Involuntarily her eyes moved to David. He, too, seemed disturbed by this news.

'How did it start?' April asked. *Which trailer is on fire?*

'We haven't heard yet.' Jamie paused as Iris appeared at the door.

'Nicky just called on his cell phone,' Iris reported with an air of excitement. 'The fire at the trailer park – it's a case of arson.'

'Everybody get out safely?' David demanded.

'Which trailer was it?' April broke in, her heart pounding

'The last one on the row,' Iris said. *Rosita's trailer.* 'It was unoccupied except for a dog. A woman in the next trailer called the fire department, then got the dog out.'

'Rosita has a dog!' Suspicions charged across April's mind. Was someone trying to kill Rosita – or to drive her out of town – in fear that Rosita had seen him loitering about the house the night Debbie was killed? Did she see someone but is scared to tell us? *Am I jumping to absurd conclusions?*

'Let's get over to that fire, April.' David was grim. His face reflected the same suspicions. 'This one I'm covering myself.'

Chapter Fifteen

April and David hurried to the parking area, settled themselves in his car. Up to this point silent about their suspicions.

'Maybe I'm off the wall,' David conceded, 'but the hairs on the back of my neck were sticking upright when Iris told us about the fire at the trailer park.'

'It has to be Rosita's trailer,' April insisted. 'Hers is the last on the row there. And she has this great black Lab.'

'He's okay,' David reminded with a gentle smile.

'Rosita must have been at work and the kids at school. But it's arson. Why would somebody set fire to Rosita's trailer?'

'I don't know how it links to what – what happened that night,' David said, 'but my mind tells me there's some connection. And we can't afford to overlook any possible link.'

By the time they arrived at the scene, the fire in the trailer – Rosita's – was under control. A pair of firemen worked to make sure it was extinguished. The other firemen were heading back to their truck. With April at his side David approached the fire chief.

'You're sure it's arson, Tim?' David asked with no preliminaries.

'The fire was set,' Tim confirmed. 'No doubt about that. If the dog hadn't alerted the neighbors, the whole trailer park could have gone down.'

April tugged at David's arm. 'There's Rosita! She must be devastated.'

April and David strode to where Rosita stood, the Lab at her feet. She glanced up with a shaky smile as they approached.

'Rocky is a hero.' She bent to caress his head. 'I came home from work, and the fire truck was here!' She shuddered in recall. 'I was so scared until I saw him.'

'Do you have a place to stay tonight?' April asked. Her apartment was small, but she could manage to put them up somehow.

'My next-door neighbors – they're takin' us in. Until we can move back into the trailer,' Rosita explained. 'I know that the church will help me. But what is happening to our town?' Her eyes exuded bewilderment and fear. 'Murder, now somebody tries to burn down my trailer? It makes me wonder – is this a safe place to live? But where else can I go with my kids?'

'The police will track down whoever did this,' April comforted.

'But why? Why do these things happen?'

'Rosita, do you have time to take on another job?' April strived to be diplomatic. 'Could you do my apartment once a week?'

Rosita's face lighted. 'Yes! I can come on Tuesdays or Thursdays. When would you like me to start?'

For a few moments the two women focused on business arrangements. David left them to talk with the two police officers who had been questioning other residents of the trailer park.

'Oh, the school bus will be here soon.' Rosita was anxious again. 'The kids – they'll be so scared when they see the fire truck and the police car.'

'They'll see you and Rocky.' April tried for a confident smile. 'They'll know you're both all right.'

Rosita gazed tenderly at Rocky. 'They'll be so proud of him. If he hadn't barked so loud and carried on the way he did, all the trailers could have burned down. People could have been hurt.'

But who had set the fire? April probed in silence. Why? She couldn't erase from her mind the conviction that somehow this case of arson was connected to Debbie's murder. What was Rosita afraid to tell them?

David joined April and Rosita, paused to pat Rocky for a moment.

'You don't have to worry that this will happen again,' he told Rosita. 'The police chief is posting a man here around the clock for the next two weeks. Whoever set this fire will get the message. You'll all be okay.'

But it was Rosita who was the target, April pinpointed. Again she asked herself, what was Rosita afraid to tell them?

The following evening – at night court – Beth was arraigned, along with an unsavory cluster of petty thieves, a drug dealer and his buyer, and a pair of ageing prostitutes. Knowing it was futile, April offered a spirited defense. Beth was ordered held for a grand jury hearing. Along with David and Bob, April watched in anguish while Beth was led away again.

Out in the cold night air – with a group of children singing Christmas carols close by – David suggested the three of them go in for coffee at a nearby coffee shop that was open until midnight.

'What a rotten Christmas this is!' he muttered as they walked into the lightly populated coffee shop. Christmas lights outlined the windows. Wreaths hung about the walls. Mobiles of smiling Santas hung from the ceiling.

They settled themselves in a booth at the rear. David exchanged guarded greetings with a group of men seated in a nearby booth.

'What do you hear about Clark?' Bob asked when they'd ordered. 'Will he be home for Christmas?'

David flinched, ignored the question. 'Beth asked me about him when I saw her today. With all her grief she worries about Clark.'

'That's Scott's brother-in-law?' April asked, recalling some talk of Clark and Elaine.

'That's right.' David nodded. 'Scott said their two kids are very upset about Debbie.'

Bob frowned in thought for a moment. 'Scott understands that he and Beth mustn't show a divided front now, doesn't he?'

David nodded. 'I'm not sure what they were battling about, but from little things Beth dropped I suspect it was about his promoting a deal for Kensington Womenswear. Like me, she sees it as bringing in jobs at the bottom of the barrel. Jamie's hoping for something better. The town's been in such an economic slump that Scott feels any new jobs should be welcomed.'

'David, you understand we're going to try to postpone the trial as long as possible.' April's eyes sought for approval. 'We need time to make our case.'

'Sure.' But April sensed his frustration.

'We must bring Beth out of her lethargy,' April told David. 'And I think you're the key to that.'

'How?' David was puzzled.

'She's concerned about how all this will reflect on you. She loves you so much.' *But Beth will never know how much I love her.* 'I know it's a rough deal – but let her know that her being cleared will reflect well on you in this town.'

'I'll do anything that'll help Beth. You know that.'

'We'll dig into every lead you gave April,' Bob reassured David. 'We'll check out every person in this town who might have been nursing a grudge against you, against Scott – and against Beth. We'll find Debbie's murderer.'

'First thing tomorrow morning I'll go over to talk with Beth,' April pursued. 'Pick her brain. We can't overlook any small clue. It could go back to her high school years – or even earlier. Some sick kid who's been nursing what he or she considered a slight all those years ago.' She paused in thought. 'It would be reaching too far, I suppose, to consider Scott's sister and brother-in-law might be the object of somebody's hate. No,' she rejected before David or Bob could reply. 'If Clark or Elaine was the subject of a grudge, then their kids would have been the target.'

Their waiter arrived with coffee and danish. They abandoned conversation until he left their booth.

'Scott sent a memo over to the paper late this afternoon.' David sighed. 'Beth's going to be upset. The doctors at the hospital have come up with answers about Clark. He won't be coming home for Christmas. He needs a liver transplant.'

Bob was shaken. 'This town is a living soap opera. When will these crazy things stop happening?'

'Tell Beth about Clark,' David told April. 'She'll be upset – but she'll want to know. Tell her before she reads about it in the paper.'

They lingered at the coffee shop until Bob suggested calling it a night.

'I like to be home before the kids go off to bed. You know, kiss them goodnight and all . . .' His voice trailed off. April read his mind. Debbie's death had made them all conscious that tragedy could lie just around the corner.

'I'll drive April home,' David said. He'd picked her up at her apartment to go with her to the night court session. 'You run along, Bob.' David reached for the check.

In the car en route to April's apartment David talked compulsively about Beth. Oh yes, April told herself, David and his wife had been fine parents. Thank God for that.

'Beth was the best thing that ever happened to us,' David said as he pulled up before April's apartment complex. In the darkness of the car April felt more than saw his eyes focus on her. 'Were you ever married, April?'

'For seven years. It was doomed from the start. We were both in law school. I was alone in the world – scared of being alone, I suppose. We grew apart through the years. The relationship became ugly. I divorced him. He's remarried.'

'But you have no regrets,' David prodded while they sat in the car.

'Oh no. It was a relief to me to be free of him.' She hesitated, sensing his need to talk. A need reflected in her. 'I know we've just had coffee – but it's been a traumatic evening. Would you like to come in for more coffee?' He wouldn't take that the wrong way, would he?

'I was hoping you'd ask,' he confessed. 'I'm too wired to sleep for a long time yet.'

They left the car, went to April's apartment. He glanced about the living room with an air of approval, then hesitated. 'May I turn on the TV for the late news? Just to hear the headlines . . .' She understood; he suspected – feared – the news of Beth's being charged would be first on the list.

'Go right ahead. I'll put on the coffee.' All at once she was tense. *How can I be feeling this way about David at a time like this?*

From the kitchenette she heard a newscaster report that Beth was being held for a grand jury hearing. 'A trial date is to be scheduled shortly.' Without waiting to hear anything further, David switched off the TV. For David and her this was the darkest period of their lives.

They lingered over coffee – both loath to say goodnight.

'You and Bob will have to carry the ball.' Almost a note of apology in David's voice. 'I didn't mean to doubt your professional skills, April. It's just that I'm so damn scared. Not because of what's come out so far,' he added with a touch of defiance. 'They don't have much of a case at this point. But I'm terrified of what they might dig up as evidence – things that can be twisted around to appear what they're not.'

'We both know Beth couldn't be guilty.' April strived to sound professional. 'My instincts have never failed me. And they tell me that in some fashion whatever Rosita is concealing from us is important. I'd like to do some digging into her background.' She hesitated. 'It'll be expensive, but I believe a private investigator could be helpful.'

'April, I don't care what it costs!' A tic quivered in his right eyelid. 'Hire a PI – let him dig into Rosita's background.'

'I'll talk to Beth about her. Beth might be able to point us in the right direction.'

'I realize we've known each other only a short time . . .' David's eyes held hers. 'And I know this isn't the time to talk about personal feelings. But when this nightmare is over, I want to get to know you far better. I want you to be an important part of my life.'

'I feel that way, too,' April whispered. 'I never expected to feel this way about any man.'

But how will David feel about me if he learns that I'm Beth's mother? Will he hate me for giving up my baby? I couldn't bear to have him hate me . . .

Chapter Sixteen

April sat with Beth in the tiny, drab cubicle provided for attorney/defendant conferences. She felt sick at the need to probe when Beth was in such a precarious mental state. But she proceeded because she knew it was urgent.

'Then you know of no one who might hate Scott,' April concluded.

'Scott is Mr Congeniality,' Beth said with rare cynicism. 'At least, in public. Everybody in town thinks he's wonderful.'

'A neighbor reported that the two of you were constantly fighting,' April continued with guilt. She made a point of not mentioning the neighbor by name. 'Was it because you were against his promoting Kensington Womenswear?'

'I wasn't against Kensington – I was for the dot-com company that Jamie was promoting. Everybody knows garment manufacturers pay low salaries. The dot-com company was a much better deal for the town. But Scott was desperate to promote Kensington. He was spending every free moment he could manage with some man who was in town representing them.'

'Oh, your father asked me to tell you . . .' April shifted to another approach. 'The doctors have finally come to a decision about your brother-in-law's condition.'

'How is Clark?' Beth seemed to emerge from the fog that embraced her much of the time. 'What did the doctors say?' Her eyes clung to April.

'It's very serious,' April said gently. 'He's to be put on the list for a liver transplant.'

'Will he receive one fast enough?' Beth was fearful. 'Elaine must be so upset.'

'I don't know any more.' April was apologetic.

'Tell Dad to let me know what's happening.' Beth's face was tense. 'I only see you and Dad. Scott doesn't come here – and that's the way I want it.' A touch of defiance in her voice now. 'But Clark and Elaine and their kids are very dear to me.'

'I'm sure your father will keep you advised.' It wasn't good that Scott didn't visit Beth, April thought. In a small town like this word would get around that they were estranged. But then Della Comstock had already stressed that, hadn't she? Not good for Beth. 'He's working out a schedule of visitation rights with Jeff Goodwin.'

'Clark's kids must be so frightened. Such sweet kids.' Beth's face was tender. 'And I can't even be there to comfort them . . .'

'Beth, you know Rosita Rivera fairly well, don't you?' April was fishing.

'I know she's a good person. She's had such a rough life.'

'She and her husband came up here from Mexico, didn't they?'

'Yes. First they lived in Texas for a while. They were legal immigrants,' Beth defended them. 'And then they heard about farm jobs up here – and left Texas. But why are you asking me about Rosita?' Beth was puzzled.

'Someone tried to burn her trailer. There was some damage.' April rushed to reassure her as Beth gaped in shock. 'Neither Rosita nor the children – nor their dog – was hurt. A church group is helping to restore the trailer. Meanwhile neighbors have taken them in.'

'Why would anybody want to burn Rosita's trailer?' Beth winced. 'I know we have a few people in town who resent the migrant workers. But to burn her trailer?'

'Sick people.'

'I hope Dad runs a story about that. This is a nice town – we shouldn't allow such things to happen.' All at once Beth seemed to be withdrawing into herself again. Her baby should not have been murdered in this nice town – but it happened.

April and Bob were frustrated at spending sixteen-hour days in their search for answers, yet coming up with nothing. One by one they had to discard possible suspects – all with alibis for the night that Debbie was murdered. The normal Christmas atmosphere was tainted this year.

Each day April went to visit with Beth – ostensibly as her attorney working on the case but ever conscious of a need to be with her. Each day she brought another magazine, fruit, a candy bar. Aching to take her daughter in her arms and comfort her.

'We're going to clear you, Beth,' she repeated rashly each day. She asked questions – with a hope of latching on to some bit of information that would be useful. 'Bob and I are working very hard.'

'Where are all those people who claim to admire Beth?' David taunted. 'Why do they turn angry when we ask questions? Why do they read the lies the *Ledger* persists in spreading?'

April forced herself to read David's competition. The hate it spewed forth each day was scurrilous, yet both she and Bob realized it would not be useful to attack the other newspaper. Like David, she sensed that as days passed doubts were creeping into the minds of many in town about Beth's innocence. At the same time sympathy engulfed Scott.

David had hired a private investigator to check on Rosita's background – and that, too, seemed difficult to pin down. Rosita and her husband had been just another pair of Mexican immigrants yearning to improve their lives. Still, Rosita appeared to be a threat to someone. That someone who'd set fire to her trailer in hopes of frightening her out of town. How was this linked to Debbie's murder? The reason continued to elude April.

Just four days before Christmas Eve – which April knew David dreaded – Elaine returned to town. April was at the newspaper office in yet another meeting with David when Elaine came to see him.

'Elaine, it's great to see you.' David left his seat to embrace her. 'We've all been with you in spirit.' His eyes were questioning as he prodded her into a chair.

'The kids were getting upset – I've never been away from them overnight until now. Clark insisted I come home to be with them.' Elaine took a deep breath. 'I can't tell you how shocked and disturbed I am about Debbie. With Clark so sick I couldn't come home for Debbie's funeral. Clark and I felt so bad about that . . .'

'We understood,' David said gently.

'Nobody can be serious about the charges against Beth?' Elaine's eyes pleaded for reassurance.

'She's being held on a charge of murder.' David's voice deepened in rage. 'She's to go on trial late next month.' The latest date April and Bob had been able to secure. 'But what's the word about a transplant for Clark?'

'He isn't about to receive a transplant any time soon.' Elaine struggled to continue. 'He's at the bottom of the list.'

'Why?' David was astounded.

'The hospital claims he's an alcoholic. That he has a history of heavy drinking.' Elaine shook her head in disbelief. 'Clark, who never touches a drop. Not since his first year in college when he got so sick after a drinking binge. You know, the usual college scene. But I can't make anybody believe that.' She hesitated a moment. 'I'm bringing you my problems when you have such grief of your own.'

'There must be some way to prove Clark isn't an alcoholic. April, isn't there some legal angle?' He swerved to Elaine –

all at once conscious the two women had never met. 'Elaine, this is April Winston, who's handling Beth's case along with Bob Allen. April, you've heard us talk about Elaine, Scott's sister.'

'Yes, of course.' April's smile was warm. 'Despite her own problems, Beth's so upset about Clark's illness. She asked to be kept up to date on what's happening.'

'Nobody could want a finer sister-in-law than Beth. I've told Scott that endless times.' Elaine's eyes clung to April's. 'You're going to clear Beth, aren't you?'

'We won't consider anything else.' April managed a smile. *Will we clear her?*

'April, what about this business with the hospital?' David pursued. 'Is this a legal matter? Can you and Bob tackle this?'

'I'll talk to Bob.' April glanced at her watch. 'I have to run now. I have a scheduled meeting with Beth.' She turned to Elaine. 'Bob and I will dig into this before the day is over. I'll get back to you,' she promised.

In the cubicle where she was allowed to confer with her client, April told Beth about Clark's problem in acquiring a liver transplant.

'I don't believe it!' Beth gazed at April with a blend of shock and rage. 'Everybody knows Clark doesn't drink!'

'Elaine says the hospital staff concluded he's an alcoholic.' April sighed. 'Bob and I are getting together this evening to try to find some precedent for legal intervention.'

'That could take months. Clark doesn't have months. There must be another way.' Beth clasped her hands in agitation. 'The schools close for the holidays tomorrow . . .' April sensed wheels spinning in Beth's head.

'Yes?' April waited for her to continue.

'Help us,' Beth pleaded. 'Beyond the legal way.'

'How?' April was puzzled.

'Tell Dad he must corral a busload of teachers – two

busloads,' she amended with an air of excitement. 'Let the teachers who've worked with Clark for the past dozen years go to that hospital and tell whoever's in charge of the transplant situation that they *know* Clark isn't an alcoholic!' Her eyes darted about in thought. 'Can you give me a notebook – paper – and a pen? I'm allowed to have that?'

'I don't see why not.' April reached into her purse, withdrew a notebook and pen, handed them to Beth.

'I'll write a plea for Dad to run on the front page of the *Sentinel* tomorrow morning,' Beth explained. 'I can do it in a few minutes, if you can wait?'

'I'll wait,' April said with a surge of love. In the midst of her own heartache Beth was anxious to help her brother-in-law. Her daughter was a very special person.

April sat in silence while Beth wrote her urgent plea for local teachers to come to Clark's aid. The atmosphere was electric. Her own life on the line, Beth was trying to save Clark's.

'There'll be assembly at the schools tomorrow morning,' Beth said urgently. 'Have this read there. The teachers will help!'

Ten minutes later April was charging into David's office. He was in deep conversation with Jamie.

'I'm sorry to break in on you this way,' April apologized, 'but I've just left Beth.'

'How is she?' David asked and grimaced. 'How can I expect her to be?'

'She's worried about Clark. She has an idea that she thinks might be helpful . . .' In a few words April explained Beth's plan, gave David the brief, impassioned article Beth had scrawled.

'I always told Beth she'd be a great reporter,' David said, reading as he talked. 'But thank God I'm familiar with her handwriting. She scribbles worse than doctors.' But his face reflected the great love he felt for Beth. 'This goes front page center tomorrow morning.'

April's gaze moved from David to Jamie. 'How do we put Beth's plan into motion?'

'Easy.' David turned to Jamie. 'See who has to be notified that we'll need at least two school buses.' He checked his watch now. 'School won't be out for half an hour. I'll go to Clark's school, call an emergency meeting in the auditorium. We'll have teachers headed down into the city in forty-eight hours. Jamie, you'll drive one of the buses. I'll get someone in the press room to drive another.'

Jamie seemed ambivalent. 'I have to be in Manhattan tomorrow. Remember, I told you? I have a meeting with the dot-com group.' His face brightened. 'But I can be back in town tomorrow night, drive a bus the next morning.'

'How does it look for them?' David asked, then turned to April. 'Jamie's talking about the company he's hoping to bring into town. The one that'll provide two to three hundred good jobs – as opposed to Scott's garment factory deal.'

'They've gone public,' Jamie said. 'They've raised a lot of capital. And they're real bright and hard-working. They'd be an asset to the town. I want to come in to the next town council meeting with all the figures.' His smile was dry. 'Scott will be coming up with his group – and seven hundred jobs. I think it's fairly certain the council will make a decision at the meeting next month.'

'All right, let's get cracking.' David was brisk. 'Check out the school bus situation, Jamie. But first, set this up to run in tomorrow morning's paper.' He handed Beth's article to the town to Jamie. 'I'll go over to the school and rustle up bodies for the trip to the hospital.' He turned to April. 'I realize you've got a lot on your plate, but could you contact Elaine and tell her what's happening?' He scribbled a phone number and an address on a notepad on his desk, ripped the page and handed it to April. 'She'll feel a little better once she knows.'

'I'll make time,' April promised.

*   *   *

April called Elaine on her cell phone, for a moment suspected she wasn't at home. Then the phone was picked up at the other end. She heard the raucous shriek of a vacuum cleaner in the background.

'Hello?' An uneasy tremor in Elaine's voice told her that phone calls were traumatic in the current situation.

'Elaine, this is April Winston. Would it be all right if I dropped by for a few moments? Now?'

'Sure, come on over,' Elaine said after a moment. But April heard unease in her voice.

Elaine knew she was part of Beth's defense team, April pinpointed. Did Elaine know that Scott and Beth were estranged – and worried that she might be questioned about this? That rag – the *Ledger* – had been blunt about that. Still, it was unlikely Elaine had been reading the Magnolia papers down in New York. Why was Elaine wary of her coming over? Was she disturbed at the prospect of having to take sides between Beth and Scott?

A few minutes later April parked before the pretty, gray-blue ranch house with a jaunty shingled sign that said this was 'The Millers' Nest'. As she walked up the flagstone path, the front door swung wide. Elaine's smile seemed forced. But then she could hardly feel in a happy frame of mind under the circumstances, April reproached herself.

'I have some news,' April began gently as she and Elaine walked into the small, pleasant living room. Now she launched into an account of Beth's plan to help Clark, and how David was moving to put this in motion.

'Sitting there in jail Beth worries about us. That's so like her . . .' Elaine's voice broke. 'I told Scott he was the luckiest man in the world to be married to her.' Elaine struggled to continue. 'I can't find words to tell you how much we appreciate what she's trying to do for us. We've felt so lost. So helpless.'

'I'm sure David will bring teachers together who'll fight for Clark. This is a close-knit town – people will fight for their own. And at the same time,' April promised, 'Bob and I will look into the legal aspects.'

'There's no way a jury in this town will convict Beth,' Elaine said with sudden intensity. Everybody loves her. She's always trying to help somebody.' Elaine's eyes pleaded for reassurance. 'They won't convict her, will they?'

'By law the prosecutor must prove beyond a reasonable doubt that she's guilty.' Beautiful words, April thought while she sought for composure. 'But we must be realistic. What Bob and I have to do is to discover who murdered Debbie – and bring him or her to justice.'

'That's wrong!' Elaine's voice was strident. 'Beth adored Debbie. She would have done anything to protect her!'

'Elaine, do you know of anyone who hated Scott?' She was his sister – she should know this, April thought with a touch of desperation. 'Anyone who might be vindictive enough to have killed his child?'

Elaine seemed stunned by this question. 'No.' Her voice sank to a whisper. 'Scott has no enemies. He's always been such a charmer.'

'If you think of someone,' April urged, 'call me – no matter what the time of day or night. Call me. It's terribly important.'

The days were racing past, April taunted herself. And at this point she and Bob had nothing to take to trial. Nothing except their conviction that Beth was innocent.

Chapter Seventeen

In his one business suit and a tie, Jamie sat in the thirty-eighth floor mid-Manhattan office of Burt Melrose and began his impassioned sales pitch. He needn't have bothered to dress, he thought in a corner of his mind. Burt wore jeans and a cotton turtleneck.

Burt had just told him that Melrose.com had its capital – they were ready to roll. The next meeting of the Town Council was just two weeks away. He was impatient to bring in a deal they could see was better for the town than Kensington Womenswear.

'Jamie, you don't have to sell me,' Burt chided. 'We're sure Magnolia is a great site for us. Financially we're in the best of shape. But we must be assured that we have a long-term lease that'll cost us no more than seven dollars a square foot. We're not asking for any tax abatements,' he stressed.

'On a long lease like that, the council will want provisions for escalations,' Jamie pointed out. That made sense, didn't it?

Burt Melrose considered this for a moment. 'We can handle that. We'll accept a clause that agrees to rent increases in line with annual inflation. How's that?'

'A deal,' Jamie agreed, began to perspire from tension. So he was taking a lot on himself. He'd have to make the council understand that was the way to go.

'We'll hire local people at strong salaries. A few top management people will come in with us – but I can guarantee, the way business is building, a minimum of three hundred full-time jobs at substantial salaries. For us it's important not to tie ourselves up with exorbitant rents.' He shuddered. 'You don't want to know what we're paying here.'

'I'll present this at the meeting.' Jamie was exhilarated. 'I'll get the Town Council to approve the lease at your figures. They'll understand that you're not asking for any tax abatements. I'll do the groundwork before the meeting. After the meeting,' he predicted, 'we'll have the deal sewed up.'

Jamie left the office, picked up his car at the garage, and headed back for Magnolia. Now he had to convince the council that Melrose.com would be a great addition to the town. They ought to see the advantage of acquiring upscale jobs that would keep their young people in town. Now most of them chased off to cities where the future looked more promising.

He'd buzz Ned Jenkins as soon as he got into town. Ned had been bitching about the tax abatements Kensington was demanding. This was a far better acquisition for Magnolia. No tax abatements, no giveaway sales on the property. The rent would be a steady income for the next twenty years.

But Jamie's exhilaration dissipated as he sped up the thruway. Now his thoughts focused on Beth. It was inconceivable that she wouldn't be cleared, he told himself – yet he was terrified for her. He couldn't sleep nights – thinking about her in a jail cell.

Hour after hour he'd talked with David about the trial. David was so frustrated. The lawyers were coming up with nothing substantial to clear Beth. He could hear David's voice now: *I know April and Bob are working like hell for Beth – and they're both bright. Still, I wish I could get through to Beth that we should bring in some big-wheel attorney with heavy trial experience.*

He ached to be able to comfort Beth. To hold her in his arms and convince her she was going to be fine. He'd suspected for months – since Debbie was a few weeks old – that Beth and Scott's marriage was in trouble. Even before the *Ledger* ran its ugly stories about this. Not that either Beth or Scott said anything, he analyzed – but he'd sensed it in little things that slipped past her. And it disturbed him – and David – that while people in Magnolia seemed to be so sympathetic towards Scott, that sympathy seemed not to extend to Beth. Could they – knowing all the things she'd done for this community – believe she could be guilty? Not everybody, he agreed – there were people in town who were furious that she'd been charged with murder. But the jury pool would include the others, also.

He was halfway to Magnolia when his cell phone rang. The caller was David.

'How'd you make out in New York?' David asked.

'Good,' Jamie said. 'I figured I'd drop by the hardware store to talk with Ned Jenkins before I came to the office. Okay?'

'Sure.' David was brisk. 'We'll need two school buses tomorrow. You can get them?'

'Two are being allotted to us. You rounded up that many?'

'We've got 'em.' A touch of apprehension now. 'But there's a new problem. Elaine talked with the hospital people. They've been checking records – I guess because some people here in town have been calling down there, dressing them down for listing Clark as an alcoholic. They claim they have court records proving he's been arrested three times for driving under the influence and about a dozen times for disorderly conduct when he was drunk.'

'No way!' Jamie searched his mind for an explanation. 'David, it has to be somebody with the same name.'

'I can't get hold of either Bob or April – they're both out of their office. Anyhow, you'll be driving down to the city again in the morning. Maybe we'll have some word by then about this court record mix-up.'

'I'm about an hour out of town. I'll stop by to bring Ned Jenkins up to date on Melrose.com, then come into the office.'

*   *   *

Ned Jenkins looked up from the sales figures on his desk to see Jamie Lawrence striding down the aisle of the store to the office at the rear. Bright young twerp, he thought – but maybe not as sharp as Scott Emerson. The two of them weren't fooling anybody. Both of them were after the town council seat Jamie held now.

'Got a few minutes?' Jamie asked, his smile ingratiating.

'I can handle that,' Ned drawled. 'What's up?' He relished being on the Town Council. The one place – besides the store – where he was kingpin.

'I've just come back from a quick trip down to New York.' Jamie slid into the chair before Ned's desk. 'I had a meeting with Melrose.com. They've got their capital – more than they anticipated. They're making an offer to take over the Taylor property for twenty years at a rental of seven dollars a square foot, and—'

'That's low rent for a big outfit,' Ned drawled. Normal for this town – but peanuts compared to New York.

'There'll be an escalation clause, keyed to inflation. They'll make all the necessary renovations – and there're a lot to be made,' Jamie reminded. 'And' – he paused, leaned forward with a glow of satisfaction – 'they're not asking for any special concessions. If I can bring them a twenty-year lease at seven dollars a square foot, they'll sign and start renovations immediately. They figure that could take around three months. That means at least a dozen construction jobs in town. And they'll be hiring around three hundred skilled workers – with substantial salaries.'

'It's something to think about,' Ned agreed. 'Stall them until the next meeting. We'll discuss it then.'

Ned waited until Jamie was out of sight, then dialed the radio station. Scott was on the air, the receptionist reported.

'Tell him to call me when he's clear,' Ned instructed.

An hour later Scott called.

'We need to talk about Kensington,' Ned told him. 'Something else has come up. Can you drop by before we close for the day?'

'I can be there in about an hour,' Scott said. 'That's my dinner break.'

At just past five thirty Scott strolled into the store. Ned was dealing with a contractor who was a major account.

'Go sit in the office,' Ned instructed. 'I'll be with you in a bit.'

'Sure.' Scott flashed his charismatic smile. He was holding up well, Ned thought – with his baby dead and his wife in jail. 'I'll have dinner while I'm waiting.' He held up a paper bag from the Chinese take-out across the street.

Ned finished with the customer, joined Scott in the office. 'I hear there's a busload of teachers going down to New York tomorrow morning to campaign for a transplant for your brother-in-law. That should be good news.'

'Two busloads,' Scott said. 'Clark's hanging on by a thread. My sister's a nervous wreck.' Scott took a deep breath. 'Not much of a Christmas for my wife and me . . .'

'Better times are coming,' Ned commiserated. What could you say to a man whose wife was to be tried for murder?

'What's up?' Scott asked, wolfing down an egg roll.

'I talked with Jamie Lawrence earlier today,' Ned said. 'He's got this big dot-com company in New York who's pining for low rent.'

'Wouldn't it be smarter to sell?' Scott lifted an eyebrow.

'I'm not sure,' Ned demurred. 'If the town really starts growing – and we're hoping for that – the value can skyrocket. And' – he paused for dramatic effect – 'they're not asking for any tax concessions.'

'They'll bring in what? Two hundred jobs? Kensington guarantees seven hundred.' Scott leaned forward, a glint in his eyes. 'And we can make sure they'll buy all their supplies from Jenkins Hardware.'

Ned contrived an inscrutable expression. Sometimes he figured Scott Emerson was too sharp for his own good.

'I'll give it some thought,' he told Scott.

'Kensington won't hang on forever,' Scott warned. 'They've been talking with other towns.'

'Be at the next council meeting. We'll make a decision then.'

On Friday morning – despite the early hour – scores of Magnolia residents gathered to see the two busloads of teachers off for the New York hospital where Clark Miller was being treated. Last-minute Christmas preparations had been pushed aside. The Christmas spirit had taken over. Clark Miller needed their help.

April stood with Elaine beside one of the two buses while teachers climbed aboard. In a moment Elaine, too, would join the cavalcade. At Christmas time, April thought tenderly, Magnolia was fighting to provide the most precious of gifts: the gift of life.

'Beth should be here with us,' Elaine whispered, her eyes wet.

'In spirit she is.' April reached to embrace Elaine. The bus was about to depart. 'Clark will get his transplant,' she predicted with a tremulous smile. 'He'll enjoy many more Christmases.'

Later in the morning April received a phone call from the private investigator hired to check on Rosita down in Texas. He'd been instructed to call her or Bob if he couldn't reach David.

'I'm sorry,' he apologized. 'I've gone as far as I can. I keep running into blank walls. It's like I told you. She and her husband lived in this little town of Chickasaw, Texas. He was trying to organize workers at the factories. They got run out of town. Nobody will say why, but it's pretty clear his union activities were the problem. Wish I could be more helpful, but there it is.'

When Bob came into the office, April told him about the call.

'I'm not giving up on Rosita,' April insisted. 'I'm still getting vibes about her. Why can't she be honest with us?'

'Even up here she's scared.' Bob was sympathetic. 'And life isn't easy for her.'

'I'll catch up with David and tell him. He'll be disappointed.'

'Oh, Nicole said she wants you and David over for dinner tonight. Will you tell him?'

'Sure. A special occasion?' April was curious.

Bob grinned. 'You might say that. It's our wedding anniversary. Remember? You were there. Tell David we'll be expecting him.' He glanced at his watch. 'I've got to get to court.'

April arrived early at the Allen house. Nicole was ecstatic over the gift April had brought. She cradled the thick volume in her hands.

'You remembered me talking about her new cookbook.' Her eyes were bright with affection. 'But where did you find it? I didn't see it anywhere in town yet.'

'I made a few calls, drove over to a mall near Albany,' April explained.

'You were always one to go the extra mile,' Nicole murmured. 'You're like David in that.' Her eyes seemed to be asking questions.

'I take that as a compliment,' April said lightly, walking with Nicole into the kitchen.

'He was wonderful to Jane in those last years, when she was so sick. In such pain.' Nicole hesitated. 'I think their marriage had gone cold long before – but he was there for her.' And April remembered that David said he and his wife had grown apart. Again, Nicole hesitated. 'Women were always attracted to David. It was weird – even at Jane's funeral they were already chasing after him. But he wouldn't give anybody a tumble. Until now . . .'

'Oh?' April pretended ignorance.

'April, you must know,' Nicole chided. 'David's mad about you.'

'It – it isn't something to talk about at a time like this.' But her heart was pounding.

'Anyhow, I wanted you to know – Bob and I think it's great.'

The doorbell rang. That would be David, April realized.

'Would you answer that?' Nicole reached for the oven door. 'I should check on the roast.'

Within minutes Bob, too, arrived. The four adults and the children gathered at the dinner table.

'I'm beginning to feel like a boarder,' David told Nicole with a wry smile. 'When this is all over – and I pray it'll be soon' – he took a deep breath – 'I owe you and Bob a lot of dinners.'

The four adults shared a tacit agreement not to discuss the trial nor Clark's problem in the presence of the children. As soon as dinner was out of the way and Marianne and Neil went off to the den to do homework, they settled in a corner of the living room.

'I've been digging into the DWI claim and the disorderly conduct arrests,' Bob reported. 'One of the guys downtown is checking it through their computer network. I figure we'll get Clark's fingerprints, prove that the arrest records belong to another Clark Miller.'

'Elaine's going down with the buses. I'll tell her to bring back a full set of Clark's fingerprints,' David said. He rose from his chair to go to the phone.

'Wait a bit,' Nicole suggested. 'Bob's source should be calling soon. Maybe these were charges that were made twenty years ago – when Clark was a teenager.'

'How're you doing with your list of suspects?' David asked Bob with rare brusqueness. The others knew he meant those people who could be considered to dislike Scott.

'I'm almost done,' Bob admitted. 'It's a short list.' His tone was apologetic. 'Scott's only been in town four years – and he's so popular.'

'I still ask myself, what is Rosita hiding?' April said slowly. 'The PI hasn't come up with anything yet beyond the fact that she and her husband worked in a factory in some small town in Texas. He thinks they were fired because Rosita's husband was trying to organize the workers. Which leads us nowhere.' April shook her head in bafflement. 'My gut keeps telling me Rosita could help us – but she's scared.'

The phone was a jarring intrusion. Nicole darted to pick up.

'Hello? Oh, just a minute.' She turned to Bob. 'It's for you.'

The others waited expectantly while Bob carried on a brief conversation with the caller. He put down the phone with an air of satisfaction. 'That was my contact down at the police precinct. They tracked down the business about Clark. It was a guy with the same name – and would you believe this? – in Magnolia, Utah.'

'Go down to the precinct and pick up the printouts,' Nicole told Bob. 'Take them to Elaine. Clark's young and otherwise healthy. That'll move him up the list for a transplant fast.'

'Fax the printouts to the hospital,' April instructed.

'I know Beth will be angry at me for suggesting this again,' April said to David when Bob had left to go down to the precinct and Nicole had gone out to the kitchen to put on more coffee, 'but I think Scott ought to see Beth. It's not good for word to be circulating around town that they're estranged. I know the *Ledger* has been blatant about this – but we should refute it.'

'I'll talk to Scott,' David said after a moment. 'And to Beth. I understand your thinking,' he admitted, 'but something went terribly wrong between them. I suspect it can't ever be mended.'

Chapter Eighteen

It seemed to David on Saturday that the whole town was holding its breath while the battle for a liver transplant for Clark was being waged. Even the shops seemed less busy on this day before Christmas Eve – normally the busiest day of the year. In his role as radio announcer Scott thanked the listening public for its efforts to help his brother-in-law.

Late in the afternoon Elaine arrived at David's office to report that Clark was now high on the list for a transplant.

'They'll keep him there in the hospital until a transplant is assigned to him. He's in intensive care, but the doctors say they can keep him stable. We have to pray now that his body will accept the transplant.'

'Beth will be so relieved,' David told her.

Elaine closed her eyes for a moment in anguish. 'Dear God, I wish I could do something to help. If I could, I would – you know that, David.'

Did she know that Beth and Scott's marriage had been on the rocks before Debbie was murdered? *Hell, I didn't even know.* But yesterday April had approached Scott, then Beth, to persuade both to show a united front. God bless April for throwing her heart and soul into Beth's defense.

'Sure.' David snapped back to the moment. 'How're the kids holding up?'

'They've been so scared. They're still scared,' she admitted. 'I guess they will be until they see their daddy home again. I can't wait for that day.' Tears welled in her eyes. She managed a shaky laugh. 'But I will, of course.'

'We're running the latest news in tomorrow morning's paper,' David told her. 'Along with your letter of thanks.'

'The kids in Clark's class have been so sweet. They've bombarded the hospital with cards for him.'

'It'll be a great day in this town when Clark is well again. He's one of the best-liked teachers in the school.'

'It'll be a great day,' Elaine added, 'when this insanity is over, and Beth is cleared.'

'Amen.' But his smile was strained.

David was about to leave the office for the day when April called.

'David, we need to talk.' Her voice was taut. 'When will you be clear?'

'I'm just about to break for the day.' All at once he felt encased in alarm. 'Shall I come to your office?'

'Please.'

Driving to April and Bob's office, David searched his mind for the reason for this summons. April had sounded distraught. What had the DA's office come up with now?

Sandy greeted him with a somber 'hello'. Bob always said Sandy was the office barometer. She knew something rotten had happened.

'David, I didn't mean to frighten you,' April greeted him as he strode into her office. 'But something has come up.'

'What?' David was grim.

'Sit down,' April said gently. 'I gather you haven't seen this afternoon's *Ledger*?'

'No.' It must have hit the news-stands no more than twenty minutes ago. He read the rag these days – to seethe at the ugliness they spewed forth about Beth. 'What did they dredge up now?'

'They're running a story about Scott's going to a divorce attorney about three weeks ago. They're claiming he dropped the suit when – when Beth was arrested. Because – they claim – as long as he and Beth are married, he couldn't be forced to testify against her.'

'I don't believe it!' David was ashen.

'I caught up with Bob on his cell phone. He knows the lawyer the *Ledger* mentioned.' April took a deep breath. 'He's some creep with a shady practice.'

'They paid him a bundle to lie like that!' David swore under his breath. The DA would latch on to this like a tiger.

April abandoned her plan to visit Beth first thing in the morning, postponed dinner to drive to the police precinct. While a drunken prisoner in a nearby cell shrieked profanely, April sat with Beth in the cubicle assigned for attorney–client conferences and told her about the article in the *Ledger*.

Beth gaped in shock. 'They're lying!'

April forced herself to continue. 'Bob talked with Scott. He isn't denying it. He claims he withdrew the suit so that he couldn't be forced to testify against you.'

'That's insane!' A vein throbbed in Beth's forehead. 'I was the one who wanted a divorce. He begged me not to divorce him. He said it would wreck his career. What is he trying to do to me?'

April's mind was charging into directions that unnerved her for the moment. 'He won't get away with it, Beth.' She reached across the table for Beth's hands. Ice-cold now, like her own. 'I promise you that.'

April paced about her living room, as she'd been doing at intervals during the past two hours. Now she stopped, gazed in ambivalence at the phone. It was too late to call David again. But she was haunted by painful questions. Why had Scott lied that way? Beth wasn't lying. All right, phone David. Tell him now about her meeting with Beth.

With a sense of urgency she punched in David's number, waited for him to reply. She glanced at her watch again. Had he gone to bed early tonight? He'd admitted he was getting little sleep these last days.

'Hello?'

'David, I know it's late to be calling,' she apologized.

'It's never too late for you to call.'

'I decided not to wait until morning to talk with Beth. I was with her this evening.' She took a deep breath, reported on what had transpired.

'This came out of left field,' she admitted, 'but somewhere there's a thread that ties this all together. I think we ought to sit down and try to work this through. Why is Scott lying that way?'

'Could I come over now?' David asked urgently.

'Please.'

As always in crisis April put on coffee. It was something to do, also, until David arrived. Why was Scott lying like this? The question ricocheted in her mind. No power on earth could make her believe that Beth was lying.

While she waited for David to arrive, she tried to hack her way into Scott's brain. Was he trying to tighten the case against Beth? Could he believe she'd killed Debbie? And in a corner of her mind she remembered Beth's expressing this thought.

She heard the soft swoosh of the coffee completing its cycle, went into the kitchen. Moments later a car pulled up into the parking area. She was at the door when David charged up the path.

'You're troubled by this business with Scott,' David guessed, walking into the apartment with April. 'As I am.'

'We must discover why he's lying this way.'

'Not everybody will believe he's lying,' David warned.

'We believe,' April said defiantly, heading into the kitchen for coffee. She paused now, turned to face David with her own fear. 'Does Scott believe that Beth killed Debbie – and means to help in her prosecution?'

David gaped at April in shock. 'How could he believe something so insane?'

'Can you think of any other reason?' She didn't want to consider the repercussions. He couldn't be forced to testify against Beth – but would he waive that privilege? What other damaging facts would he offer?

'He'd have to be out of his mind to believe that. He knows how she loved Debbie. He knows what a fine mother she was . . .'

'We have some tough work ahead of us.' April fought for composure. Jeff Goodwin would grab at this newest development, add it to the broken appointment with the psychiatrist. He would arrive at absurd conclusions. 'Of course, they have no real hardcore evidence,' she said with an edge of defiance. 'Sit down, David. I'll bring us coffee.'

She returned with the coffee tray to find David pacing the small living room.

'There's another unpleasant development.' He paused, his face grim. 'Jamie called me just an hour ago from the airport in New York.' April remembered now that Jamie was flying down to Florida this evening to spend the holidays with his parents. 'The big city tabloids are latching on to the case. Why should they be interested?' he flared.

'When a child is involved, the tabloids can build up a fever of interest – and that sells papers.' But she was disturbed that the case was spreading beyond Magnolia.

'They'll distort everything like crazy!' David predicted.

'Somewhere there's a single fact that would put this whole thing into focus.' She managed a shaky smile. 'Sit down, David, and have your coffee. We need to dig deeper, find some answers.'

'You don't know how I feel,' he said passionately. 'My child sits there in jail – and I can't do anything to help her.'

'I know how you feel,' April whispered. 'Every minute of every hour of every day I cry inside a little. My baby is hurting – and I can do nothing for her.' She felt a surge of shock. *What am I saying? Why is David looking at me that way?*

'That's why I keep thinking I've known you somewhere.' His eyes searched her face with a startling tenderness. 'You're that lovely little teenager we saw in the hospital. So frightened, so anguished. I felt so guilty that we were taking your baby.'

'I never meant to tell you. You mustn't tell Beth!' she exhorted. 'She mustn't know. She must hate me for giving her up . . .'

'I often thought of you through the years.' David's eyes were saying unnerving things. 'Eventually the feeling of guilt ebbed away – but I remembered your face. I often wondered how life worked out for you. You gave us such happiness, April. Beth was the center of our lives.' He reached for her hand. 'This is not the time to say what's in my heart – but I've already told you, I want you to be a part of my life.'

'I want that, too.' Her eyes caressed him. She'd never felt this way about any man. 'But for now we must concentrate on clearing Beth.'

'Whatever it takes we'll do it,' he vowed, pulling her into his arms. 'I've wanted to hold you this way since the evening I met you at Bob and Nicole's house. I think I knew then – before all this insanity happened – that I loved you.'

But both knew that their personal lives must remain on hold – until the nightmare was over.

Chapter Nineteen

April awoke to the sound of church bells ringing in the distance. She'd overslept, she thought with dismay – then realized this was Sunday. Her mind darted back to last evening. How could she have been so careless – to confess to David that she was Beth's birth mother! But he hadn't been shocked or repulsed. It was as though Beth was another tie between them.

All those years ago he'd understood her pain at giving up Beth. He hadn't thought she was selling her baby. He knew she had to agree to adoption. And he'd been – he was – a wonderful father.

Last evening, in his arms, she'd felt reborn. He was so sweet, so warm, so charming. They'd known each other such a little while, yet it seemed as though she'd been waiting her entire life to meet him. But both their lives would be over if she couldn't prove Beth's innocence.

She heard a delivery truck pull up outside. Last-minute Christmas presents being delivered, she surmised. Tonight was Christmas Eve. The loneliest night in the year for those who were alone. Every Christmas Eve she used to ask herself, *What is my baby doing this evening? Does she have a big Christmas tree, lots of presents? Is she happy?* But this Christmas Eve she sat behind bars in a jail cell.

Yesterday Nicole had called and asked her to go to church with the family this morning. Why had she said no? It was as though she felt she didn't deserve to go to church when she was doing so little to clear Beth.

She'd made up her mind to go to see Beth this morning, though there was little she could say. She knew that David would be going to see Beth this afternoon. He'd debated about taking her a tiny Christmas tree, then discarded this as a harsh reminder of her situation.

She'd been so lucky that David and his wife came along to adopt Beth. But did Beth ever wonder about her birth mother? Did Beth feel only contempt for a mother who gave up her baby?

Suddenly restless, she tossed aside the covers, left her bed. Sunday and Monday were two wasted days, she fretted. Questions plagued her now. Why did Scott lie about starting divorce proceedings? Was he convinced that Beth had killed Debbie? So vindictive that he'd try to help the prosecution?

She was to spend Christmas Eve with Bob and Nicole and the kids. The hours between – except the time she'd be with Beth – would drag. There were Christmas presents for Nicole and Bob and the kids to be wrapped – but how long would that take? She'd searched her mind for some small gift to take to Beth, settled on two books. But could Beth focus on reading in her situation?

This would be a painful evening for David, she thought compassionately. Not the Christmas Eve he'd anticipated. The newspaper didn't publish on Christmas Day – he wouldn't even have that diversion.

Nobody should be alone on Christmas Eve, she thought rebelliously. She remembered the parade of Christmas Eves when she'd sat alone. There'd been invitations, yes – but Christmas Eve had been a time of penance, when she sat alone and grieved for her baby. And now her baby desperately needed her – and what was she accomplishing?

As arranged with Nicole, April went to the Allens' house at twilight. 'Come over early and keep me company while I put on dinner,' Nicole had said. 'Bob's taking Marianne and Neil ice-skating on the pond, and then they're hearing Christmas carols at the community center.'

Juggling packages, she left the car at the curb and walked up to the house – like the others on the block, colorfully adorned with Christmas lights. Still, despite the outward signs of a joyous holiday scene, a pall hung over the town.

Should she have dressed more festively, she asked herself in sudden concern. Were slacks and a sweater too informal for Christmas Eve dinner? But this was just family, she comforted herself.

April rang the doorbell. In moments Nicole swung the door wide.

'Did you buy out the town?' she effervesced, drawing April into the house. Nicole, too, wore slacks and a sweater. Informal was okay.

'I'd searched my mind for days for a gift for Beth – and ended up taking her books,' April said wryly. 'I couldn't think of anything else.'

'What she wants,' Nicole said, her eyes moist, 'nobody can give her.'

'What about Elaine and her kids?' April asked as they headed for the ceiling-high Christmas tree in the living room. 'Where are they this evening?'

'Oh, they left this morning for New York, to be with Clark this evening and tomorrow. One of the nurses on Clark's floor was going home for the holidays and offered Elaine her apartment.'

'Thank God for that.' April deposited her four packages at the foot of the tree beside the others. She paused for a moment. 'It must be a rough evening for David. I hate to think of him being alone.'

'He won't be alone.' Nicole offered an impish smile. 'He's coming over here for dinner.'

'You didn't say anything . . .' Of course, she'd wondered that Nicole hadn't invited David, too.

'I suppose I took it for granted you'd know he'd be here

with us, considering the circumstances.' Again, an impish smile. 'Anyhow, I thought it'd be a pleasant surprise.'

'What's for dinner?' April was disconcerted. Nicole was harboring romantic ideas again. But she wasn't off base. It was just that the timing was wrong.

'Oh, it isn't Christmas without a turkey. The kids like it so much at Thanksgiving we do a repeat for Christmas. It's in the oven, roasting nicely. Now let's throw everything else together.'

April was setting the table when the others arrived. The children rushed into the kitchen to report to Nicole on their ice-skating at the pond and the Christmas caroling afterwards. Bob went to the fireplace to ignite the logs already laid there. David crossed to April.

'You're looking beautiful,' David told April. Clearly he was pleased at her presence. 'Beth told me you'd been to see her, that you brought her books.' His eyes were tender. 'She likes you very much.'

'She's not to know,' April whispered. 'You promised.'

'When you're ready, you'll tell her.' He reached for her hand, pulled her down to the sofa with him.

The logs in the grate were wrapped in flames. Bob stood back and inspected the fireplace in satisfaction, then turned to April and David.

'I went to see Scott's shitty divorce lawyer,' he told them. 'I figured he might loosen up over a drink.'

'Did he?' David demanded.

'No.' Bob sighed. 'But he was real belligerent at being questioned. He's sticking to his story.'

'Dinner in five minutes,' Nicole called from the kitchen. 'Kids, go wash your hands.'

'So we know Scott's out to paint Beth as a murderer.' David was struggling for control. 'The bastard thinks Beth killed Debbie!'

'We'll dig into this later,' April said gently. 'When Marianne and Neil have gone to bed.' This was Christmas

Eve. For the sake of the children they must push aside the ugliness that haunted them.

The atmosphere at the dinner table – and afterwards as they gathered in the living room before the Christmas tree and Marianne and Neil made wild guesses about the contents of the gaily wrapped parcels – was almost festive. At last Nicole sent the children off to bed.

'Let's take time out,' Nicole urged the others. 'We'll wake up tomorrow with clearer heads. So Scott's jumped to the wrong conclusions. We'll dig to the root of this nightmare and come up with answers. Now, who besides me would like a cup of hot cider?'

It was close to one a.m. when April – seeing Nicole smother yawns – suggested they call it a night. In a flurry of warm wishes April and David left the house and headed for the parking area.

'I know it's late,' David said, 'but could we have more coffee at your place?' His eyes told April he dreaded being alone.

'Why not?' Her smile was unsteady.

'I'll be right behind you.' He opened the door to her car, reached to squeeze her hand for a moment. 'I thank God for your coming to Magnolia.'

In her apartment, David followed April into the kitchen, lingered at her side while she put on coffee.

'This is the first time in her life that Beth and I have been apart at Christmas.' His voice was husky with anguish. 'I can't believe she's alone tonight – behind bars. And that bastard Scott!' He clenched a fist in fury.

'David, we'll find a way to clear Beth.' *This could have been my first Christmas with my baby.* 'I know the situation seems rough now – I'm convinced we're on the right track. We don't have answers yet, but I have a feeling things are about to fall into place.'

'Having you here holds me together,' he told her. 'And I know how terrible this is for you.'

It seemed so natural, she thought, for David to pull her into his arms this way. All their fears in retreat for a moment when their lips met. Hungrily sweet at first, then passionate. They parted. David's eyes searched hers, pleaded for more. Her own eyes luminous in consent.

But all the while a small voice taunted her with the reminder that this might be all they'd ever have.

Chapter Twenty

Jamie hurried from his desk in the city room to David's office.

'I've finished the article,' he said with blend of satisfaction and faint defiance. 'Here.' He handed David the page he'd been laboring over much of the afternoon. He was hoping the paper would run it in tomorrow morning's edition.

David had been ambivalent about running the article when they'd discussed it this morning, Jamie recalled. Still, he felt it was urgent to jump the gun on the Town Council. He knew Scott was liked by most of the board members – they might lean in his favor, ignore the facts in the case.

Jamie stood before David's desk and watched for his reaction as he read.

'It's great,' David acknowledged. 'You're sure the company's got strong capital? This won't backfire?'

'I've seen their records.' Jamie nodded with conviction. 'They're dying to get moving here. Manhattan rents have hit the ceiling – and they don't need to be there.'

'The Town Council may be pissed,' David warned. 'You're presenting this to the public before they've had a chance to evaluate your plan.'

'People need to know their options,' Jamie insisted. 'Melrose.com will bring in jobs with substantial salaries. It'll help keep our young people in town,' he reiterated for the hundredth time. 'Kensington will offer barely above minimum wages.'

'We'll give it a run,' David agreed. 'Beth's all for it, you know.'

'We worked together on this,' Jamie acknowledged. There, that surprised David. 'Scott was furious that she didn't go along with his plans for Kensington. He didn't like it when Beth and I started the local committee to campaign against sweatshop-made merchandise.'

'In the midst of all this craziness,' David said tenderly, 'Beth still thinks about the welfare of this town.'

'Beth's special.' Jamie's face revealed his love. 'When you see her next, tell her she's always in my thoughts.' They both knew that – under the circumstances – it was unwise for him to try to visit her. 'How's the case coming?'

'All the DA has is circumstantial evidence.' But David seemed frustrated, Jamie thought – and was frightened for Beth. 'April and Bob are scrounging for evidence to clear her. Damn it!' David slammed on his desk with one fist. 'The law says she's innocent until proven guilty beyond a reasonable doubt – but a lot of people here in town are forgetting that.'

Jamie lingered in the pressroom until the first copy of the following morning's *Sentinel* came off the press. His article was right in the center of the front page. He read it with relish and left to go home. He hoped David would show it to Beth in the morning. With all her problems, she'd be pleased.

He slept a restless four hours before he was awakened by his alarm. With reluctance he left his bed, headed for the bathroom to shower. It wasn't the first time he faced a new day after only four hours' sleep, he derided himself. He was impatient to hear some reaction to his article.

As on many mornings he decided to forgo breakfast at home. He'd stop off at the Happy Days diner on Main Street instead. He walked out of the house into a cold and blustery morning. He realized how the temperature had dropped when it took three tries to get his two-year-old Camry motor to turn over.

He parked a few doors down from the diner. None of the stores along Main Street had opened yet, but the diner was well occupied. The Christmas-decorated steamed-over window lent an air of sybaritic comfort, he thought as he walked inside. The aromas of freshly brewed coffee and bacon sizzling on the grill filled the room. Several regulars sat at the counter. Other early risers sprawled in booths.

Jamie greeted patrons whom he knew, settled himself in a booth for two. He spied copies of the morning's *Sentinel* being read here and there.

'You got a front-page article in this morning's paper. Did you stay up all night writin' it?' the good-humored middle-aged waitress who'd been at Happy Days forever joshed.

'Not quite,' Jamie told her with a grin.

'Hey, I've got a kid I'm strugglin' to put through State. I'd sure as hell like to see him land a job right here in town,' she admitted. 'Somethin' that'll pay more than seven bucks an hour.'

A man at the counter swerved on his stool to join the conversation. 'Look, every kid can't go to college.' A hint of belligerence in his voice. 'So mine don't dig all this computer crap. What good will it do her?'

'Not every job will require computer skills,' Jamie soothed. 'The company will need less skilled workers, too.'

All at once there was a lively discussion among the patrons. Most, Jamie noted with satisfaction, had great respect for a company like Melrose.com. Let this be reflected on the town council.

Jamie's waitress returned to refill his coffee mug. 'If this company comes to town,' she said with an air of excitement, 'will you put in a word for my kid? He's already talkin' about movin' down to New York. He talks about somethin' called Silicon Alley.' She grimaced. 'Why the hell can't families stay together these days?'

Fighting yawns, Jamie headed back for his car. He glanced at his watch. He wasn't due at the newspaper today, but he was anxious to learn if any calls had come in about his article. There was always a core of local people who'd call in to express their opinions.

At this hour – shortly past eight a.m. – there was little activity on Main Street. Two black Labs and a dog of mixed lineage strolled in the area of Jamie's car. He paused to pat each for a moment. All had license tags – they weren't strays. His mother – when she was here in town – was active in rounding up strays and finding homes for them, he remembered lovingly. As a small boy he'd cherished this habit.

His thoughts focused on Beth as he drove away from the center of town and out towards the newspaper's headquarters. So fast life had become a nightmare for her. And for him, he acknowledged, because he'd loved Beth since high school days – when she was a sophomore and he was a senior.

Normally he enjoyed this drive out to the edge of town. The landscape thinning as he proceeded. The two-lane road was set between slight hills on either side. He made a habit of driving slowly because raccoons, squirrels, feral cats had a habit of darting across the road as though it belonged to them.

All at once he was conscious that the brakes of the car were not responding. *Why am I moving so fast? My brakes are shot!*

Now he saw the young doe that was scampering down from an incline directly in his path. He swerved to avoid her – and at the same time aborted his increasing speed. He was conscious of a searing pain as the Camry smashed into the hill. And then nothing . . .

David leaned anxiously over Jamie's hospital bed.

'He looks a mess,' David said, white and shaken. 'You're sure he suffered just minor cuts and bruises?'

'That and a minor concussion,' Jamie's doctor insisted.

'We'll keep him here for a couple of days for observation – but he'll be fine. Relax, David.'

'He's coming out of it.' David's eyes clung to his face.

'We had him under sedation,' the doctor reminded. 'He'll be a little groggy for a while.'

'I swerved so I wouldn't hit the doe . . .' Jamie's voice was unsteady.

'Yeah.' David smiled. 'I've done it myself, but I didn't plow into a hill.'

'My brakes were shot,' Jamie said. 'Maybe that doe saved my life.' He hesitated. 'The car was inspected just ten days ago.' He seemed to be struggling to continue.

David leaned forward, suddenly alert. 'What are you trying to tell us, Jamie? You believe the brakes were tampered with?'

'You've got it.' Jamie was grim. 'The car is two years old. It was inspected ten days ago. Have somebody check the brakes. A hundred to one they were cut.'

In a hastily called meeting with David and Bob, April listened to David's report of Jamie's accident.

'I had the mechanics check out the car – and reported to the cops.' David's face was taut with rage. 'Somebody meant to kill Jamie.'

'Why?' Bob was astounded. 'Why would anybody want to kill him?'

'I've been thinking about that ever since I left the hospital.' David squinted in space. 'I can only come up with the fact that somebody was pissed about his article in this morning's paper. But why?'

'My gut reaction is that this is somehow tied up with the fire in Rosita's trailer,' April began.

'And to Debbie's murder,' Bob pounced. 'Somewhere there's a link.'

'David, who would be hurt by that article?' April challenged. 'Anybody you can think of?'

'Somebody who's promoting Kensington Womenswear,' David began and stopped. 'I'm not referring to Scott,' he protested. 'Somebody involved with Kensington. Scott said they're very anxious to put this deal through.'

'Somebody in town who's going to benefit from their coming,' Bob surmised.

'The contractor whom they'll hire to build their extension,' David pinpointed. 'Let's see if anybody's been approached. We—'

'They've talked to somebody,' Bob broke in. 'They'd need figures to know what they were letting themselves in for.'

'All right.' April felt a surge of excitement. 'Let's work on that theory. You two set up a list and follow through.' Her mind was racing. 'I'm going to have another talk with Rosita. I've always suspected she was holding something back.'

April drove over to the trailer park. Nobody was in Rosita's trailer. Rocky, her black Lab, sprawled on a mat before the trailer. At the sight of her he ambled over for a pat.

'Hi, Rocky. You're guarding the house?' she crooned, a long-time lover of anything on four feet.

She glanced about, saw a young woman with a toddler emerge from a nearby trailer.

'Are you drivin' to town?' the young woman asked hopefully. 'It's awful cold to be walkin'.'

'I should be in a while,' April told her. 'Do you know when Rosita will be home?'

'She's workin' today. She won't be home until around four.' The young woman's eyes were questioning. She tugged at the scarf about her throat.

'I'll give you a ride into town,' April told her. No point in sitting around here for over an hour. 'Hop into the car.'

An hour later April returned to the trailer camp. She crossed to Rosita's trailer, offered the anticipated scratches behind the ears to Rocky. There was no response when she knocked on the door. Rosita had not arrived.

School was out, April realized. Where were the kids? Then she remembered. Rosita had an arrangement whereby her kids stayed with a neighbor on days when she was at work. Rosita was a good mother, she thought compassionately.

She sat in the car – growing colder by the minute. Then she spied Rosita emerging from a car at the edge of the road. She'd been given a lift home.

Rosita seemed startled to see her there. She waved, hurried over to the white Mercedes. 'You're waiting for me?' An odd wariness in her voice.

'Yes, Rosita.' April left the Mercedes. 'Could we talk?'

'Sure.' But Rosita was uneasy. *What is she afraid of?*

Rosita unlocked the door to her trailer. The two women walked inside.

'I'll light the stove.' Rosita reached for a match to ignite the kerosene stove that served to heat her trailer. 'Please, Miss April, sit down.' *Why is she so nervous?*

'Rosita, the police are still trying to track down the arsonist that torched your trailer,' April began. She'd noted that a police officer sat in an unmarked car across from the trailer park. 'And now they're concerned that somebody tried to kill Jamie Lawrence.'

Rosita gaped in alarm, crossed herself. 'That nice reporter at the *Sentinel*? Why?'

'We suspect whoever tried to kill him also torched your trailer.' April tried to sound matter-of-fact. 'Maybe even killed Beth's baby.' All at once Rosita was trembling. *She knows something.*

'Why would anybody kill Debbie? I keep asking myself that . . .' Rosita's voice dropped to a whisper.

'Rosita, you used to live in Texas, didn't you?'

'Yes.' It was a fearful admission.

'Where in Texas?'

'A little town across the border. Chickasaw. But we were legal immigrants. We had papers. Why do you ask this?'

A touch of defiance in her voice now. 'We belong in this country.'

'I'm sure you do, Rosita,' April comforted.

'The people at the church – they're good to us. But we know to some people we're dirt. We don't belong here.'

'Of course you belong here.' April was startled. But Rosita was right. There were people in town who resented the migrant workers. Did she believe that was why her trailer was torched? David had talked with deep anger about how migrant workers had their mailboxes vandalized, the windows of their shabby houses broken. How they were taunted by clusters of teenagers. Two migrant workers had been beaten up last year.

'We do work that your Americans don't want to do,' Rosita pursued. 'Most of us work for wages Americans would laugh at. Not me,' she said hurriedly. 'My ladies pay me what's right. Not like in Texas,' she added with contempt. 'My husband and me – we worked for two dollars an hour. And we had to take it, because how else would we keep a roof over our heads and food on the table?'

'Rosita, most people here in Magnolia like you very much.' April's mind was racing. Jamie wrote an article about Kensington Womenswear, located somewhere in Texas. Rosita's husband had tried to unionize workers in a small town in Texas – where she and her husband had worked for sweatshop wages. The same town?

'Can I – I make you a cup of tea?' Rosita's air of defiance ebbed away. 'It takes a while to get warm in here.'

'Thank you, no. I just stopped by to see how you're doing,' she fabricated. 'I saw the policeman on duty outside. I'm sure you're safe.'

Is Kensington Womenswear operating in Chickasaw, Texas? How does this tie in with Debbie's murder?

Chapter Twenty-One

April and Bob sat with David in his office and rehashed what they had discussed earlier.

'We suspect there's a link between the fire at Rosita Rivera's trailer and the attempt on Jamie's life.' Bob frowned in thought. 'Okay, we may be way off base – but it's all we've got to run with right now. But how does that tie in with Debbie's murder?'

'Let's take one step at a time.' April's mind was in high gear. 'Start with the fire and the tampering with the brakes of Jamie's car. Find the link there, and I'm betting it'll lead us on. It'll—'

'How do we do that?' David broke in. His gaze swung from April to Bob, back to April again. 'What's the next step?'

'I think I should go down to Chickasaw, Texas,' April began. 'That'll—'

'I don't like that!' David rejected. 'It could be dangerous. Maybe we could hire a private investigator.'

'That'll take time to set up.' April dismissed this. 'I can fly down to El Paso, rent a car at the airport and drive to Chickasaw. I'm a reporter,' she plotted, 'doing research on immigrant labor.'

'April, you could run into trouble.' David turned to Bob. 'Tell her it's too dangerous!'

'I've known her too long to expect her to accept that,' Bob said wryly. 'She's a stubborn woman.' But he, too, seemed uneasy.

'I won't take chances,' she promised.

'You don't go near Kensington Womenswear,' David ordered. 'We know how badly they want to set up here in town. We're guessing they're behind Jamie's "accident". They expect Scott to persuade the Town Council to offer them a great deal. A lot of money is at stake. You don't go near Kensington,' he repeated.

'I won't go near them,' April soothed. He was so afraid for her. 'We need to know what links them to Rosita and to Jamie – and how that ties in with Debbie's murder.'

'We all have a pretty good idea what links them to Rosita.' Bob was blunt. 'They must have driven Rosita and her husband out of town for trying to organize their workers. And the article Jamie wrote must have infuriated them.'

'They wouldn't be reading the *Sentinel*,' David scoffed, then paused. 'Or would they, considering they want to move here?'

'It's like we said, cutting the brakes on Jamie's car could be the work of somebody in town who wants Kensington to come here.' Bob squinted in thought. 'April, going to Texas could be a wild goose chase.'

'I'm going. You two check among the local contractors – see what you dig up. I'll be on an early-morning flight to New York, en route to El Paso. From the looks of the map it'll be about a fifty-mile drive to Chickasaw.'

'I keep asking myself why Rosita Rivera landed here in Magnolia,' Bob confessed. 'The same town where Kensington Womenswear wants to set up shop.'

'One of those crazy quirks of fate,' David said, his eyes moving to April. 'They happen.'

While David went on his usual visit with Beth, April shopped for dinner makings. David would come to her apartment after his visit with Beth. He was so grateful that he was able to see Beth every day – one of the perks, she mused, of being the publisher of the town's major newspaper.

While she waited in line at the supermarket, she focused on

the task ahead. Use a pseudonym, her mind instructed. Okay, her mother's name, she decided. She'd be Claire Bolton, a staff writer of a small magazine.

Now she remembered Bill Andrews – who'd lived in the next apartment when she first moved to New York. He was struggling to get his magazine moving – and suddenly was hit with a crazy lawsuit. She took on his defense pro bono, and he'd been so grateful.

What was the name of Bill's magazine? Right away she remembered. He'd moved up in the world these past few years. Not a major magazine yet – but solid now. They exchanged Christmas and birthday cards each year. He'd invited her – and she'd gone – to the cocktail party when he'd moved into fancy new quarters a couple of years ago.

Call Bill. Ask him for a press pass or whatever ID she'd need to be researching an article for his magazine. This trip must appear authentic. And make sure her wardrobe was suitable. Her taupe pantsuit and a tailored blouse – only someone sharp would recognize the expensive tailoring. And the old camel polo coat that should have gone to Goodwill years ago.

At the apartment she put away the salmon steaks in the refrigerator and the frozen vegetables into the freezing unit. Popped the two Idahos into the oven. She checked her watch. Would Bill still be at the office? Try him.

She found his office phone number in her book, called. Moments later he was on the line.

'April, how great to hear from you!'

'It's awful how we let so much time go by without getting in touch.'

'I was anxious when I didn't hear from you at Christmas – but I figured you were probably off on a cruise or skiing in Switzerland.'

'I totally skipped the Christmas card scene this year,' she apologized in sudden recall. 'My life was chaotic. I've moved out of the city. Let me give you my new address and phone number.'

Now she briefed him on her decision to leave the law firm and to go into partnership with Bob in Magnolia. She explained her need for some cover in approaching a company in Texas.

'I'm tracking down information for a murder case,' she explained. 'I need your advice about how to represent myself as a staff writer for a magazine.' She paused. 'Your magazine.'

She listened to his instructions. She would be on staff at his magazine, Bill told her. The article? Statistics on the reception of immigrant workers in small border towns in Texas.

'Stress that you're showing both sides of the story. Workers from south of the border are taking over jobs that would go to local workers. Of course,' he said with a chuckle, 'in many cases these are jobs the other workers don't want to take on. As a matter of fact,' he pursued, 'we recently did an article about a situation in a northern Westchester town where immigrant workers – some legal, some illegal – have come up in search of jobs. Some well-heeled suburbanites are angry that they gather on street corners early every morning and wait to be hired by local contractors. Angry that they live packed together in tiny quarters.'

'Bill, I know this is an imposition – but I'm fighting against time. Could you have someone from your office meet me at the airport in New York with a press card plus a copy of that article? I'll be waiting for tomorrow's ten a.m. flight to Atlanta.'

'Tell me what you'll be wearing,' Bill began. 'Oh, I have a snapshot of you from the cocktail party when we moved to the new quarters. I'll give that to Tiffany, our receptionist. Hold on,' he said, and April heard him calling to Tiffany. Moments later he was back on the line. 'I caught her,' he reported. 'I'll give her the snapshot. What gate will you be at?'

'The ten a.m. flight to Atlanta,' she told him again with a

surge of relief. She'd be able to handle this. 'And thanks so much, Bill.'

'Hey, I owe you,' he said affectionately. 'Anything you need, you just call.'

April set the table in the dining area. The Idahos were almost done, vegetables waiting in the steamer to be started. All right, pack what little she'd need. The pantsuit would see her through – just add an extra blouse, pack nightwear and fresh underthings and knee-highs. Toiletries, make-up, an umbrella that would fit into her purse. She'd just finished this task when she heard the doorbell. David was here.

She hurried to admit him. Why did she feel this comforting sense of relief at having him here?

'How's Beth?'

'I think her situation is finally sinking in,' he admitted, shedding his coat. 'She's beginning to be scared. Up till now she was just dazed – plus furious at Scott.'

'Better that than apathetic,' April comforted.

'All along she's been worried about Clark, of course – and feeling guilty that she wasn't able to take in the kids so Elaine could stay down in New York while Clark waits for a transplant.' He sighed. 'Iris said the neighbor who's been caring for the kids is leaving for Florida in a couple of days – her daughter's expecting a baby.'

'I hope you like salmon steaks.' April reached for David's hand.

'Salmon steaks are great.' He kissed her hungrily. 'Can dinner wait for a while? I need to hold you in my arms and make love.'

Just past six a.m. – the sky still night dark – April and David left her apartment for the long drive to the Albany airport. Settling herself beside him in what he called his 'long in the tooth' Chevy, April knew he was alarmed for her yet determined to hide this.

'You're sure you're not making this trip just to get away from this damn cold?' he joshed. 'It's probably thirty degrees warmer in El Paso.'

'I'll be equipped.' She indicated the smart taupe pantsuit beneath her coat. 'It'll just be a matter of shedding.'

'I'll miss you.' He reached to hold her hand for a moment before inserting the ignition key.

Her smile was tender. 'David, I'll only be there two days.' But in the current crisis two days seemed a lifetime.

They'd sat up late last night. David was candid about his discomfort at her making this trip, yet – along with her – he knew they must pursue any hint of a clue that would clear Beth. They'd made love with a sweetness and passion that had brought tears to her eyes. How ironic that in the midst of such anguish they could find such joy. And she knew David shared her guilt at this.

'You'll call me when you reach El Paso?' he prodded.

'I'll call you,' she promised.

'Where the hell will you stay in a crummy little town like that?' he demanded with fresh alarm. 'You couldn't locate a motel chain within twenty miles of Chickasaw.'

'We don't know that it's a crummy little town,' she scolded. 'And even Chickasaw will have a local hotel of sorts.'

'Of sorts,' he grumbled. 'I'll be worried until you're on a plane headed back for civilization.'

They stopped at a roadside diner for a quick breakfast. By the time they emerged, pink streaks of morning had broken through the night sky. At the Albany airport April picked up her reservations. They had at least ten minutes before her flight could be boarded. They stood at a window and watched the sun rise. This morning a glorious orange ball.

'I can't believe that five weeks ago I didn't know you existed,' David murmured, his eyes making love to her.

'I was waiting all these years for you.' And for Beth, she thought. All she wanted of life – but so precarious.

David held her with touching urgency for a moment before she left him to board her flight.

'Be careful,' he pleaded.

'I'll be careful.' She managed a smile. 'But there'll be no problems. I'm just a reporter out to do a story.'

Chapter Twenty-Two

April arrived at LaGuardia, searched for the gate for her flight. At the waiting area she was immediately approached by an ebullient young woman. Tiffany, Bill's receptionist, she assumed.

'You're April,' Tiffany said with an air of excitement. She held up a snapshot of April and two members of Bill's staff.

'Right,' April acknowledged, and Tiffany handed her a manila envelope – relieved that this mission was accomplished. 'Thanks so much.'

'You'd better get your boarding pass – you should be taking off in a few minutes.'

'Right.' April smiled in apology. 'I'm sorry to have dragged you all the way out here.'

'I live ten minutes away,' Tiffany bubbled. 'I got a chance to sleep late. Have a great trip.'

April joined the line waiting for boarding passes. Everything going to schedule so far. No delays.

She would leave here at ten a.m., arrive in Atlanta at twelve thirty. She was familiar with Hartsfield – she'd be able to find a restaurant to have a decent lunch in the course of her one-hour layover. She'd land in El Paso at three ten p.m. Central Time. Check into a hotel, look around the town, start asking questions.

The day dragged as she shuttled between planes. She stared out the window beside her seat on each plane but saw nothing. Her mind sought for answers that seemed so elusive. Yet instinct told her they were close to fitting together the pieces of the puzzle.

How did Scott fit into this latest development, she probed. David said he wanted to bring Kensington Womenswear into Magnolia to show the town how much he was contributing to its future. That he was wildly ambitious for a career in politics. Or was he counting on a financial reward for his efforts?

But why the lies about his wanting a divorce? He was deliberately handing the prosecution damaging evidence. *He wants Beth to be convicted. Why? How can he believe she killed Debbie?*

He couldn't be forced to testify against Beth – but the story was out there. A prospective jury pool had heard every damaging word. What were the chances of their getting a change of venue? Nil. And that story was creating disturbing doubts in the minds of people in town. They remembered the harrowing story of several years ago about a seemingly loving young mother who'd murdered her two small sons.

At the Atlanta airport she forced herself to eat lunch. It helped to pass the one-hour layover. On impulse – with a few minutes to spare – she phoned David.

'April, be careful there in Chickasaw,' he urged yet again. He hesitated. 'We tracked down a contractor who's given quotes to Kensington on the extension they plan. Not one of my favorite local businessmen,' he conceded. 'He's been involved in a couple of shady operations. Bob's deep in follow-up. This guy could be the one we're looking for. Maybe you ought to turn around and come home . . .'

'Bob'll track down the contractor. I'll focus on Chickasaw. David, we can't afford to drop even the slightest lead.' And this was fragile, she conceded in a corner of her mind. How were they to link what happened to Rosita and to Jamie with Debbie's murder?

'You're right, of course.' But apprehension lurked in his

voice. 'Call me when you've checked into the hotel. I need to know where you are.'

'David, I have to run. My flight's ready to board.'

In El Paso she picked up her car rental. As she'd anticipated, the temperature was at least thirty degrees higher than in Magnolia. She deposited her winter coat on the back seat of the car, unbuttoned her jacket. This was Magnolia in early summer. All right, head for Chickasaw.

The road was lightly traveled. Within forty-eight minutes she was approaching the town. It was absurd, she rebuked herself, to feel this sudden anxiety. Nothing bad was going to happen. She just might pick up clues that would lead to Debbie's murderer.

This wasn't just another case. Her precious granddaughter whom she'd never seen had been murdered. Her precious daughter was going to trial for that murder. She felt herself breaking into a cold sweat. The opening date of the trial was terrifyingly close.

On the few occasions when she had defended a client charged with murder she'd fought hard. But there had been cases she'd lost. She couldn't face losing this one. She'd do anything to clear Beth. If that meant putting her own life on the line, so be it.

Her hands tightened on the wheel. She was approaching what appeared to be the main street of a very small town. She drove past a gas station, a general store, a diner, a tavern. On the opposite side of the street she saw a drugstore, what appeared to be an old-fashioned ice-cream parlor, and what must be the local supermarket – though 'super', she thought, was hardly the proper designation.

There must be a hotel around, she thought in sudden alarm. The last motel was twenty miles back. With a sigh of relief she spied a three-story red brick structure with a wrought iron balcony on its second level. Seedy, yes – but a sign swinging in the slight breeze indicated this was the Chickasaw Hotel.

She parked, reached for her weekender, and headed for the Chickasaw Hotel. A blonde with dark roots stood behind a counter in the tiny lobby, glanced up with a smile.

'Hi.' Her heavily mascara'd eyes telegraphed her curiosity at April's appearance.

'Would you have a room for the night – possibly two nights,' April amended.

'We got a room – with a private bath,' the blonde added with a touch of pride and pushed the hotel register towards her. 'You here to sell to the new beauty parlor that opened up?'

'No. I'm a reporter.' April was conscious of lively interest as she signed the register. 'I'm doing a story on immigrant workers in border towns in Texas.' As planned, April rattled off a list of tiny towns in the area, as supplied by a friendly clerk at the car rental office.

'Oh, we got immigrant workers.' A hint of distaste glowed in the hotel clerk's eyes. 'They come and they go. You're in room nine, one flight up and to your left.' She pointed towards a staircase at the side.

'Where's a place where I can have an early dinner?' April asked, accepting the key the blonde extended. The tavern she'd seen appeared unappealing. 'Nothing fancy,' she added with an ingratiating smile. 'My magazine doesn't go in for lavish expense accounts.'

The blonde chuckled. 'Honey, you don't have much choice in this town. 'There's the tavern that's open for lunch and dinner and drinking. Then there's Mabel's Diner. That's open for breakfast, lunch and dinner. Mabel closes at eight p.m. sharp. It's on the next block.'

'Thanks.' April paused for a moment. 'I understand you have a good-sized manufacturing business here in town. Kensington something or other?'

'Our major employer.' Again, April sensed distaste in the blonde. 'They don't hire locals much, though. I mean, folks that were born here.'

'Looking for cheap labor?' April asked with a show of sympathy.

'You got it.' She debated for a moment. 'Don't go nosing around Kensington. That's asking for trouble.'

'I'd better settle in my room and then go out for an early dinner.' April chuckled. 'It's great to be warm. It was freezing where I come from.'

Walking up the flight of stairs to her room, she focused on the fact that Kensington obviously had an abundance of cheap labor. So why were they so hot to move to Magnolia? Instinct told her that here in Chickasaw – right on the Mexican border – Kensington wasn't paying even American minimum wage to their workers.

And then – as she unlocked the door to her room – an ugly suspicion hit her over the head. Kensington expected to tap into the migrant worker supply in Magnolia. Farms in the area – as in other parts of the country – used migrant labor from south of the border. Seasonal work. Kensington would offer them year-round work – at the pittance they earned on American farms.

There'd be no jobs – even at minimum wages – for the unemployed in Magnolia. Didn't Scott realize that when he talked so grandly about bringing a major manufacturer into town? Here was something for Jamie to take to the town council.

Was she allowing herself to be distracted from her real objective? Somebody in Magnolia wanted to scare Rosita out of town – and that same somebody wanted to silence Jamie. The link between Rosita and Jamie was clearly Kensington Womenswear. But how could that be tied in with Debbie's murder? Logic said it wasn't. Instinct told her it was.

April's hotel room was small and drab. An effort to enliven it for out-of-town guests consisted of a pair of Utrillo prints that hung on one paint-hungry wall. A vintage air-conditioner jutted out one of two windows. So it wasn't a suite at the Carlyle. She'd be here for only one or two nights.

In sudden alarm she glanced about for a phone. There, on the night table beside the bed. She called the operator, asked for David's private line at the newspaper. She knew he would remain there until he heard from her.

'Hello?' The tension in his voice told her he'd been anxious for this call.

'I'm in Chickasaw,' she told him. 'Let me give you the number.'

'Be careful,' he said yet again. They both knew not to speak about her objective lest someone be listening in on her call.

'Sure,' she promised. 'How's the weather up there?' A safe topic of conversation.

They talked a few minutes about impersonal subjects. Then April asked the question that had been hovering at the back of her mind. 'Oh, did you have any luck in finding a contractor to build that extension?'

'Too many,' he said. 'All of them eager to give me quotes. But Bob and I will follow them all up.'

'Great.' Another time-consuming effort, she thought in frustration. Time was what they didn't have.

She unpacked her weekender, left to seek out Mabel's Diner. She was conscious of curious – admiring – stares from a sprinkling of male passers-by. She found the diner on the corner of the next block. Christmas lights still adorned the large, square window. She opened the door and walked inside.

Here and there a table was occupied. Three stools at the counter were straddled by what she suspected from the good-humored repartee being exchanged with the counterman were regulars at Mabel's Diner. With the precision of Rockettes from New York City's Radio City Music Hall three heads simultaneously swung around to inspect her. One whistled in approval.

With a faint smile April sat at a small table by the wall, reached for the menu. A ponytailed waitress – somewhere in her late teens and with a sassy smile – sauntered over to the table.

'Tonight's special is grilled chicken.' Her eyes appraised April's designer suit with approval. 'You get two vegetables and a baked potato with it. The soup's clam chowder or bean. You'd do best with the chowder.'

'I'll have the chowder.' April's smile said she appreciated this advice. 'And skip the vegetables.' A hundred to one they'd be boiled to death. She preferred her vegetables steamed.

'Yeah.' Her waitress giggled. April guessed that other diners before her had sent back vegetables. 'What're you drinkin'?'

'Coffee. Decaf,' April began and paused as her waitress shook her head. 'Tea,' April amended. Now she remembered that random checks by a TV channel in Manhattan had indicated that many restaurants served regular coffee as decaf. 'Decaf tea.' For weeks she'd been sleeping badly. Without caffeine maybe she could break that cycle tonight.

When her waitress returned with her clam chowder, April made a point of admiring her lush ponytail.

'Thank you,' she chirped, plainly in a talkative mood. 'The boss is a real creep.' She glanced about to make sure he wasn't in earshot. 'He said folks didn't like my hair flyin' around. I oughta wear a hairnet. Ain't that gross? He belongs in another century.'

'Somebody I knew back home told me to be sure to eat here,' April confided. 'Maybe you know her,' she added. 'Rosita Rivera. She said she used to live here.'

'She ain't much of a friend.' A wariness in the waitress's eyes now. 'She and her old man got run out of town. She shoulda told you this was no place for a tourist. Fights are always breakin' out. And it ain't local folks' fault.'

'I'm not really a tourist,' April confided. 'I'm a reporter doing a story on immigrant workers in Texas border towns.'

'You don't want to hang around here.' She sent a swift glance about the lightly populated diner now, lowered her voice to a whisper. 'Don't get mixed up with the folks over at Kensington. That's askin' for trouble. Bad trouble.' All at once she was nervous. 'Eat your chowder before it gets cold.'

All right, she understood that Kensington would be a bad scene for Magnolia – that their big boys played rough. But could they be involved in Debbie's murder?

Did they have some threatening hold over Scott? Was he being blackmailed to fight to get them a deal in Magnolia? Had Debbie's murder been a nasty warning to him that his own life was at stake?

Chapter Twenty-Three

Tomorrow morning, April plotted, she'd ask the desk clerk if Chickasaw had a newspaper. If not, discover what newspaper was published in a nearby town and read by local people. Go back five or six years – when Scott had not yet moved to Magnolia. Search for some connection between him and Kensington.

April lingered briefly over dinner. Conversations were loud and friendly – but she'd pick up nothing of value here. She returned to the hotel, called David. He was still at the office. They both knew to be cautious about what they said.

'Oh, some good news,' David reported. 'Elaine just heard. Clark is to receive a liver transplant in the morning. She's probably in New York by now. We knew he'd been pushed to the head of the list, but nobody expected a liver to be available so fast.'

'That's wonderful, David! We'll all be praying for him. Oh, I was wondering,' she said casually, in the event someone was eavesdropping, 'do you know where Scott went to school?'

'I think Beth mentioned that he went to Columbia Business School.' He paused. 'I don't know much about his background. Just that Elaine is his older sister. They've never seemed very close. When are you coming home?' he prodded.

'Oh, I don't think I'll be using material from Chickasaw for my article,' she improvised. 'I expect I'll fly out tomorrow afternoon.' She couldn't say, *I want to check local newspapers for something on Scott.*

'I miss you,' David said.

'I miss you, too.'

April wished she had brought along a book to read. The evening hours in her drab hotel room would drag. She switched on the ancient TV set, watched the evening news from El Paso. Far earlier than normal she went to bed – knowing she faced insomnia. In the morning she'd check on local newspapers. She'd call El Paso to make reservations for a late afternoon flight.

Celia Logan left the hospital later than usual tonight – well after visiting hours were over. Marcia was becoming cantankerous. That meant she was getting better, thank God. How had she picked up a case of pneumonia when she was there because of a fractured ankle?

She hurried across the hospital parking area to her car – eager to be out of the sharp cold of the night. Turning into Spruce Lane she noticed an unfamiliar car sitting in front of the Emerson house. She squinted to read the words strung across the side. Her vision wasn't what it used to be.

She tensed in sudden comprehension. Somebody from one of the supermarket tabloids was in the house talking with Scott! Didn't Scott know better than to talk to one of those reporters? She'd heard that a couple of them were nosing around town.

She put the car in the garage and went into the house – enjoying the sybaritic warmth that greeted her. With the way oil prices were climbing she ought to keep the thermostat lower, she rebuked herself. But this was one of the few luxuries she and Marcia allowed themselves. The temperature zoomed down – the thermostat went up.

She went out to the kitchen to make herself a cup of tea. She debated about watching the late news. Nothing good on the news, she thought wryly. Still, it was her nightly habit to watch. But sitting in the living room before the TV set, she found her thoughts going back to the car that sat in front of the Emerson house.

She left her chair to cross to the window. The car was still there. This case was going to be dragged out before the whole country. What the devil was Scott telling that reporter about Beth?

With a surge of impatience she strode to the phone, hesitated for a moment. It was awful late to be calling David – but he'd want to know what was happening. With grim determination she reached for the phone book, found his home number. So it was late – he'd want to hear this.

She waited, hearing the ring at the other end. On the fifth ring she was about to hang up when David's voice came to her.

'Hello?'

'David?'

'Yeah.' He was instantly alert.

'This is Celia Logan. I know it's late to be calling, but I thought you'd want to know. A car belonging to one of those supermarket tabloids is sitting in front of Beth and Scott's house.'

'Hell!' David grunted. 'Thanks, Celia. You bet I want to know.'

April was awakened after lying sleepless for hours by a shrill whistle somewhere in the distance. She glanced at her watch on the night table. It was seven a.m., daylight just arriving. But by early evening, she comforted herself, she'd be homebound.

Leaving her key with the desk clerk, she asked about a local newspaper. There was none.

'We got one in the next town – twelve miles away,' the clerk said and gave her driving instructions.

'Oh, what was that shrill whistle around an hour ago?' she asked curiously. 'The volunteer fire department?'

'That was Kensington calling its workers to the plant. Six

mornings a week at seven a.m.' The desk clerk grimaced. 'Can you believe we have to put up with that every morning? There was a court case. They won.' Her eyes indicated she suspected a pay-off.

'It's awful,' April commiserated. That was like in southern cotton mill towns at the turn of the century, she recalled. She'd written a paper on that back in college.

She ignored the curiosity of the newspaper office when she asked for back issues. She covered four years – scanned the papers for some mention of Scott Emerson. There was nothing.

All right. She'd go back home, scout further. Talk to Elaine, her mind ordered. Scott's sister should be helpful. And call down to Columbia Business School – pretend he'd given the school as a reference. Put together a breakdown of his life before Magnolia.

Driving back to Chickasaw she plotted her day. Try for a flight around four or five p.m., she told herself. That would give her time to do more checking. The local library, that little women's specialty shop she'd noticed last evening – and a trip to Kensington Womenswear.

She parked at the hotel, went to her room to call the El Paso airport about a late afternoon reservation. There was a flight leaving at four p.m., with a brief layover in Dallas. Plenty of time to visit the local library, buy a tee shirt at the women's shop – and ask questions.

Luck was on her side. The tiny library was open today. She pretended to be looking for Texas guidebooks, contrived to engage the friendly librarian in conversation.

'We don't have much call for that,' the librarian confided. 'This isn't exactly a tourist town.' Her eyes were curious.

'I'm here to do some research for an article,' April explained and launched into her plotted conversation.

Right away the librarian was contemptuous about the influx of immigrant workers – and particularly harsh towards Kensington Womenswear.

'This was a nice town before they came here seven years ago.' Her eyes exuded resentment. 'Before they opened up, they talked a lot about all they were going to do for the town. And do you know, they even got some kind of tax abatement? All they did was bring in folks who'd work for almost nothing – but the town had to provide extra services. There's a big battle now about bilingual education at the school. You know what that'll do to our taxes.'

April left the library and walked to the women's shop. The only saleswoman there was a partner, she said in the course of casual conversation. She brought out a stack of tee shirts in various colors for April's inspection.

'Are they made here?' April asked with a show of interest.

'Lord, no!' the woman scoffed. 'I wouldn't buy from them if it meant I had to go out of business.'

'I'll take these two,' April decided and reached for her purse. It was clear residents of Chickasaw resented the presence of Kensington. The powers that be of Kensington realized it was time to move on. But not to Magnolia, April promised herself.

Leaving the shop she was conscious of hunger. Cross over to Mabel's for a quick lunch, then head for the Kensington plant. Over a white western omelet she asked the waitress on duty for directions to the plant.

'Sugar, you don't want to go out there,' the waitress clucked.

'I'm doing an article for a magazine,' April explained. 'I just want to ask them a few questions.'

'They won't be answering,' the waitress predicted. 'Real nasty people.'

The day was growing more humid. Even her lightweight pantsuit was too warm, April fretted. But in a couple of hours she'd be heading for El Paso and her flight back home. Not much being accomplished here.

Driving towards the Kensington plant, she noted that

houses on either side of the road were growing far apart. Rundown, paint-starved houses that said this was a depressed area. Now she saw acres planted in winter vegetables. Farmers moved slowly beneath the hot sun.

Then a large, rectangular building came into view. A sign announced that this was Kensington Womenswear. A chain fence surrounded the structure. It appeared more a prison than a manufacturing plant. April felt a chill dart through her body. Was this what they meant to bring to Magnolia?

She drove up to the barred entrance, leaned out to talk with the guard on duty.

'Hi.' She tried for a friendly approach. 'I'd like to interview someone in your promotion department – for a magazine article I'm researching.'

'We don't have no promotion department.' The guard was inspecting her with lively interest. 'But I'll call the boss.'

'Thank you.' She managed a dazzling smile.

A few minutes later the guard returned. His face was hostile. 'The boss – he says get lost. He ain't got no time to talk to you.'

Chapter Twenty-Four

April boarded the four p.m. flight out of El Paso, was restless during the hour layover in Dallas. Her flight was scheduled to arrive at LaGuardia at eleven forty-five p.m., Eastern Time. How sweet of David to insist on driving all the way down to pick her up.

Her face lighted when – at last – she was walking towards David at LaGuardia. She wished wistfully that she had some helpful news.

'You shouldn't have made this long drive down to New York,' she scolded after a warm embrace.

'I found a decent diner just off the expressway where we can have a bite and talk.' His eyes were full of questions as he took her valise from her.

'I wish I had more to report. But one thing is clear – Kensington must not locate in Magnolia. It would be a disaster.'

'And Scott never attended Columbia Business School,' he told her. 'I drove down early this afternoon, went up to the school to check. They have no record of Scott's having attended any of the Columbia schools. I always suspected he was a liar. April, what is he hiding?'

'He may have substituted Columbia for some little-known school – for the prestige involved.' She was striving for logic. 'But let's discuss that when we're out of here . . .'

In silence now they hurried through the usual airport throngs to the parking area, settled themselves in David's car.

'Kensington is on Chickasaw residents' shit list,' April began bluntly. 'I talked with a woman at the hotel, a saleswoman in a shop, and to a waitress at the local diner. People in Chickasaw resent the immigrant workers who make up the Kensington workforce. No locals are hired. They're after cheap labor.'

'Below minimum wage,' David surmised, grimacing in distaste. 'And they figure on doing the same thing in Magnolia – drawing from our migrant farm workers.'

'Chickasaw is getting too hostile for them. They figured it was time to move on. Magnolia seemed perfect for them – available migrant workers, a big tax break if Scott swings the deal.'

'I had a call last evening from Celia Logan,' David began as they drove out of the airport parking area and towards the Long Island Expressway. 'She saw a company car belonging to one of those supermarket tabloids sitting in front of Beth and Scott's house.'

'Scott's allowing himself to be interviewed?' April was cold with shock. 'Is he that hungry for money?'

'He's setting Beth up as unstable.' April saw David's hands tighten on the wheel. 'First, he pulled that business about Beth's breaking the appointment with the psychiatrist. Damn it, he made that appointment without consulting her – of course she broke it. Then he tells us Beth should plead temporary insanity – implying he believes she's guilty. Next he comes up with lies about his being so desperate he was talking with a divorce lawyer. And now this interview.'

'David, could Celia have made a mistake?' Once the trial began, the town would be overrun with city news teams, she thought and shuddered at the prospect. 'Maybe it was a car from the radio station . . .'

'I drove over there. I circled around several times. Nutty, maybe, but I was mesmerized by seeing that car sitting out there and knowing some reporter was in there interviewing

Scott. And being handed a bunch of lies. Why, April? Why is he doing this?'

'Could Kensington have something on Scott?' A supposition that hit her earlier. 'Maybe murdering Debbie was a warning to him to play their game. From what I heard down in Chickasaw, they'll do anything to get what they want – and they're desperate to make a deal to set up in Magnolia.'

'Both Beth and Jamie have been fighting to bring the dot-com company here,' David followed this thought. 'They're against companies that use sweatshop labor. Kensington wants the two of them out of the way – and they're leaning on Scott to make sure this happens.'

'It could be that.' April felt a surge of excitement. 'Now we've got to discover what Kensington has on Scott, expose both him and Kensington.'

'But will that help Beth?' All at once David was skeptical.

'Let's search for evidence that someone from the Kensington mob killed Debbie as a warning to Scott.' April's heart was pounding. 'We'll dig into Scott's background, ferret out whatever ugly secret he's been hiding. That's how we'll clear Beth.'

'And we've got to do it in about fifteen days,' David pointed out apprehensively.

'Let's find out if someone from Kensington was in Magnolia the night Debbie was murdered. We know the company had somebody in town. Beth told me Scott was spending his every free moment with him. We can't ask Scott,' April conceded. 'But he must have stayed at a local hotel or at one of the motels.'

'Bob may be able to track that down,' David pinpointed. 'Ten to one Scott introduced the Kensington rep to one of the Town Council members – looking for support for the deal. We'll check with him first thing in the morning.' David leaned over the wheel, stared ahead. 'There's the exit to the diner I told you about – it's open twenty-four hours.'

Several eighteen-wheelers sat on the parking lot before the brilliantly lighted diner.

'Where truckers eat, the food is good,' David said. 'And remember, we've got a long drive ahead.'

They settled themselves in a booth that provided privacy. A good-natured waitress, who'd been exchanging raucous remarks with a pair of ebullient drivers, came over to take their orders.

'Did you see Beth today?' April asked when she and David were alone again. One of the perks of being a big shot in a small town was that he could manage to visit her daily.

'You know I did,' he chided tenderly. 'She's thrilled with the news about Clark. She—'

'Oh, he went into surgery this morning!' April recalled. 'Has there been any word about his condition?'

'He was still in surgery when I left Magnolia. Everybody's keeping their fingers crossed. The doctors felt he was a great subject for transplant. His age, his general health . . .'

'How's Beth holding up?' April felt sick every time she visualized her sitting in a jail cell.

'She's furious at Scott – the business about the divorce. She's trying to figure out why he's lying this way. I didn't tell her about that tabloid rag interviewing him.' David reached across the table for April's hand. 'We've got barely fifteen days before she goes to trial. It scares the hell out of me. I feel so damn helpless.'

'We've got to use every hour of those days.' April fought to conceal her own fears. 'Let's track down the Kensington rep or reps who were in town when Debbie was murdered. Let's dig into Scott's background, discover what Kensington might have on him. As I see it, Scott's life before he moved to Magnolia is a blank page. Let's fill it in. I have a gut feeling that Scott will lead us to the murderer.'

April was pleased that the roads were all but deserted as they sped towards Magnolia. She sat with her head against David's shoulder – finding comfort in his presence. In all her years of practicing law she'd never approached a trial with so little ammunition – and this was a trial that meant so much to her.

David was in a reminiscent mood. He talked with much love about small incidents in Beth's life. Her first birthday party at three. Her first day at school. His pride in her brightness, her eagerness to help others even as an early teenager. He remembered how happy he'd been when she'd chosen to go to the state college in Albany – which meant she could spend many weekends at home.

'Beth and Jamie were right for each other,' he said in frustration. 'And then Scott burst into town – and she couldn't see anyone else. I prayed he'd find somebody else. God knows, most of the girls in town were smitten. But he chose Beth – and she was out of her mind with joy.'

'How's Jamie doing?'

'He's out of the hospital, insists he'll be back on the job tomorrow. He said a few cuts and bruises wouldn't keep him out of action.' David took one hand from the wheel to rest it on April's knee. 'We need all the help we can get.'

They drove into Magnolia – bedded for the night. Only the tavern on Main Street showed signs of life.

'Beth's probably lying awake, staring at the ceiling,' David said in anguish. 'I'm her father – I should be able to do more for her.'

'You're doing everything you can,' April insisted. 'We're going to win this case.'

'From your lips to God's ear,' David said softly. 'That's what my mother used to say in moments of crisis. And I thank God you came along. You give me strength.'

'We give each other strength.' It was almost as though the three of them – David, Beth, and she – were a family.

'We've made great time coming home,' he pointed out as he pulled up before April's apartment. His eyes were questioning. 'I don't suppose I could come in for coffee?'

'Please do.' Her eyes were a caress. 'I need you, David.'

* * *

Later – lying in his arms and too wired to sleep – she tried to envision the course that lay ahead. They knew the only way to clear Beth was to find Debbie's murderer. And time was breathing down their necks.

One day, David kept insisting, Beth must learn that she – April – was her birth mother. How would Beth feel about that? Would she demand, why did you give me away?

Will she hate me?

Chapter Twenty-Five

Over a hasty breakfast April and David plotted their day. April would work on discovering if someone from Kensington was in Magnolia the night when Debbie was murdered – and once she had established that, do a follow-up. David would dig into Scott's background. They'd check with each other – and with Bob – in the course of the day.

'I'll head for the hotels – plus the motels on the roads that lead into town,' April plotted. 'I'll fabricate something about having misplaced the address for Kensington Womenswear in Chickasaw and I'm trying desperately to track this down. I'm working with the Chamber of Commerce, who're talking to the firm about relocating here.' Her smile was wry. 'If a desk clerk tells me nobody from Chickasaw, Texas, registered with them around the date I mention, then I'll just apologize and say I was mistaken about where he had stayed while in town. If I handle it right, I should come up with the dates the rep was in Magnolia.'

'I'll head over to the radio station,' David said while April poured a second round of coffee for them. 'I'll—'

'The station?' April broke in. 'Where Scott works?'

'I've been close with Ted Abrams – the station owner – through the years. We've worked together on several campaigns for civic improvement. I'll say the *Sentinel* is preparing to run a human interest story on Beth and Scott, but I don't want to bother Scott with questions at such a traumatic time. I'd just like to see his résumé – the station must have it on file. That should give us a lead to his past.'

'Elaine will be in New York for a few days at least.' April was wistful. Elaine should be a gold mine of information. She could elicit important facts without seeming intrusive. Words were already forming in her mind: *Did you and Scott grow up in a small town like this? You did? Where?*

'I should call the hospital and ask about his condition.' David was thoughtful. 'We'll run a small box on the front page each day to report on this.'

'Call now,' April persuaded.

'I should wait until late in the day to get the latest news – before tomorrow morning's edition goes to press.' David hesitated. 'Hell, let's check now. I'll call again later.'

The hospital reported only that Clark had received a transplant the previous day. His condition was critical but stable.

'They're waiting to see if his body accepts the transplant.' David sighed. 'It'll be a waiting game for a few days.'

'But he's stable.' April clung to this.

David glanced at his watch. 'I'd better get cracking. I want to get over and talk with Ted before Scott's around. As I recall, he won't be in until noon today. I'll pop into the office for a few minutes, then head for the station.'

'Jamie, what the hell are you doing here? You ought to be in bed resting.' David hovered in the doorway of Jamie's small office.

'I'm fine.' Jamie grinned. 'As long as I don't drag around anything heavier than my laptop.'

'And what do you mean to do with your laptop?' David said with transparent gruffness.

'We don't have a phone number for the apartment where Elaine is staying down in New York, so—'

'What's your laptop got to do with Elaine?'

'I thought it might be a good idea to drive down there to interview her at the hospital for tomorrow morning's edition. You know, a report on Clark's condition, what their plans are in the coming weeks . . .' Jamie flashed a hopeful smile at David.

'Should you be driving that much?' David was ambivalent.

'No sweat.' Jamie's eyes pleaded for approval.

'Let me bring you up to date,' David hedged. 'April's back from Chickasaw. We did some intense digging at an early morning meeting. We want some background on Scott. Nobody seems to know anything about him before his arrival here. He's talked about going to Columbia Business School – but I discovered that was a lie.'

'That might have been just to impress,' Jamie said, yet David sensed his skepticism. April, too, had pointed that out – but he'd suspected she didn't believe that.

'Maybe. But we need to go back, build up a picture of Scott's life pre-Magnolia. I'm going to talk with Ted Abrams, see if I can get a look at Scott's résumé. It must be in the station's personnel files.'

'Maybe I can get something from Elaine – if Abrams doesn't come across,' Jamie pursued. 'Like where did she and Scott grow up. That would be a starting point, wouldn't it?'

'That's what we need.' David was emphatic.

'Wouldn't Beth know that?'

David sighed. 'I remember her saying he called his home town "a dead-end graveyard". He never gave it a specific name or locale. She said he'd had an unhappy childhood – his parents were a pair of alcoholics. He tried to erase those years from his mind.'

'I could head down to New York in about an hour,' Jamie said. 'I'm sure I'll find Elaine at the hospital. We could go for coffee and talk. I'll be back in time to do the story before the morning paper goes to press.'

'Okay,' David capitulated. 'Go for it.'

David lingered at the newspaper only long enough to handle necessary business. Now – conscious of the passage of time – he hurried over to the radio station. The receptionist directed him to go right to Ted Abrams' office.

'Hi.' Ted greeted him with a warm smile. 'Haven't seen you for a while. You missed the last Rotarian luncheon.'

'I've been derailed from the usual socializing.' He was sure Ted knew what he meant.

'I hope things work out well.' A guarded glint in Ted's eyes now. 'What's up? You have some new project you're ready to launch?'

'The newspaper is on the slow track for now.' Did Ted think he could worry about some new community project at a time like this? 'Actually, I'm working on a series about Beth and Scott. You know, the human interest angle.'

'Yeah, I know you're facing rough sledding right now,' Ted commiserated, yet David still felt a certain wariness in him. Damn! He'd watched Beth grow up through the years. His younger son was in Beth's classes. He couldn't believe she was guilty.

'I don't want to bother Scott with questions at a time like this.' What did Ted think about the nutty stories in the *Ledger*? 'Nor Beth,' he added. 'I need some general information – like where Scott went to school, where he grew up, where—'

'I think you should talk to Scott about that,' Ted interrupted. 'I wouldn't know these things. Oh, he went to school in New York – Columbia College, then the Columbia Business School.'

'That's right.' David nodded in recall. But that was a lie. 'If you could dig up his résumé from your personnel file—'

'We don't hang on to résumés.' Ted dismissed this with a touch of impatience. David got the message: Ted didn't want to be involved in whatever was being set up. 'You'd better talk to Scott.'

In his parents' treasured 'pre-owned' Cadillac Seville – his own car laid up for heavy repairs – Jamie removed the bandage on his forehead, replaced it with a band-aid. That looked less intimidating, he told himself as he glanced into the rear-view mirror. Still, it was unnerving to remember that somebody had tampered with his brakes. Hoping he'd die in the accident sure to happen?

He turned on the car radio when he arrived at the thruway. He didn't want to fall asleep at the wheel. He'd slept little these past two nights. Sure, he was concerned a little about the accident, he conceded – but most of all he was anxious about Beth. It unnerved him to hear some people in town talk as though they were sure she killed Debbie. *How can they believe that, knowing Beth?*

Despite his impatience to be talking with Elaine – maybe learning something that would help clear Beth – he was conscious of the stark, gray winterscape on either side. Beautiful in an awesome fashion, he thought. It reminded him of the times he and Beth had gone for a day of skiing when they were both home from college – once on Thanksgiving weekend, once during the Christmas holidays.

He'd never liked Scott – and it wasn't just because of Beth. There was something in Scott that sent out warning signals to him. But only in the past three months had they become openly hostile – because of Scott's trying to shove Kensington Womenswear down the Town Council's throat. And he knew Scott was dying to oust him from his seat on the council.

Midway into Manhattan he swung off the thruway to grab an early lunch. All he'd had for breakfast was three cups of coffee. He was haunted by the way the days were rushing past – and Beth's trial coming terrifyingly close. David insisted April and Bob were working hard at her defense – but what did they have to show? David was scared to death. So was he.

Then he was off the thruway and heading into Manhattan. He had made good time, he congratulated himself. Under other conditions he'd linger in town after he saw Elaine, go to a museum, have an early dinner. He could knock out the story about Clark on his laptop in forty minutes, he guessed. But this wasn't a time to play. Let him spend a while with Elaine, then head back for home.

Abandoning the hope of finding a parking spot, he left the car in a nearby garage and hurried to the hospital. As he'd anticipated, Elaine was there – in the reception area on Clark's floor.

'Jamie!' She leapt to her feet with a welcoming smile. 'How good to see you.'

'How's Clark?'

'He's doing fine. The doctors are so pleased. Of course, he's not out of the woods yet . . .'

'He's going to make it,' Jamie predicted. 'You know that everybody back home is praying for him.'

'Clark and I are so grateful. The town's been wonderful to us.'

'I don't suppose I could see him?'

'No.' Elaine was apologetic. 'I can only see him for a few minutes at a time – with all kinds of precautions. This isn't a time for him to pick up germs.'

'I figured.'

'When he leaves here, he'll go to rehab for about a month, the doctors say – and then, God willing, he'll come home.' She glowed in anticipation.

'Could we go somewhere and have a snack?' Jamie asked.

'The hospital cafeteria? I like to be close by . . .'

'That's fine,' he approved.

While they waited for an elevator to take them up to the top-floor cafeteria, Elaine asked about Beth.

'She's hanging in there,' he reported. 'It's insane.' He gestured in exasperation.

'It'll be a fast trial. She'll be cleared with no sweat.' A hint of bravado in Elaine's voice now.

How much did Elaine know about Beth and Scott's marriage? He hesitated. No, don't bring up my feelings about

Scott. He's her brother – she'll just be defensive. 'Crazy things are happening.'

'But everybody knows how wonderful Beth is.'

The elevator slid to a stop. The door opened. Jamie and Elaine abandoned conversation as they joined the other passengers.

In the sunlit cafeteria they joined the line, made their choices, and headed for a table for two that flanked a huge picture window.

'I'll have to return home tomorrow night,' Elaine told Jamie with a wistful smile. 'The neighbor who's been caring for the kids has to leave to be with her daughter, who's expecting. Of course, I miss being with the kids – but I felt this was a time when I should be with Clark.'

'Will his rehab place be close to home?' Jamie asked sympathetically.

Elaine's face brightened. 'Close enough so the kids and I can drive up on weekends.'

'Fill me in on Clark's treatment, anything you can tell me about the rehab scene,' Jamie said. 'Folks in town are eager to know how he's doing, when he'll be able to return to teaching. How you and the kids are handling the situation.'

'Sure.'

Elaine began a detailed story of Clark's days in the hospital, what lay ahead, how she and the children were coping. Jamie made notes on his laptop. He pushed aside guilt that he was waiting to elicit information about Scott.

'That's about it,' Elaine wound up.

'Why don't we do a little background on you,' he began ingenuously.

'Jamie, I've lived in Magnolia for a dozen years,' she protested. 'What's there to know about me?'

'Did you grow up in a small town like Magnolia?' he asked with a show of pleasant curiosity.

'Right.' *Why does she suddenly seem guarded?* 'The only time I lived in a real city was when I went to college.'

'Was your home town in New York State?'

'Yes.' She reached for her coffee, seemed reluctant to pursue this line of conversation. 'Are you driving back home today?'

'That's the plan. Where did you grow up?' he pursued with a warm smile.

'No place you ever heard of,' she dismissed. She was silent for a moment. 'Tell me about David. How is he holding up?'

'You know David. He never lets on how upset he is – but we see his pain. He's scared to death every waking moment. His whole world centers around Beth.'

Why is Elaine so evasive about her home town? Her home town and Scott's. What happened back there that we should know about?

Chapter Twenty-Six

April glanced at her watch as she settled herself in her car again. It was almost five p.m. – another day wasted, when they had so little time. She'd inquired at both local hotels, checked with three motels and had come up with nothing. Damn! A Kensington rep must have stayed somewhere in town. Not with Scott and Beth – she'd asked Beth about that before she started on this rat race.

All right, drive further out towards the thruway, she told herself. He probably arrived at the Albany airport, rented a car and drove towards Magnolia. Perhaps he checked in at a motel further away from town than she'd considered.

She stopped by two chain motels. Desk clerks were wary of her efforts. No results there, she thought in frustration. He might have stayed at one of these. She'd never know. Try one more, she resolved, then head for home.

Two miles down she spied a sign that read 'Paradise Inn Motel'. Privately owned, she noted. Small but well maintained, though the name was blatantly extravagant. Not exactly rushed with guests at the moment.

She pulled off the road, parked, went into the office. The woman clerk was reading a paperback romance novel but put it aside with a warm, welcoming smile.

'I'm not here to register,' April said with an air of apology. 'I'm with the Chamber of Commerce back in Magnolia – and did something so stupid.' She pantomimed eloquently. 'I lost the address of a firm down in Texas that's considering a move to Magnolia. Their rep told me he stopped at a small, charming motel about a dozen miles from town. This was about a month ago. A Mr Mitchell or Glover – I can't really remember his name.' She made a pretense of dismay. 'But I know the firm. It's Kensington Womenswear, from down in Texas.'

'Yeah, a guy from Kensington something or other was here.' The desk clerk grimaced in distaste. 'He complained about everything. One of those . . .'

'I heard he was a creep.' April was sympathetic. 'Then you have his address?'

'I'll get it for you.' She fumbled in a file drawer beneath the desk, came up with a folder. 'Him I remember because he was such a pain in the butt. Nothing was ever right.' She searched through the folder's contents. 'Here's his registration. I'll write down his address for you.' She reached for a notepad.

'And his name, please?' April sighed. 'I have such a terrible memory for names. Oh, and the dates he was registered.'

'Jamison,' she repeated. 'RD Jamison, Chickasaw, Texas. And here're the dates right here . . .'

April gazed at the sheet of paper the desk clerk extended. Yes! The Kensington rep had been in the area the night Debbie was murdered.

Back on the road April called Bob at the office on her cell phone.

'A Kensington rep was in the vicinity of Magnolia the night Debbie was murdered,' she reported. 'RD Jamison. He stayed at the Paradise Inn Motel for three nights!'

'Okay, let's check out RD Jamison,' Bob said crisply and sighed. 'But I don't think you should fly back down to Chickasaw. Let's talk to David about putting that PI down in Texas on this.'

'Have you and David come up with any background on Scott?'

'David bombed out at the radio station. We're waiting to see if Jamie came up with anything in his interview with Elaine. David said he phoned from New York to say he'd be here around dinner time. David said he sounded kind of excited – but he didn't say what he'd learned from Elaine. Come straight to the house. Nicole's expecting all of us for dinner. We'll have a conference afterwards.'

April arrived at the Allens' house just as Nicole returned with Marianne and Neil. The children were shipped to the den to start homework.

'I don't know . . .' Nicole sighed as she and April headed for the kitchen. 'We want to give our kids all the advantages, but sometimes I think we overschedule them. Shouldn't there be time just to do nothing – maybe dream a little, lie around and read just for the pleasure of it?'

'We don't live in that kind of world anymore.' April frowned in thought. 'Look at the way some kids fasten themselves to their computers – forgetting about socializing.'

'Neil doesn't have the computer bug yet,' Nicole said and crossed her fingers. 'We limit how much time Marianne can use our computer. Just the way we limit how much time she spends watching TV.' Now Nicole shifted the conversation. 'How did you make out today?' Nicole followed every step of their operation, at regular intervals made contributions.

'I've got a name. RD Jamison. I was about to give up,' April admitted, 'but decided to try one more place. I found out long ago that persistence pays off.'

'Bob told me that Jamie drove down to New York to interview Elaine for a story in tomorrow's paper. He and David are hoping Jamie comes up with something about Scott's background.' Nicole seemed to be debating inwardly. 'April, are the three of you running around in circles? I mean, David's chasing after contractors, you're in pursuit of this rep from Kensington, and all of you are hoping for some lead on Scott's background.'

'We're desperate.' April nodded as Nicole pointed to the coffee maker. 'Do you realize how close we are to the trial?'

'I think you ought to put all your efforts to looking into Scott's past. That's where you'll find answers.'

'My thought, too,' April confessed. 'But we're having a devil of a time finding a starting point.'

'Let's see what Jamie brings to the table.' Nicole managed to sound optimistic. 'We'll sit down after dinner and dig.'

David and Bob arrived simultaneously, closeted themselves in a corner of the living room while the two women focused on dinner preparations. April marveled at Nicole's culinary skills.

'You don't miss being totally involved in lawyering,' she guessed.

'I love it – but not on a full-time basis,' Nicole admitted. 'I like being here for the kids. Later – when they're in high school – I'll get back to it. I find the greatest relaxation in cooking, preparing interesting dishes. I enjoy dividing my life this way.' But now her eyes were troubled. 'Marianne and Neil are so upset about Debbie.'

'That's understandable.'

'They can't believe Beth is about to go on trial for murder. How do I make my kids accept that in this imperfect world right doesn't always win?' But right must win in the case of Debbie's murderer, April thought rebelliously.

'Nicole, you think – the way I do – that Scott is going to lead us to our murderer?'

'Absolutely. And I keep asking myself, why did Jamie sound so excited when he talked to David earlier today? If he'd come up with something substantial, why didn't he tell David in his phone call?'

'Maybe he was concerned about privacy. He ought to be showing up soon – unless he's run into bad traffic.' He'd said they were not to hold up dinner until he arrived, April remembered. But a place was set for him.

They were just sitting down at the dinner table when they heard a car pull up into the driveway.

'Jamie.' David tensed, exchanged a loaded glance with April, then with Bob. 'I'll get the door.'

'Marianne and Neil, I know you're anxious to get to the TV to see that program you talked about,' Nicole said. 'Just tonight you can take your plates and go watch on the set in the den.'

'Thanks, Mom!' Marianne gestured to Neil to join her in this unexpected escape.

The others at the table looked up expectantly as David and Jamie joined them. Dinner forgotten for the moment.

'Tell us,' David ordered. 'Why did you sound so excited when you called?'

'It was nothing Elaine said,' Jamie warned somberly. 'It's what she didn't say. I came right out and asked – casually, of course – where she and Scott had grown up. I tried again – and she stonewalled me. She wouldn't tell me. Why was she so evasive? What happened back there that she doesn't want us to know about?'

'There's got to be a way to find out.' An edge of desperation in April's voice. 'I'll talk to Beth about that again tomorrow. Oh, one new item . . .' She struggled for a show of optimism. 'The Kensington rep was in town that night.' No need to be more specific; the others understood. 'A man named RD Jamison. He spent three nights at a small motel about a dozen miles out of town.'

'I'll put the PI down in Texas on it tomorrow.' A vein pounding in David's forehead betrayed his anxiety.

'Let me go check on the Internet.' Nicole rose to her feet.

'What'll you find on the Internet?' David challenged.

'Let's see if RD Jamison is a felon. We'll know in minutes. But eat while you're talking,' Nicole admonished. 'I slaved for hours over that chicken casserole.' She paused, grinned. 'Well, at least at hour.' Now she strode from the dining area and towards their home office.

'There's got to be a way to get a background check on Scott.' David grunted in frustration.

'Jamie, did Elaine say when she's coming home?' April asked.

'Tomorrow night.'

'Then the next morning I'm going to talk with her,' April said with a calm she didn't feel. *By the time Elaine is back in town the trial will be just eight days away.* 'I must make her understand how important it is that we know where she and Scott grew up. I must make her realize what's at stake.'

For a few minutes they dissected what they knew about Scott. Again, April stressed she would talk with Beth about his origins. 'Maybe something fresh will pop into her mind.'

Nicole charged into the dining area with an aura of triumph.

'We know something about RD Jamison,' she told the others. 'He's a felon. He spent time in prison first for insurance fraud and then for assault with a deadly weapon. Not exactly the kind of person we'd want to see living in Magnolia.'

'I know it's a wild card,' David admitted, 'but Bob, let's you and I focus on Jamison's activities here in town. Let's check again on whether anybody in the neighborhood saw a strange man in the area that night.'

'We've interviewed everybody,' Bob reminded.

'Maybe we skipped somebody,' David pursued. 'Somebody who was out of town the day we questioned the neighbors. Let's do it again,' he insisted. 'And while we're doing that, April, you'll be searching for a motive – that we feel is tied in with Kensington.'

'We need to know what Elaine is hiding from us.' April reiterated Jamie's thought. 'What happened back in that town where she and Scott grew up that gave Kensington blackmail fodder?' All at once she couldn't bear the prospect of waiting another two days to confront Elaine. 'I'm driving down to New York early tomorrow morning,' she told the others. 'I'll get an answer from Elaine. And when I have that, I'll drive to that town – wherever it is – and I'll come up with answers.'

Chapter Twenty-Seven

Just past seven a.m. April and David sat in a diner on the road that led to the thruway. Half a dozen patrons sat at the long counter. Another few occupied booths. The windows were steamed because the temperature this morning had zoomed downward.

'I'll stop by and see Beth on my way to the newspaper,' David said. 'And take her a decent breakfast. Thank God I have enough pull in town to see her every day.' He grimaced in pain. 'But not enough pull to keep her out on bail.'

'We're going to get her out of this horror,' April vowed, yet in her heart she was fearful.

'I still think you ought to call Elaine to make sure she won't be heading home earlier today. You could pass her on the thruway . . .'

'No.' April shook her head in conviction. 'I want the element of surprise. I mustn't give her time to build up a defense against me.'

'What kind of blackmail could be so strong as to let Scott protect the murderer of his child?' David shook his head in bewilderment. 'To try to frame his own wife for that murder?'

'A threat of his own death? Or some bizarre disgrace? You've said he was obsessed with acquiring political success. What did Beth tell me?' April searched her mind. 'The White House by the time he's forty-eight?'

'Beth said that was his mantra. He was furious because

I wouldn't put the newspaper behind him for a run for the Town Council. The first rung up the ladder.'

'And he'd fight against anything that might stop his success,' April guessed.

Ten minutes later they'd finished breakfast and headed for their cars. For a heated moment David held April close.

'Drive carefully,' he told her. 'You're precious cargo.'

At intervals traffic was heavy – April impatient. She would go directly to the hospital, she plotted. Elaine spent the whole day there, to be available for the brief periods when she was allowed to see Clark. Was David right? Should she have phoned first to make sure Elaine wasn't already en route home?

By the time she left the thruway and was headed towards Manhattan snow began to fall. She inspected the sky with anxious eyes. Were they in for a snowstorm? She mustn't get stuck in the city.

She knew not to bother trying to find a parking spot. She drove to the garage within short walking distance of the hospital, left the car and headed for her meeting – hopefully – with Elaine. Clark was still on the critical list but stable, she reminded herself.

At the hospital she went directly up to Clark's floor. She searched the small reception area with alarm. Elaine was nowhere in sight. She was about to go to the nurses' station to enquire when she saw Elaine walking down the hall.

'April, hi . . .' Elaine seemed uneasy.

'How's Clark doing?' April asked with a warm smile.

'He's doing great,' Elaine told her. 'The doctors are very pleased.' Questions in her eyes now. *She's trying to figure out why I'm here.*

'Could we go somewhere for coffee?' April struggled to appear casual. 'What a creepy day.'

'We can go up to the cafeteria.' All at once Elaine seemed tense. 'It's right in the building.'

'Fine.' April smiled in approval. 'This isn't a day to

go chasing around town. The snow is already beginning to stick.'

The two women walked to the elevator. 'Snow in the city is beautiful when it's coming down,' April said, 'but a dirty mess the next day if it sticks.' *Elaine knows why I'm here. She's nervous, building up a defense. Why?*

In the cafeteria – almost deserted at this hour – they went directly to the coffee urn. With coffee in tow they headed for a table in a private corner.

'How's Beth holding up?' Elaine asked when they were seated.

'She's grieving, of course,' April said gently. 'And so upset at Scott.'

'What's Scott done?' Elaine was defensive – and April reminded herself that this was her brother. From what Beth had said, she gathered there were no other close relatives.

'He's allowed himself to be interviewed by one of those supermarket tabloids. I dread to see what they do to Beth.' April paused. 'He's claiming he'd been talking to a divorce lawyer just before – before Debbie's murder.'

'I didn't know about that.' Elaine was shaken.

'He's hinted to the police that she's mentally unstable.'

'Beth?' Elaine gaped at her in shock. 'Never!'

'Elaine, the only way we're going to be able to clear Beth is to find the murderer. The police are doing nothing – they're convinced Beth is guilty.' April took a deep breath. 'Bob and I are working on the assumption that somebody out there is carrying on a vendetta against Scott. They're hurting those close to him – Debbie and Beth.' April's mind was charging ahead. 'Then somebody set fire to Rosita Rivera's trailer and—'

'Rosita?' Elaine was startled.

'Do you know her?'

'She cleans for me – once every two weeks,' Elaine said. 'But how does Rosita figure in this?'

'She and her late husband worked for an outfit down in

Texas that Scott is representing to the Town Council. And then there was the attempt on Jamie Lawrence's life.'

Elaine's face was drained of color. 'When?' she gasped. 'How?'

'Several days ago he was driving when his brakes failed. He wasn't badly hurt, thank God – but the mechanics discovered his brakes had been cut. It was an attempt on his life. He was fighting to keep Scott's outfit out of town. We suspect that somebody may be blackmailing Scott. That he's afraid to come out and say whom he suspects of murdering Debbie.'

'Oh, my God,' Elaine whispered. 'Where will this end?'

'Elaine, Beth's life is at stake. She could be sent to prison for life – for a murder she didn't commit. She could be sentenced to death. Help us unravel this vendetta. Where did you and Scott live before you moved to Magnolia? Where did the two of you grow up?'

The atmosphere was all at once electric. April sensed the inner battle going on within Elaine, her ambivalence. She held her breath, waited.

'I have to tell you,' Elaine whispered. 'I have no choice. We lived in a small town much like Magnolia. Upstate, close to the Canadian border.' She paused, seeming to fight to utter the name. 'A town called Cedar Grove.'

Driving back to Magnolia, April inspected the sky with growing anxiety. The snow had stopped, but the cluster of gray clouds hinted at more to follow. Could she reach home before a serious snowstorm?

She called David on her cell phone. Iris picked up.

'David's out of his office,' Iris reported. 'But he should be back in fifteen minutes.'

Now April called Bob.

'He's in court. He'll be there most of the day,' Sandy reminded April.

'If he calls in, tell him we know Scott and Elaine's home

town. Elaine gave me the name. I'll be home in about three hours,' April estimated. 'I want to go up there first thing tomorrow morning.'

'I'll tell him,' Sandy promised. 'That's great!'

Fretting with impatience, she waited fifteen minutes to try David again. Instinct told her they were hovering at a breakthrough.

'David Roberts,' his voice came to her.

'David, I know where Scott grew up. In a small town further upstate. Cedar Grove. Elaine couldn't bring herself to tell me any more – but there are answers there we need. I know that, David!'

'We're coming up with nothing here. You're right. Cedar Grove must hold the answers.'

'I want to go there first thing tomorrow morning. We'll—'

'We can't afford to wait. I can leave the office in Jamie's hands for a couple of days. We'll go up together tonight – if you're up to it,' he amended.

'I'm up to it.' *We can't afford to waste time.*

'I'll do the driving,' he plotted. 'We'll stay over at a motel near town, start looking for answers first thing in the morning.' He hesitated. 'April, maybe I should go up alone. The weather forecast is predicting heavy snow. I can handle this.'

'I'm going with you,' she insisted. 'I have to stay with this . . .' Her voice broke. 'My daughter's life is at stake.'

'*Our* daughter's life,' he said gently. 'We'll go together.'

Snow began to fall again. The weather forecast was right, April conceded. They were in for a heavy snowstorm. But the snowplows would be out on the roads soon, she reassured herself. Maybe traveling would be slower – but by late tonight she and David would be just outside of Cedar Grove. Early in the morning they'd drive into town. First stop, the local newspaper.

She ordered herself to slow down. Already the roads were becoming icy. So she'd arrive in town half an hour later than she'd expected. She'd arrive in one piece. Beth needed her alive – not lying in a hospital somewhere after a crack-up.

She'd forgotten how early twilight arrived this time of year. It was almost night when she drove into Magnolia. She and David ought to leave as soon as possible – while the roads were passable. Already the trees were lined with white. The snow gave no sign of letting up.

She found David pacing in his office.

'I've checked on Cedar Grove,' he told her. 'We take the thruway north. I've packed a bag.' He reached to pull her close for a moment. 'We'll go to your place so you can pick up what you'll need, then we'll hit the road.'

'I'll need boots and my down coat. The temperature's sliding downward.'

'Bob just called. I told him what's happening. We'll keep in touch with him, of course.' He hesitated. 'Bob's uneasy about our driving in this weather.' David's eyes were somber. He was nervous for her, April thought.

'If it was Marianne or Neil's life at stake,' she said softly, 'Bob would be driving tonight. Let's get moving.'

David followed her in his car. April left her car in her garage, went with him into her apartment to pack what she'd need for a couple of days.

'Let's have an early dinner here,' she suggested. 'Something quick. Diners on the road might close if the weather gets worse.'

They settled for cheese omelets and coffee, ate with unaccustomed speed and stacked the dishes in the dishwasher. In less than an hour after she'd driven into town, they were on the road in David's car.

'This is a night when I'm damn happy I've got four-wheel drive,' he said with determined optimism. 'The roads may get lousy, but we'll get through.'

'The snowplows are coming out up here.' She sighed with a relief when they saw the first plow moving like a prehistoric monster on to the strip of road ahead of them.

'Even with the snow we should be there in less than four hours.'

They soon realized her prediction had been overconfident. Though traffic was light, it was sluggish. Still, April remembered, David had checked with the AAA before they'd left. There were two motels at the edge of town. Neither was apt to be fully occupied on a night like this.

'We know we're on to something,' April insisted as they inched their way up the thruway. 'Why else would Elaine be so distraught?'

'Why couldn't she have come right out and told us who's out to destroy Scott? Why do we have to play these games?'

'We're going to discover something about her family that's terribly painful,' April guessed. 'She couldn't bring herself to take that extra step.'

Per AAA instructions they left the thruway and headed west. 'The motels should be about a dozen miles ahead,' David said. 'We're almost there.' He took one hand from the wheel to squeeze April's in encouragement.

At close to midnight – squinting through the falling snow – they saw the neon sign of a small motel.

April read the lighted 'Vacancy' sign with relief. They had a place to stay for the night.

'Get the flashlight from the glove compartment,' David told her as he swung off the road. 'There's a good chance we'll lose power before the night's over.'

Chapter Twenty-Eight

April and David slept little in the course of the night. At one point she was conscious that power had been lost. Total darkness engulfed the area.

'Awake?' David's voice was soft.

'Yes.' April felt his arms draw her close in comfort. 'Power's out here. Will the businesses be closed?' she asked in sudden alarm.

'They'll manage to stay open. These small towns are hardy. What time is it?' He reached for the flashlight on the night table, sent a beam of light on the clock he'd placed there earlier. 'It's just past six. Nothing will be open yet.' His impatience reached through to April.

'Let's get up and head for town. By the time we get there we'll find a diner open – place to have breakfast. Maybe ask questions.'

Grateful for the warmth of their unit, they prepared for the day. The first faint light lit the sky by the time they left their unit and went to check out. Even now they could hear the sound of snowplows on the road.

'There must have been at least eight inches already,' David surmised as they made their way to the car. Unexpectedly he grinned. 'I'm glad I keep waterproof boots in the car once winter arrives.'

For a few moments April was afraid the car wouldn't start up. Then the faint, welcome sound as the motor crept into action.

'Okay, Cedar Grove, here we come,' David proclaimed.

But let the town not be closed up because of the weather, April prayed.

They drove into a winterscape of awesome beauty. The boughs of trees laden with snow. A magnificent serenity cloaked the atmosphere. Birds chirped. Squirrels darted along ice-edged utility wires like tightrope performers. By the time they arrived at the edge of town they saw the first glints of sun breaking through the clouds. Now they approached the town. A replica of small towns throughout the country, April thought – her eyes sweeping over the array of small shops, still closed at this early hour. No sign of sidewalks being swept clean of snow. Would they open later?

'Main Street,' David decided, reading her mind. 'Ah, and there's a diner – down at the end on the left. It looks like it's open.'

David parked before the diner. Emblazoned in red neon was a sign that pronounced it 'Open.'

Through the steamed-up window they saw that a handful of patrons were already being served. Three men at the counter joshed about earlier snowstorms.

'Hey, this is nothing. Remember last winter when we hit thirty-four inches? This'll give us a little work,' one of the men conceded.

'Let's stop loafing and get out there and shovel,' another scolded. 'We ain't makin' no money sittin' on a stool and drinkin' coffee.'

'It's cold out there,' the third complained. 'We need to warm up.'

Only one booth – up front and flanking a radiator – was occupied. A middle-aged couple sat devouring breakfast with gusto. At intervals the woman reached out to touch the radiator with a sigh of pleasure. 'Ooh, that feels good!'

April and David headed for a booth at the rear. A forty-ish waitress sauntered over with menus.

'Everybody's complaining about the weather,' she drawled. 'It's winter. What do they expect?'

'It's beautiful,' April said. 'If you're dressed for it.' And she was.

'Folks around here are getting ulcers at the way oil prices are rising,' the waitress chatted while they inspected the menu. 'And those with gas furnaces . . .' She whistled eloquently. 'Gas is costing four times what it cost last year.'

'Wood stoves and fireplaces will get a good workout if we have the severe winter the forecasts are talking about,' David predicted.

'I told my brother and sister-in-law last spring, start cutting wood for the winter,' their waitress said. 'Already we heard we'd have a cold winter. And it takes a year for wood to dry out to burn right. But he wouldn't listen,' she sighed. 'They could have saved themselves a bundle.'

April read curiosity in her eyes about their presence here.

'We're heading to Canada for a family wedding,' April improvised.

'The snowplows have been out all night,' David picked up. 'We should make decent time today.'

April settled down to order, and David joined her. Her mind charging ahead, she decided to do some exploring.

'We got off the thruway when we realized we were near Cedar Grove,' April fabricated. 'I thought it would be interesting to stay over at a motel and come into town for breakfast. Friends back home used to live here. Oh, years ago. Maybe you knew them?' She contrived a dazzling smile. 'Elaine and Scott Emerson. At least, she used to be Elaine Emerson – now she's married to Clark Miller.'

'Yeah . . .' A guarded glint in the waitress's eyes evoked a sudden excitement in April.

'You knew Elaine?' she asked ingenuously. 'She's a wonderful person.'

'I was a year ahead of Elaine in school.' The waitress seemed to be in some inner debate. 'How's she doing?'

'Her husband is a doll – he teaches in the junior high back home. And they have two adorable kids.' Now April's voice grew somber. 'But they've been through a rough time. Young as he is, Clark had a serious liver problem. Some bug he picked up in Africa when he was in the Peace Corps. He's had a transplant, thank God – and it seems to be taking well.'

'Elaine had enough tragedy in her life without that,' the waitress commiserated – clearly upset. 'I mean, her parents being murdered that way.' She paused. 'You knew about that?'

'No,' April said, feeling the shock that had invaded David as well as herself. 'Elaine probably wanted to put that behind her.'

'It happened when Elaine was in her last year at college. Scott was fourteen or fifteen,' the waitress continued. 'They never found out who did it. They figured it was some drifter coming through the town. The house was a shambles, the police said. They figure it was a robbery – somebody figuring Mr and Mrs Emerson had money stashed away in the house. They were a well-fixed family.'

'How awful.' April was shaken. 'No wonder Elaine never mentioned it.'

'When you see Elaine, tell her Laurie Jackson back in Cedar Grove asked about her. I wish her the best – she deserves it.'

April waited to speak until Laurie was out of hearing. 'David, is what's happening in Magnolia a follow-up on the murder here in Cedar Grove?'

'I don't know what to think anymore,' David admitted. 'But I'm certain there's a link. We'll dig into the local newspaper morgue.' His eyes focused on a newspaper lying on a table just beyond theirs. The *Cedar Grove Gazette*, April noted. 'They've got a newspaper.'

'I doubt if the office opens before eight thirty or nine,' April pointed out. 'We have to stall over breakfast.'

'We'll ask for issues that date back fifteen to thirteen years,' David plotted. 'Laurie Jackson said Elaine was a college senior when her parents were murdered.' He glanced at his watch, grunted in impatience. 'It'll have to be a leisurely breakfast,' he agreed.

They were relieved that the chef was slow in preparing their orders. They ate with deliberate slowness – almost afraid to discuss the situation lest they give themselves away. Over second cups of coffee David plotted their approach – in words so soft April had to lean towards him to hear.

'We're doing research for a book on small towns in this country in the latter half of the twentieth century,' he improvised. 'Small town newspapers are usually cooperative with writers.' He chuckled. 'At least the *Sentinel* is. It seems sometimes that half the world is talking about writing a book.'

At eight thirty a.m. sharp they left the diner – hoping the newspaper office opened early. Before heading for the car they picked up a copy of the *Gazette* at a just-opened shop. In the car they checked for the address. Judging from the street addresses they gathered the newspaper was situated at the far end of Main Street.

The newspaper was located in a two-story red brick building that was kept in top-notch condition.

'They do all right,' David surmised as they walked up the short flight of stairs to the entrance. 'This is no depressed town.'

They were met with mild curiosity, supplied with microfilm copies of the years they'd requested.

'The microfilm machines are in the room to the right.' The clerk was cordial. 'And you can make copies for twenty-five cents a page.'

The room indicated provided two microfilm machines plus one photocopy machine. April and David each sat before a microfilm machine, inserted the first of the reels. Both churning with impatience as they viewed nothing of interest.

'David, here!' April's heart began to pound. She beckoned him to read over her shoulder.

Here was the story of the murder of Carl and Phyllis Emerson – Scott and Elaine's parents. April scrolled down to read the follow-up on the following date.

'All right, make copies,' David ordered. 'I'll go back and see what I can come up with – and make copies.'

Not allowing themselves to communicate about their findings, April and David read on. The atmosphere was supercharged. Then they scrambled for quarters to make copies. Fighting to conceal her excitement, April went out to the clerk to acquire more quarters. At last April was finished. She noted that David was now rewinding the film. They'd talk when they were out of here.

In the dank, cold car they sat and compared what they had discovered.

'Why did Scott lie that way about his parents?' David asked in astonishment. 'They weren't alcoholics! His father was a respected judge. His mother served on philanthropic committees. They were model citizens!'

'Perhaps he was looking for sympathy,' April offered. 'You know, playing the kid from a rough background who rose above it. And Scott,' she pointed out grimly, 'was hardly a model boy. He was suspended from junior high school just months before the murder.'

'Why was he suspended?'

'He and another boy pulled a fire alarm. I suppose that could have been just a silly escapade,' April conceded.

'I'd like to see where they lived.' David was thoughtful. 'We need an old phone book – the year of the murder,' he pinpointed.

'We'll probably find it at the local library. If it's open at this hour.'

'Let's go ask questions.' David gazed along the street. 'Let's try the pharmacy. It seems to be open. My throat's scratchy,' he improvised. 'Let's go buy some cough drops. And ask questions.'

In the pharmacy they learned that this was one of the two

days in the week when the library opened at ten a.m. Back in the car they settled down to read the local newspaper – until it was ten a.m.

'Let's hope the library has phone books that go back twelve or thirteen years. If not,' David said thoughtfully, 'then we'll head back to the diner for an early lunch and talk with Laurie Jackson.'

At exactly ten a.m. they pulled into the parking area beside the small but charming library, located in what was once a white colonial residence.

'Okay,' David said briskly. 'Let's find out where the Emersons lived. And keep your fingers crossed that a neighbor of that period still lives there.'

If the librarian was surprised that anyone would request phone books of years ago, she gave no indication of this.

'We have them on microfilm,' she said with a touch of pride. 'Would you like more than one year?'

'The 1986 phone book would be fine,' April said with a casual smile.

They retreated to a pair of microfilm machines, threaded the reel of film, and searched for their quarry.

'Here it is.' April pointed to an entry. 'Carl Emerson, 345 Maple Avenue.'

'Where the hell is Maple Avenue?'

'No sweat,' April soothed. 'I'll ask the librarian.'

Ten minutes later they were searching for house numbers on Maple Avenue, a neighborhood of pleasant, large houses.

'There it is.' April pointed to a well-maintained white colonial set on a lavish plot. The landscaping hinted of many years of care.

'Not quite what Scott described,' David said drily as he pulled up at the side of the road.

'Nobody's home,' April judged. Neither the driveway nor the path to the house had been cleared of snow.

'Now where is a friendly neighbor when we need her – or him?' David's eyes swung to the house on the left, then to the right. 'Somebody Up There is looking after us,' he whispered and nodded towards the fifty-ish woman who had emerged from a white brick house on the right. Let's go make conversation.'

They left the car and approached the woman, who was gingerly making an effort to shovel the snow from the path to her house.

'Good morning,' April said as the woman looked up with an air of mild curiosity. 'We were just wondering. The house next door' – she nodded towards what had been the Emerson house – 'is that where Elaine Emerson used to live?'

'Yes.' Her eyes widened in surprise. 'Why do you ask?'

'We're friends of hers from down below,' April explained, striving to sound casual. 'We were headed towards Canada when we got caught in the snowstorm. We stayed at a motel off the thruway, and then I realized we were near Cedar Grove – where Elaine used to live. I thought it would please her if we looked up her old house.'

'Elaine was such a sweet girl. My husband I watched her grow up.' Now the woman next door frowned. 'But that brother of hers – he was a bad lot.'

'Why don't you let me shovel a path for you.' David smiled ingratiatingly. 'That's man's work.'

'Oh, I couldn't ask you to do that . . .' But her eyes were wistful.

'I need the exercise,' David insisted. 'You two chat and I'll clear a path in no time.'

'My husband's out of town on business,' she explained and turned to April. 'Why don't you come inside and have a cup of coffee with me? And we'll make sure there's coffee for your husband.'

'That would be lovely. Did you know the Emersons well?' April asked.

'Phyllis and I were very close. She and Carl were fine people – more than anybody could say about that spoiled brat of a son.' The Emersons' neighbor hesitated. 'While

Phyllis was alive, I never repeated a word she said to me. But that boy was always in trouble. Always gave them such grief. But it's so cold just standing here,' she apologized. 'Let's go into the house and warm up.'

April's hostess introduced herself as Nora Martin. 'Bill and I have lived here since the day we got married almost thirty years ago. The Emersons had been living next door almost ten years by then,' she reminisced while she led April down a long hall to a large, pleasant kitchen.

Nora talked about Cedar Grove while she poured coffee – kept warm on the coffee maker. She was fourth generation, loved the town. 'It's a quiet, almost serene town most of the time.' She paused. 'I expect you know about the Emerson murder?'

April nodded. 'It must have been a terrible shock to the people here.'

'Oh, we'd never experienced anything like that.' Nora shuddered in recall. 'And nothing since.' With delicate china coffee cups on a tray, along with a plate of cookies, Nora guided April down the hall and into the pretty antique-furnished living room to the left.

'I understand the murder was never solved,' April sympathized.

'That's what the police say.' Nora's eyes went opaque. *What does she mean?*

'You don't believe that?' April asked, her heart pounding. *No, it's wrong to think this way. I'm jumping to wild conclusions.*

'It's not for me to say. But it was a horrible experience. Carl and Phyllis were such fine people. Elaine was special.' Nora's eyes softened. 'After it happened, she dropped out of college to come home and take care of everything. She even managed to find the money to send Scott off to boarding school. Oh, everybody thought he was such a charmer! Except those who knew what he was really like. Bill and I were worried about Elaine's finances. We knew that Carl and Phyllis had to sell all their stocks, take a second mortgage on the house to bail him out of that last escapade – just a few months before the murder.'

'He was in serious trouble?' April's mind was chasing down bizarre paths.

'He broke his parents' hearts when he got into trouble with a young girl in town. He beat her and raped her. Her parents were drunks, riff-raff. They took Carl and Phyllis for almost everything they were worth.' She hesitated. 'When first our cat and then our dog was poisoned, I asked myself if Scott had done that. We never found out.' All at once she seemed disconcerted by these revelations. 'Tell me about Elaine. Is she happy? After what she's been through, she deserves the best.'

Chapter Twenty-Nine

To distract Nora Martin from her anxiety at being so candid, April launched into a report on Elaine's current situation.

'Clark is a wonderful person. His students adore him. And the doctors are optimistic about his condition. The whole town's keeping their fingers crossed for him.'

A knock at the door told them David had finished shoveling a path to the house. Nora hurried to bring him into the house, brought him coffee, urged him to try the cookies. Yet April sensed Nora was relieved when they left the house.

April was eager to return to the privacy of the car and to report what Nora had told her.

'Drive around the corner and then pull up somewhere so we can talk,' April said, faintly breathless.

'We can talk while I drive,' he chided good-humoredly.

'Not with what I have to tell you.' She was grim. 'Of course, I may be jumping too far ahead . . .'

'You talk and I'll listen.' He swung around the corner and pulled up at the side of the road. The area was deserted except for a pair of amiable dogs romping in the snow.

April repeated what Nora Martin had told her about Scott. The unspoken accusations. She watched him as she talked. She wasn't alone in her suspicions.

'We mustn't jump to wild conclusions,' he warned. 'But yes – I know what you're thinking. It's an horrendous possibility – but we must follow it through.' He squinted in thought. 'But how do Rosita and Jamie fit into this puzzle?'

'I'm convinced there's a connection,' April confessed. 'I can't even conceive of what it could be at this point.' Her mind searched for answers. 'David, I need to talk to Beth,' she said with sudden urgency. 'Let's go home.'

April and David drove straight to Magnolia – too anxious to pursue their suspicions to stop for lunch.

'We're probably way off track,' David warned as he swung off the thruway, headed for the road that would take them into Magnolia. Already the day was waning. 'I know – we both jumped to the same conclusion. But Scott was out of town that night. I'm sure the police checked it out.'

'I checked it out,' April admitted. 'He could have hired someone,' she added after a moment.

'Not Scott.' David dismissed this. 'He wouldn't want to be tied in with a second party. Damn it, he couldn't be in two places at once!'

'We'll see.' Questions were taking shape in her mind. 'But first let me talk with Beth.'

'Afterwards meet me at Bob and Nicole's.' He glanced at his watch. 'Bob will be heading home very soon. I'll pop into the office for a few minutes, then head there.'

David dropped her off at the shop where each day she bought a magazine to take to Beth. From there she went to the small grocery where she shopped for fruit or cookies. Thank God, she thought while she waited for Beth to be brought to the tiny conference room, that David had the pull in town that provided them with small privileges.

In the last three or four days she'd sensed that Beth was becoming terrified of the coming trial – now so close.

'You're so good to me,' Beth said tenderly when April handed over the latest magazine and a box of cookies. 'You barely know me and you're so kind. Dad tells me how hard you're working for my defense.'

'You're special, Beth.' April fought back tears. What

would Beth say if she knew the truth? 'Now let me bring you up to date.'

She began to report her findings about Scott's parents. 'So you see, they were highly respected people in Cedar Grove.'

'Why did Scott lie that way?' Beth stared at her in bewilderment.

'Maybe he just wanted to forget the past.' Now April forced herself to tell Beth about Scott's troubles as an early teenager. To tell her that Scott's parents had been murdered a dozen years ago.

'Oh, my God. Our whole marriage was built on lies.' For a moment she closed her eyes, as though to blot out the memory. 'So quickly I knew I'd made a horrific mistake when I married Scott – but I tried to make it work. And then when I was pregnant, I thought he would change. He was forever jealous of Jamie. I suppose people in town told him how we'd gone together from high school days.' She paused. Her voice dropped to a whisper. 'He – he even questioned that Debbie was his child. Oh, at moments he liked the image of a family.' An unfamiliar bitterness crept into her voice. 'He thought it was good for his political career.'

'Beth, why does Rosita dislike Scott?' A shot in the dark, April thought – but worth pursuing.

Beth hesitated. 'Rosita cleaned for me at intervals. Not regularly, because Scott was anxious about our saving money. Rosita was so grateful for any additional income. I told her she wasn't to clean the windows – that was man's work. But she insisted. She was on the outside cleaning the windows a few weeks ago when Scott and I were having another of our fights.' She paused, prodded herself to continue. 'Rosita saw him slap me. He told me never to have her clean for us again.' Another pause. 'That was the day I asked him for a divorce.'

* * *

Jamie decided to make a quick stop at the supermarket before heading home from the *Sentinel.* Everything was running on schedule at the paper. No crises arose in David's absence. But he missed David's daily reports of his visits with Beth. It was frustrating that he couldn't see her. That would play right into Scott's hands.

He'd been hoping all day that David would call in with some news of what he and April were discovering in Cedar Grove. He'd listened to radio news about road conditions further upstate. The snowplows and sanders were clearing the roads, of course. Still, he doubted that driving conditions were great.

Viewing the abundance of cars in the supermarket parking area he realized this was the before-dinner rush hour. Damn, that meant lines at the checkout counter. All right, pick up what he needed and get out of here.

He was conscious of avid conversation among those waiting in line – and then he saw the front page of the tabloid rag that David said had interviewed Scott. He felt encased in ice as he read the headline above a photograph of Beth: HUSBAND ADMITS WIFE UNSTABLE.

Clenching his teeth, he reached for a copy of the tabloid and tossed it on the checkout counter along with the contents of his shopping cart. Impatient to be out of the supermarket and on his cell phone.

On the off chance that David had returned to the *Sentinel* in the brief period since he'd left, he punched in David's private line.

'Yeah.' David's voice was electric. He'd been waiting for a call from someone else, Jamie guessed.

'David, you know that rag that interviewed Scott? It's on sale in town . . .'

'Where are you?'

'The parking lot at the supermarket,' Jamie told him.

'Meet me at Bob and Nicole's house,' David ordered. 'I've already alerted Bob that we need to talk. I'm heading there now. April should be there shortly. She's gone to talk with Beth.'

'How was Cedar Grove?' Anxiety crept into Jamie's voice.

'That's what we need to talk about.' David was grim. 'But not when you're on a cell phone.' David always warned that the whole world could eavesdrop on cell phone conversations.

'I'm heading for Bob and Nicole's house now.' *What happened in Cedar Grove? David sounds so uptight.*

'What's going on?' Nicole demanded of Bob.

'David wouldn't talk on the phone.' Bob sighed. 'He sounded awfully upset.' He glanced about with a sudden awareness of quiet in the house. 'Where are the kids?'

'In the den devouring pizza and watching TV. I figured you'd want them out from under foot when David gets here.' Nicole paused at the sound of a car pulling up in the driveway. 'That's probably David now.'

While David emerged from his car, they saw Jamie pull up behind him. The two were exchanging brief words.

'A taxi's stopping here,' Nicole noted in astonishment and watched while April emerged.

'David must have dropped her off to see Beth. Her car was back at her apartment,' Bob interpreted, hurrying to the front door.

In a surge of excitement the five of them headed into the living room – each knowing astonishing revelations were about to be revealed.

'The kids are having their favorite dinner – pizza,' Nicole told the others. 'They're in the den – eating and watching TV. We can talk.'

When April finished her report on her meeting with Nora Martin, she was conscious that Bob and Nicole, along with Jamie, had jumped to the same conclusion as she and David.

'We may be way off base,' David cautioned. 'Still, we must explore this.'

'Could Scott have set fire to Rosita's trailer? Could he have cut Jamie's brakes?' Nicole hesitated a split second. 'He could have,' she insisted.

'Mrs Martin was uneasy about speaking so bluntly,' April admitted. 'But it was clear she believes Scott murdered his parents.'

'But he was out of town the night that Debbie was murdered,' Bob pinpointed.

'Or so he managed to make us believe,' David shot back. 'Oh, I know – the police surely checked it out, along with April.'

'He was trying to set up the perfect alibi.' April's mind was in high gear. 'Maybe he did check into the motel – then backtracked into town on foot to rent a car. Leaving his own car there as evidence that he was at the motel all night. If he'd driven away, the night clerk would have heard him leave.'

'He's won the annual marathon the last three years,' Jamie jumped in. 'Maybe he rented a car, drove back into town' – he paused, forced himself to continue – 'killed Debbie, and went back to turn in the rented car. A hike back to the motel – and he thought he was home free.'

'What was the town where he was supposed to be?' April asked.

'Williamstown,' David told her. 'It's not quite eighty miles away. At that time of night – with no traffic – he could have driven it in little over an hour.'

'Tomorrow morning I'm going to Williamstown,' April resolved. 'As I recall, he stayed at a small, private motel called The Williamstown Arms. I'm going to ask a lot more questions this time. And I'll check with the car rental offices. He couldn't have rented a car without giving some ID.'

'I'll go with you,' David began. 'We'll—'

'It'll be easier if I go alone,' April rejected. 'I'll work up some sympathetic story . . .' She pondered for a moment. 'What about a photo of Scott? I'll need that.'

'We have some group shots at the *Sentinel*,' Jamie recalled. 'From civic affairs. But they're not the greatest,' he acknowledged.

'I have some of the wedding pictures,' David said painfully. 'We can cut out a shot of Scott.'

'Let's do that tonight. I'll head for Williamstown first thing in the morning.'

April went with David to his house to pick up a photo of Scott. She waited tensely while he unlocked the door. This was where Beth had been brought as a newborn. This was where she had lived all her life – until her marriage. Sensing her chaotic thoughts, David reached for her hand, held it tightly in his as he drew her into the spacious foyer.

'The photo album is in the living room breakfront,' he recalled. 'It's loaded with photos of Beth through the years.'

Feeling herself in another world, April sat on the living room sofa with David beside her – a photo album on her lap. This was Beth at five months, with her first two teeth. Beth and her puppy Reno on her second birthday. Beth's birthday party when she was three.

Slowly – lovingly – David identified each snapshot, as though reliving those years. The images becoming blurred for April as he continued. Tears ignored. Her baby had been blessed with parents who loved her, she rejoiced – yet all the while she feared for tomorrow.

'You'll need a photo of Scott,' David reminded, his voice all at once harsh. 'We'll find that in their wedding album.'

David crossed again to the breakfront to retrieve this second album, brought it to April.

'Oh, she was a beautiful bride,' April whispered.

'We can cut out Scott's picture from this one.' David ripped a photo of Scott and his best man from the album. 'That's

Clark, his brother-in-law,' David added. 'One of the nicest guys who ever lived.'

'That'll do,' April said shakily, hurdled back into the present.

He handed the snapshot to April, returned to the breakfront with both albums. 'I'll take you home now.'

When they arrived at her apartment, April knew he would stay with her for the night. She needed him with her, especially tonight.

Later – when she lay in the curve of his arms after making love – she voiced the fear that had been haunting her.

'David, are we out in left field with our assumptions? Did Scott come back into town in the middle of the night and kill Debbie? And if he did, will we be able to prove it?'

'We have to prove it.' David pressed his cheek against hers. 'The only way we'll clear Beth is to bring in Debbie's murderer. And Scott is the only real lead we have.'

Chapter Thirty

April stacked the breakfast dishes in the dishwasher while David made up the bed. He'd tried again – futilely – to persuade her to allow him to go with her to Williamstown. She was touched by his protectiveness towards her, his concern for her well-being.

Since her mother died all those years ago – even during the years she'd been married to Greg – she'd felt that she alone was responsible for her own welfare. She was astonished that she felt such pleasure in David's concern for her. But she was convinced she'd be more successful in tracking down needed information if she operated on her own. And so much hung on her proving that they were right in suspecting that Scott had committed an unconscionable crime.

'Be careful, April,' David exhorted as he walked with her to her car. 'Don't take any crazy chances.'

'I'm not facing any danger, David,' she scolded gently while he pulled her close. So passing neighbors would be curious, she thought. Let them be. 'This is a fact-finding expedition. And please, God, let me learn what we need to know.'

Driving towards Williamstown, she fought against impatience. She was running into the early rush-hour traffic. But all the while her mind probed what they knew thus far. Her first objective was the Williamstown Arms.

With a flurry of relief she arrived at her destination, pulled off the road on to the motel grounds. Only three cars were parked before the units. The 'Vacancy' signed was lighted.

Her heart pounding, she left the car and headed for the office. She opened the door, walked inside.

A bottle redhead glanced up with an air of reluctance from the magazine she was reading. 'Good morning.' The desk clerk managed a bright smile, meant to please prospective guests. 'How long do you plan to stay?'

'I'm not registering.' April's smile was apologetic. 'I'm trying to track down my sister's dead-beat husband. He's seven months behind in child support.' Her eyes said, *Don't men suck?*

'Yeah?' Already the redhead showed signs of sympathy.

'We know that about three or four weeks ago Scott stayed here for one night. We're trying to follow him from here on.' April dug into her purse for the photograph of Scott. 'Would you remember his being a guest here?'

The redhead leaned forward to inspect the photo April extended. 'Oh, sure, I remember him – because he was so good-looking.' Now she frowned. 'But he said his name was Michael.'

'He was using his middle name. He probably knew we were trying to track him down.' April shook her head in disgust. 'But he was here. That's important. Thanks so much.'

Hurrying back to the car, April felt a surge of excitement. They'd known he was there that night. But he'd offered a phony ID. That said loud and clear that he was up to something illicit. The desk clerk had recognized him, was witness to the false ID. Later they'd get a statement from her.

Why would he give a false ID unless he was trying to hide something? Whose ID did he use? How did he acquire it?

All right, she prodded herself back to the moment, check and see if there was a record of his renting a car in the area. A car that he drove back to Magnolia in the middle of the night. Go into town now, locate addresses of car rental agencies.

In town she found a pay phone and a local phone book at a pharmacy. She scribbled down the names and addresses of the two agencies in town, approached the cashier for direction.

The clerk at the first agency listened to her concocted story with an air of boredom, looked at the photo of Scott and shook his head.

'Never saw him here. You might come back and talk with the guy on the night shift. He comes on at four p.m.'

She approached the second agency with identical results. She debated about remaining in town till four p.m. Go back to Magnolia, drive back in the afternoon, she decided. Yet she was reluctant to admit defeat on this first go-around.

'There are just two car rental agencies in town?' she asked the second clerk.

'There's this other twenty-four-hour agency that's technically in Madison,' he explained, 'but actually it's just two miles beyond our city limits. Right on the connecting road. You might try them.'

Remembering that Scott had used the name Michael at the motel, April gave her prepared spiel to the friendly middle-aged woman clerk.

'Here's a picture of Michael,' she said ingratiatingly. 'Maybe you'll recognize him. I realize it was a while ago . . .'

'Oh yes. Good-looking guy,' the clerk commented. 'Maybe I can get the date for you.' She reached under the counter, pulled out a book, searched while April waited in soaring hope. 'Here it is. Michael Freeman.' She gave April the date that the car was rented. The night Debbie was murdered. 'Funny, he returned it at two ten a.m. We don't have many returns at that hour.'

Back in her car April called David on her cell phone. 'I have something hot,' she reported, striving for calm. 'Call Bob. If he's available, have him meet us in your office. I should be there – if there's no traffic problem – in about an hour and a half.'

'You're okay?' David asked, his anxiety seeping through.

'I'm fine. I think we've struck gold. See you in an hour

and a half,' she repeated. It would be the longest hour and a half she'd ever experienced.

She was grateful to encounter little traffic. In record time she pulled into the parking area behind the *Sentinel*, hurried from the car into the *Sentinel* building. Iris was just emerging from David's office.

'I'm sending out for lunch. Shall I add you to the list?'

'A turkey on rye toast,' April told her. This was apt to be a long conference.

'April?' David called.

'In person,' she flipped with unexpected lightness.

Bob and Jamie sat before David's desk. Jamie jumped up to pull a chair forward for her. Three pairs of eyes focused on her.

'We weren't off base in our suspicions,' April told them.

The atmosphere suddenly tense, the three men listened while she reported in detail what she had discovered in Williamstown. 'But who is Michael Freeman?' She gazed from one to the other. 'Whose ID was Scott using?'

'Michael Freeman is another announcer at the station,' Jamie said. 'We bowl together. I remember Michael being so pissed when his wallet, his driver's license, and charge plates disappeared one day – and then suddenly reappeared the next day. And then when his MasterCard bill came in about two weeks ago, there was a car rental charge in Williamstown! MasterCard reported it was a bad forgery – he didn't have to pay. But what do you want to bet that bad forgery was Scott's?'

'But how did he use Michael's driver's license?' David was puzzled.

'He replaced his photo for Michael's,' Bob figured. 'He flashed it fast, spreading his usual charm.' Sarcasm sneaked into his voice now. 'The clerk – probably a woman – just gave it a cursory glance.'

'He rented the car,' April pointed out, 'parked somewhere on the side of the road. Then late in the evening he walked back there to retrieve it, drove into Magnolia. The car was returned at two ten a.m.,' she recalled. 'Then he hiked back to the motel. For a walker like Scott, it was a breeze. I clocked the distance from the car rental to the motel. It was less than three miles.'

'Okay, let's go call on Jeff Goodwin,' Bob said briskly.

Bob and April sat waiting impatiently for Jeff Goodwin – the district attorney – to complete a series of phone calls. His last call was to Michael Freeman.

'Scott would be in a position to lift your wallet – with your driver's license and charge plates?' Jeff asked, then nodded his head to confirm to April and Bob. 'Thanks, Michael.' He listened for a moment. 'Yeah, we'll need a statement from you later.'

'Everything jibes,' Jeff conceded. 'Still, we've got a lot of proving to do,' he warned.

'But you can pick him up for questioning.' April struggled for calm.

'We'll do that,' Jeff promised. He shook his head in disbelief. 'A lot of folks in this town are going to fall on their faces in shock when they hear about Scott.'

Scott finished a news report and hurried to his closet-sized office. He was expecting a call from Texas – Kensington Womenswear knew he'd be presenting their case to the Town Council tomorrow evening. They were preparing some alternative clauses in a possible deal.

He glanced up in annoyance when the door swung open and Michael hovered there in an aura of rage.

'You bastard!' Michael seethed. 'It was you who "borrowed" my wallet and charge plates – and then returned them the next day!'

'You're crazy!' Scott leapt to his feet. 'I don't know what you're talking about!'

'You rented a car in my name! MasterCard said the

signature was a forgery. They'll find out it was you. You'll—' Michael stopped dead at the sound of police sirens somewhere down the road.

All at once Scott moved forward, slammed a fist into Michael's stomach. With a howl of pain Michael doubled up. Scott charged from his office. *Son-of-a-bitch! How did they find out? Where did I screw up? I was sure it was foolproof!*

Scott raced down the stairs and out of the building, into his car. He saw two squad cars screeching to a stop even as he stepped on the gas and lurched on to the road.

Damn it! They know my car. They're on my trail.

David was about to pull into the radio station parking area. April leaned forward, staring down the road.

'The squad cars are chasing Scott!' April gasped. 'He knows we're on to him!'

David charged ahead, ignoring speed limits, following the squad cars – their sirens screaming.

'How does he think he can get away?' David kept close behind the police cars.

'He's heading towards that same stretch of road where Jamie crashed,' April said and glanced at the speedometer. 'He must be doing ninety!'

Moments later they approached the turn in the road where Jamie had miraculously escaped serious injury or death.

'Oh, my God!' April stared in shock as Scott rammed into the same slight incline which Jamie had hit at low speed. Instantly the car exploded into flames.

David slowed down to a crawl. 'It's over, April. Scott could never survive that.'

April buried her face against David's shoulder. The detectives made a move towards the car, but it was clear there was no way they could pull Scott's body from that blazing inferno.

Chapter Thirty-One

April hunched her shoulders against the damp cold of the day while David and the police chief engaged in somber conversation. One fire truck remained at the scene, though the flaming mass that had been Scott's car had been subdued. His charred body had been removed.

Jamie had been summoned to the scene in order to report the happenings in tomorrow morning's *Sentinel*. He and the staff photographer – grim photos recorded – had returned to the newspaper.

'We have to notify the next of kin.' The police chief seemed uncomfortable. 'That'll be Beth and his sister.'

'I'll do that,' David said. He paused. 'There'll be no need to hold the body?'

'No,' the police chief agreed. His eyes were questioning for a moment. 'You'll want to arrange for an early funeral,' he surmised.

'Right.' David reached for April's hand. 'But first of all we need to talk with the DA.' He turned to April. His eyes said, *Beth's home free – thank God for that.*

'There'll have to be corroboration,' the police chief reminded, but his compassion was obvious. 'That may take a day or two. But this has to be a closed case once the paperwork is done.'

April and David returned to his car, drove to the district attorney's office. Jeff Goodwin was expecting them. He'd been briefed on what had happened when the detectives went to bring Scott in for questioning.

'We'll need about forty-eight hours to wrap this up,' Goodwin told April and David after her statement had been taped. 'It's going to take this town a while to digest what's happened.' He shook his head in amazement. 'Scott Emerson had us all fooled. We thought he had the greatest future ahead of him.'

Now April and David headed for Elaine's house – dreading what lay ahead.

'Elaine suspected Scott was guilty,' April said as they approached the Miller house. 'She was torn – terrified that Beth might be convicted, yet reluctant to betray her brother. But she gave us the all-important lead,' April reminded. 'She sent us to Cedar Grove.'

David pulled into the Millers' driveway. He and April left the car, walked up to the entrance. Dreading this encounter, April pushed the doorbell. Moments later Elaine pulled the door wide. Fear froze her for an instant.

'Something's happened to Clark?' Her face was drained of color.

'No,' David said quickly. 'This is about Scott.'

Elaine winced in pain. 'Please come in.'

April and David followed her across the foyer to the small, pleasant living room. 'Elaine, I'm sorry . . .' David hesitated a moment. 'Scott's dead. He smashed up his car – he was doing at least eighty-five. He must have died instantly.'

'There's more,' Elaine guessed, seeming to gear herself for traumatic news. 'Tell me what's happened.'

Her eyes anguished, she listened to David's report.

'Elaine, this will in no way reflect on you and Clark,' April insisted. 'You're two very special people to everybody here in town. Nothing can change that. You're not responsible for Scott's actions.'

'I knew that Scott had killed our parents – even before he confessed to me in a drunken moment. But I knew my parents would want me to protect him. They were always so sure he would straighten himself out. They prayed for that. After –

after it happened, I insisted he see a psychiatrist.' She flinched in recall. 'I sent him to three – but he never remained with any of them for more than a few sessions. When he married Beth, I thought, now he'll be all right. He'll change. I wanted so much to believe that.' Her eyes pleaded for understanding.

'The coroner will release the body quickly,' David told her. 'I'll arrange for a private family funeral. I'll take care of everything, Elaine. As soon as the arrangements are made, I'll let you know.'

From the Miller house April and David went to tell Beth she would shortly be free. David reached for April's hand as they sat at the table in the small conference room and waited for Beth to be brought to them. Despite the horror of their discoveries April felt joy in knowing Beth would be cleared.

Beth managed a weak smile as she greeted David and April. She was surprised at finding both of them here together this way, April sensed.

'Baby, it's going to be all right,' David told Beth as she sat across from him at the table. 'You'll be cleared in a matter of forty-eight hours. Just some bureaucratic red tape to be handled.'

Beth stared at her father in a torrent of emotions. Relief battled with rage. 'They know who killed Debbie?'

All at once David seemed incapable of speech. April sought for words. 'It's going to be a shock to you, Beth. Not even the police suspected him. Nobody understood except Elaine.' April saw comprehension take root in Beth. 'Elaine knew Scott was deranged. She couldn't bring herself to tell us, but she gave us the lead that broke the case.'

'Oh, my God . . .' For a moment Beth closed her eyes in shock. 'He'd screamed at me that Debbie wasn't his child. But I couldn't believe he truly meant that. I should have left him. Debbie would be alive today . . .'

'There was no way you could have prevented it,' April insisted. She reached across the table for Beth's hand. 'You have your beautiful memories of Debbie,' she said tenderly. 'Nobody can take them away from you.'

'April followed her instincts,' David told Beth – and for a moment April was unnerved. *David mustn't look at me that way – not yet. Not until we know that Beth will accept me.* 'She tracked down the facts. She proved that Scott had been in town that awful night – and how he managed to hide the truth.'

'It's so hard to believe,' Beth whispered. 'I wish – somehow – that I could know for sure that he did this awful thing.'

'Beth, we know.' David was grim. 'There's no other reason for him to have pretended to be Michael. To rent a car that he returned in the middle of the night.'

'He was Debbie's father . . .' Beth faltered. 'I wish he'd lived to face a trial – so that I would know for sure that he was the one who sneaked into the house in the middle of the night and killed our baby.'

'The district attorney is putting through the paperwork that will clear you.' April made a determined effort to re-channel the conversation. 'Another two days and you'll be out of here.'

'I'll always love you.' Beth lifted April's hand to her mouth. 'You've been wonderful, since the moment we met.'

April knew the next forty-eight hours would be chaotic. She and David were grateful that Scott's body was being quickly released. David was racing about town this morning to make all the necessary arrangements. Scott would be buried at a private family funeral the next afternoon. Secretly they were relieved that the district attorney declared the necessary formalities for Beth's release would not be completed until the morning after the funeral.

David had been blunt. 'Let Beth be spared the agony of attending Scott's funeral. She's had more than enough to bear.'

April sat at her desk and focused on the front page of this morning's *Sentinel* – dominated by Jamie's report of Beth's imminent clearance, along with Scott's involvement in Debbie's murder and his death. But April worried about Beth's state of mind – her fears that they might be making assumptions that could prove false.

April's phone rang. She reached to pick it up. The caller was Nicole. She, too, had read the morning newspaper.

'I've been out at the supermarket and the pharmacy this morning. I've talked to a lot of people. They're so ashamed of their suspicions that Beth could be guilty. Not that they all felt that way,' she added conscientiously. 'But they're shattered at learning about Scott.'

Late in the morning David came into the office. 'Everything's scheduled,' he told April. 'The funeral is set for two thirty tomorrow afternoon.' His face tensed. 'I've let it be known it's to be by invitation only.' All at once seeming exhausted he lowered himself into a chair.

Sandy breezed into the office with two mugs of coffee. 'I figured you'd be ready for these by now.' Her eyes belied her bright smile.

'Oh, Sandy, yes!' April reached out gratefully.

'I need it.' David accepted the other mug with an air of pleasure. He waited for Sandy to leave, then went to close the door. 'I want to feel alone with you,' he told April. 'Just the two of us on a desert isle somewhere . . .'

'I worry about Beth,' April said after a moment. 'Her mind tells her – as we all know – that Scott is guilty. But in her heart she wants – what?' April gestured vaguely.

'She wants someone who can say, there's no doubt – I saw him at the house that night.' David sighed. 'In time she'll understand – Scott was mentally ill.'

April's phone rang again. She reached to respond. The caller was Jamie.

'I've been trying to track down David,' Jamie said. 'Is he by any chance there?'

'He's here, Jamie. Just a moment.' She extended the phone to David.

David conferred with Jamie for a few moments, put the phone down with an unexpected chuckle.

'Jamie says the newspaper's being flooded with calls – everybody happy that Beth's being cleared.' He chuckled again. 'They call at the office because nobody can reach me at home.' He was staying with April at her apartment during this traumatic period. 'You think the town is getting the idea that we have something going between us?'

'It may be entering their minds,' April conceded.

'It'll be the first front-page wedding announcement the *Sentinel* ever offered.' A twinkle in his eyes now. 'That is, if you're accepting my proposal?'

'I was afraid you'd never ask,' she whispered.

At exactly two thirty p.m. the handful invited to the funeral home gathered together for the brief services. Afterwards April and David and Bob and Nicole – along with Elaine – went to the Magnolia cemetery for Scott's burial. Morning sun had given way to somber clouds that seemed appropriate for the occasion, April thought.

Again, the services were brief. After a few final words to the minister, they settled themselves in David's car for the ride to the Miller house for coffee.

'Was I wrong in not bringing the kids?' Elaine asked uneasily.

'No.' April was firm. 'Let them remember Scott as the uncle they saw occasionally. They'll have to know about what happened, but you'll make it clear it was a tragic defect in Scott that caused this.'

'They're impatient for Clark to come home,' Nicole guessed.

'They're out of their minds.' Elaine managed a wisp of a smile. 'He's doing so well. The doctors are delighted. And we'll always remember how this town – and Beth especially – is responsible for his being alive.'

'I understand his classes are planning a huge party when he returns to teaching,' Nicole reported.

'And tomorrow morning,' David exulted, 'Beth will be coming home.'

April's heart began to pound. David kept saying that Beth must know her birth mother – whom she already loved. But would Beth love her when she knew she'd been abandoned before she was two days old? *Do I dare take that risk?*

Chapter Thirty-Two

Together April and David waited with joyous impatience for Beth to go through the final moments of her release. Then at last she came to them.

David drew her into his arms. 'Everything's going to be fine from now on.'

'People in town are so happy for you.' April felt tears blur her vision as Beth turned to hug her. 'You must look ahead, not backwards.'

Beth clung to April. 'You've been so good to me. I'll love you always.' *Will she, if she knows the truth?*

David reached for the tote Beth carried. 'Let's get out of here.'

All at once Beth seemed frightened. 'May I go home with you, Dad? I – I can't live there again,' she whispered. April understood. She was referring to the house she'd shared with Scott – and heartbreakingly briefly, with Debbie.

'You'll come home.' David prodded her towards the exit. 'I wouldn't have it any other way.'

'Perhaps we could stop by the – the other house for a few minutes,' April suggested to Beth. 'So you can pack things you'll need for now. We'll go in together.'

'That makes sense.' David sounded almost brusque in his efforts to hide his emotions. 'And then we're to have a welcome-home luncheon at Bob and Nicole's house.' His face softened. 'Nicole remembered how you've always loved Black Forest cake.' He turned to April. 'We had a Black Forest cake at her tenth birthday party – and she was ecstatic.'

He chuckled reminiscently. 'And ever since for her birthday we'd have a Black Forest cake.'

April felt a surge of exhilaration as they approached the car. Glorious sunshine had emerged from what had been a sea of clouds. An omen for the future, she told herself.

David reached for the rear door of the car, seemed uncertain for a moment.

'Throw my tote in the back with me,' Beth said, an unexpected sparkle in her eyes. *She understands about David and me. She's pleased.*

April saw an answering sparkle in David's eyes. He, too, understood that Beth was pleased. He was relieved. He'd not been sure how Beth would react.

'Okay, old lady,' he joshed, pulling open the front door on the passenger side and patting April on the rump. 'In you go.'

April was conscious of a growing tension in the car as they approached the house where Beth had lived since her marriage. A house laden now with nightmare memories.

'We'll run in for a few minutes so you can pack some things.' April was casual. 'I'll help you.'

David pulled up before the house. He, too, dreaded going inside, April sensed.

'All right, let's get this over fast.' April reached for the door on her side. 'We have a lunch date to keep.'

'Jamie asked if he could come to lunch, too,' David told Beth. 'That's okay, isn't it?'

Beth's face lighted. 'Oh yes.'

In the house April followed Beth to the master bedroom. At the door Beth paused, as though bracing herself for ugly ghosts.

'This won't take long.' In the master bedroom Beth swung open the doors of a closet wall, pulled out a pair of large valises – flinched for an instant at the sight of them. Luggage from her honeymoon, April guessed.

'Point me to the lingerie drawers.' April reached for one

valise with a determined smile. 'I'll fill up this one while you bring down slacks and sweaters and such to go into the other. And don't forget to pack shoes and boots . . .'

For a moment Beth seemed frozen. Scott's suits hung at one side of the closet. Then – averting her gaze – she reached to bring down clothes from her side.

In silence the two women packed. Snapping her valise shut, Beth stared for an instant beyond the bedroom door to the room across the hall. Her face betraying her anguish. The nursery, April thought in sudden pain.

David appeared in the hall. 'How're you doing?'

'Just about finished.' Beth fought for composure.

'Good.' David reached for the two valises. 'I'll take these two out to the car.' David hesitated, his eyes resting on Beth. 'April has something very wonderful to tell you.'

April stared at him in momentary panic as – with an urging smile – he hurried from the room. She turned to Beth. Terrified by what David meant for her to do. Beth was waiting for her to speak.

How do I do this? How will Beth react? Will I lose her forever?

'What did Dad mean?' Beth seemed simultaneously eager and puzzled.

'I know that you were adopted,' April began, searching for words. 'Were you angry that your birth mother gave you up?'

'Oh, no.' It was a gentle reproof. 'Dad told me she was very young and very alone and very frightened. He said she loved me very much – but she couldn't take care of me.' Beth was bewildered. Then all at once her face grew luminous. 'April, you know my birth mother!'

'You don't hate her for abandoning you?'

'She did the best she could.' Beth seemed in some inner debate. 'I never told anybody this. I didn't want to hurt Mom and Dad – they were always so good to me. I never told them – I was afraid they'd be hurt. But I tried so hard to track her down. I even went to a group on the Internet that helps people trying to find their birth mothers. I tried so hard – but every road seemed closed.'

April glowed. 'You wanted to find her. You didn't hate her . . .'

'How could I do that, knowing what she'd gone through? Dad told me how she'd been left alone in the world – her father died just as she realized she was pregnant. Her mother died when she was twelve. And Dad said my father's parents had sent him away when he and my mother wanted to get married.' Beth's voice dropped to a compassionate whisper. 'I knew their whole story.'

'David told you everything.' Tears filled April's eyes, spilled over. 'Even about Tommy . . .'

All at once Beth radiated a startled comprehension. 'You're my mother! That's what Dad wanted you to tell me!'

'You're not angry with me?' April sought further reassurance.

Beth reached to draw her close. 'How could I be angry? I've wanted so much to find you. And now—' Her face grew luminescent. 'Now you're here with me.'

Later, April promised herself, she'd tell Beth about Tommy. How warm and tender and bright he was – and that he'd wanted to be there for her. Beth had a right to know that her birth father was someone special.

David greeted April and Beth with a radiant smile when they emerged arm in arm from the house and approached the car.

'The two of you get in back,' he ordered with mock gruffness. 'You have much to talk about.'

Jamie glanced at his watch. Time to get over to Bob and Nicole's house for the welcome-home lunch for Beth. He was conscious of a surge of anticipation. He hadn't seen Beth since that awful night.

He left his desk, reached for his down jacket. Now he

hesitated. Was it all right to show up in jeans and a wool turtleneck? One of the perks of working for the *Sentinel* was the casual dress code.

Would Beth remember she'd given him this sweater for Christmas five years ago? She'd knitted it herself, he remembered. He'd stopped wearing it when Beth and Scott announced their engagement. He'd kept it as a kind of souvenir of the good years – before Scott blew into town. Occasionally he'd worn it – in fits of wistful nostalgia. Feeling close to Beth when he did.

He pulled on his jacket, headed for the door. Thank God the nightmare was over. But could he and Beth go back to the years before Scott invaded this town? Don't rush, he cautioned himself. Wait for little signs that she was willing to resume their normal lives. *Am I being naive to think that can happen?*

He was halfway down the hall to the entrance when Iris called to him.

'Jamie, there's a call for David. Celia Logan. She said she'd talk to you if David wasn't available.'

'Okay, I'll take it in my office.' Jamie charged back up the hall. Damn! He didn't want to be late for the lunch. Faintly breathless, he picked up the phone. 'Hello, Celia. Jamie here.'

'Jamie, I need to get a message to David. I think it's important.' Celia's voice radiated excitement. 'I know it's late to be talking about this, but you know about my sister and her memory problems . . .'

'Sure.' What had Marcia come up with? he asked himself impatiently, glancing at his watch. 'What shall I tell David?'

'Well, Marcia was looking at this morning's *Sentinel* – with that picture of Scott on the front page. And she remembered the last time she saw him – right before she hurt her foot. Jamie, that was the night Debbie was murdered – and Marcia saw Scott going into his house. She couldn't understand why he was walking down the street – not in his car – at that hour of the night. She completely forgot about it until she saw his photo a little while ago.'

'Marcia can place Scott at the scene!' The case might be closed, he thought jubilantly, but this was the final bit of evidence that could erase any doubts in anybody's mind. 'She'll give a statement to the district attorney?'

'Oh, she'll love to do that. It'll almost be like being in one of those suspense novels she's always reading.'

'I'll tell David,' Jamie promised, 'and he'll get in touch with Jeff Goodwin. Thanks, Celia.'

April watched with an unfamiliar sense of tranquility while Bob dropped more logs in the fireplace grate, poked until flames enveloped them. Nicole was in the kitchen checking on the roast in the oven. David sprawled in a club chair and gazed with a serene smile at April and Beth, sitting together on the sofa.

'We'll have snow before nightfall,' David predicted. 'I ordered it especially for you, Beth,' he joshed. 'You've always loved snow.'

Nicole strolled into the living room. 'The roast is ready. I'm letting it sit for a few minutes before I slice it. Where the devil is Jamie?'

'Just arriving,' David said and glanced towards the picture window. 'That's his car pulling up out front.'

This would have been the most wonderful day in her life, April thought, if she could ease the pain that she knew enveloped Beth. What had Beth said earlier? *I wish I knew for sure that Scott was guilty.* How could she doubt it?

Jamie charged into the house, hovered at the entrance to the living room. He gazed at Beth with a joyous smile. Her own smile was uncertain yet warm.

'You still have that sweater I knitted for you . . .'

'I've kept it for special occasions,' he said. 'Like now.'

'I'll get lunch on the table.' Nicole exchanged a knowing

glance with April. Please, God, April thought, let all be right with Beth's world now.

'Wait a moment.' Jamie seemed to be in some inner struggle. 'I talked with Celia Logan just a few minutes ago. She wanted me to give you a message, David. I think you'll all want to know . . .'

'What was the message, Jamie?' David asked. The room was suddenly electric.

'She said her sister Marcia – you know she has some memory difficulties.' Jamie glanced about at the others. 'Marcia looked at the photo of Scott on the front page of the newspaper – and she remembered the last time she saw him. It was the night she hurt her ankle. She said she looked out the window and saw Scott walking towards the house. In the middle of the night.' He hesitated, almost apologetic at what he was about to say. 'The night Debbie was murdered.'

'Scott was there – Marcia saw him.' April turned to Beth. 'There's your proof, my darling. No more doubts to haunt you.'

'I had to know,' Beth whispered. 'Thank you for telling me, Jamie.'

'All right, let's get to the table before my roast gets cold,' Nicole ordered. 'And for dessert, Beth,' she said tenderly, 'there's Black Forest cake.'

April exchanged a heady glance with David across the room. She remembered the words of Robert Browning: *God's in his heaven – All's right with the world!* After much travail all was right with their world.